THE BACKSTABBERS

Look for these exciting Western series from bestselling authors
WILLIAM W. JOHNSTONE
and **J. A. JOHNSTONE**

The Mountain Man

Preacher: The First Mountain Man

Luke Jensen, Bounty Hunter

Those Jensen Boys!

The Jensen Brand

Matt Jensen

MacCallister

The Red Ryan Westerns

Perley Gates

Have Brides, Will Travel

The Hank Fallon Westerns

Will Tanner, Deputy U.S. Marshal

Shotgun Johnny

The Chuckwagon Trail

The Jackals

The Slash and Pecos Westerns

The Texas Moonshiners

AVAILABLE FROM PINNACLE BOOKS

THE BACKSTABBERS

A RED RYAN WESTERN

WILLIAM W. JOHNSTONE

and J. A. Johnstone

PINNACLE BOOKS
Kensington Publishing Corp.
www.kensingtonbooks.com

PINNACLE BOOKS are published by

Kensington Publishing Corp.
119 West 40th Street
New York, NY 10018

PUBLISHER'S NOTE
Following the death of William W. Johnstone, the Johnstone family is working with a carefully selected writer to organize and complete Mr. Johnstone's outlines and many unfinished manuscripts to create additional novels in all of his series like The Last Gunfighter, Mountain Man, and Eagles, among others. This novel was inspired by Mr. Johnstone's superb storytelling.

ISBN-13: 978-0-7860-4434-4
ISBN-10: 0-7860-4434-9

First printing: March 2020

10 9 8 7 6 5 4 3 2 1

Printed in the United States of America

Electronic edition:

ISBN-13: 978-0-7860-4435-1 (e-book)
ISBN-10: 0-7860-4435-7 (e-book)

CHAPTER ONE

Beneath a black sky torn apart by a raging thunderstorm, the sidelamps of the Patterson stage were lit as Red Ryan and Patrick "Buttons" Muldoon approached the town of Cottondale, some sixty miles east of El Paso, Texas.

Buttons drew rein on the tired team and shouted over a roar of thunder, "Hell, Red, the place is in darkness. How come?"

"I don't know how come," the shotgun guard said. Red wore his slicker against the hammering rain. "The place is dead, looks like."

"Maybe they ran out of oil. Long trip to bring lamp oil all this way."

"And candles. They don't have any candles."

"Nothing up this way but miles of desert," Buttons said. "Could be they ran out of oil."

"You said that already."

"I know, and that's still what I reckon. They ran out of oil and candles and all the folks are sitting in their homes in the dark, sheltering from the rain."

"Or asleep," Red said.

Lightning scrawled across the sky like the signature

of a demented god, and for a second or two, the barren brush country was starkly illuminated in sizzling light. Thunder bellowed.

"Buttons, you sure we're in the right place?" Red yelled. Rain drummed on the crown of his plug hat and the shoulders of his slicker. "Maybe this isn't Cottondale. Maybe it's some other place."

"Sure, I'm sure," Buttons said. "Abe Patterson's wire said Cottondale is east of El Paso and just south of the Cornudas Mountains. Well, afore this storm started, we seen the mountains, so that there ahead of us must be the town."

Red said. "What the hell kind of town is it?"

"A dark town," Buttons said. "Remember the first time we seen that New Mexican mining burg, what was it called? Ah, yeah, Buffalo Flat. That looked like a dark town until you seen it close. Tents. Nothing but brown tents."

"With people in them as I recollect," Red said. "Well, drive on in and let's get out of this rain and unhitch the team."

"Yeah, the horses are tuckered," Buttons said. "They've had some hard going, this leg of the trip."

"So am I tuckered. I could sure use some coffee."

Buttons slapped the ribbons and the six-horse team lurched into motion. Lightning flashed, thunder banged as nature threw a tantrum. As it headed for a town lost in gloom, the Patterson stage was all but invisible behind the steel mesh of the teeming downpour.

Cottondale consisted of a narrow, single street bookended by rows of stores, a hotel, a saloon, and a livery stable. A large church with a tall bell tower dominated the rest. The town was a bleak, run-down, and windswept place. The buildings huddled together like starving vagrants seeking comfort in each other's company. It was dark, dismal, and somber. Silent as a tomb, the only sound the ceaseless rattle of the relentless rain.

Buttons halted the team outside the saloon. A painted sign above the door, much faded, read THE WHEATSHEAF. "We'll try in here."

Red shook his head. "Try in here for what? Buttons, this is a ghost town. It's deader than hell in a preacher's backyard."

"Can't be. Ol' Abe said we have a passenger . . . what the hell's his name again? Oh yeah, Morgan Ford. He's got to be here and a whole passel of other folks."

Thunder rolled across the sky.

When it passed, Red looked around and said, "Then where the hell are all them other folks?"

"Sleeping the sleep of the just, that's where. There's a church in this town, and God-fearing folks go to bed early." He angled a look at Red. "Unlike some I know."

Red reached under his slicker and consulted his watch. "It's only eight o'clock."

"Farmers," Buttons said. "Farmers go to bed early, something to do with all that plowing they do at the tail end of a horse. All right. Let's try the saloon. Day or night, you ever seen an empty saloon? I sure as hell haven't."

The saloon was as empty as last year's bird nest. Cobwebbed and dark, the shadows were as black as spilled ink. The mahogany bar dominated a room with a few tables and chairs scattered around a dance floor. A potbellied stove stood in a corner. Red thumbed a match into flame and held it high. The guttering light revealed pale rectangles on the walls where pictures had once hung, and the mirror behind the bar had been smashed into splinters.

"Ow!" The match had burned down and scorched Red's fingers. Irritated, he repeated, "Like I said . . . we're in a damned ghost town."

Buttons had been exploring around the bar, and his voice spoke from the murk. "Three bottles. All of them empty." Lightning flared as Buttons stepped toward Red in the dazzle, and he flickered like a figure in a magic lantern show. "We've been had. This is what they call a wild-goose chase."

"I don't think the Abe Patterson and Son Stage and Express Company is one to play practical jokes," Red said. "Abe never made a joke in his life."

"You're right. Abe wouldn't play a trick on us," Buttons said. "But it seems somebody is, and if I find who done it, I'll plug him for sure."

"Unhitch the team and let the horses shelter overnight in the livery stable. I'll get a fire going in the saloon stove and boil up some coffee."

"Fire will help us dry off. Damn, Red, this was a wasted trip."

Red smiled, "It's on the way back to the Patterson depot in San Angelo. We didn't lose anything by it."

"Except a fare," Buttons said.

"Yeah, except a fare. But I reckon Abe Patterson can afford it."

Buttons closed his slicker up to the neck and stepped toward the door. Red lingered for a few moments and decided that the chairs would burn nicely in the stove. He craved coffee and the cigarettes he could build without the downpour battering paper and tobacco out of his fingers.

Button's voice came from the doorway, sounding hollow in the silent lull between thunderclaps. "Red, you better come see this. And you ain't gonna like it."

Red's boot heels thudded across the timber floor as he walked to the open door. "What do you see? Is it a person?"

"No, it's that," Buttons said, pointing.

A hearse drawn by a black-draped horse stood in the middle of the rain-lashed street. Just visible in the murk behind the large, oval-shaped windows was a coffin, not a plain, hammered pine box, but by all appearances a substantial casket made from some kind of dark wood accented with silver handles and hinges.

"What the hell?" Red said.

"I don't see anybody out there," Buttons said. "Who the hell is in the box?"

"Maybe our passenger."

"Red, don't make jokes," Buttons said. "I'm boogered enough already."

"Let's take a look out there. A hearse doesn't just appear all by itself."

Red Ryan and Buttons Muldoon stepped into the street that was suddenly illuminated by a flash of lightning that glimmered on a tall, cadaverous man who wore a black frock coat and top hat and seemed uncaring of the rain that soaked him. The man's skin was an ashy gray, as though he spent too much time indoors, and he held a hefty Bible with a silver cross on the front cover in his right hand, close to his chest.

"Well, howdy," Buttons said. "Who the hell are you?"

Lightning shimmered, turning the rain into a cascade of steel needles, and thunder boomed before the man spoke. "I am the Reverend Solomon Palmer of this town. You have come for our dear, departed brother Morgan Ford, have you not?"

Rain ran off the brim of Buttons's hat as he shook his head. "Not the dear departed Morgan Ford, mister. The alive and kicking Morgan Ford."

"Alas, Brother Ford passed away two days ago," Palmer said.

"From what?" Buttons stepped back, alarmed. "Nothing catching, I hope."

"From congestion of the heart," Palmer said. "I watched his pale face turn black and then he gave a great sigh and a moment later he hurried off to meet his Creator." The preacher clutched his Bible closer. "He was a fine man, was Brother Ford."

"He was a fare," Buttons said. "And now he isn't. There ain't no profit in dead men for the Abe Patterson and Son Stage and Express Company."

"Ah, but there is," Palmer said. He smiled, revealing teeth that looked like yellowed piano keys. "Come with me . . . Mister . . . ah . . ."

"Muldoon, but you can call me Buttons. And the feller in the plug hat is Red Ryan, my shotgun guard."

"Come with you where?" Red asked. "Me and Mr. Muldoon are not trusting men."

"I will do you no harm," Palmer said. He glanced up at the black sky where blue lightning blazed. "Only the dead are abroad on a night such as this."

"Cheerful kind of ranny, ain't you?" Buttons said. "I'll have to see to my horses before I go anywhere, and I'll take care of your hearse hoss." He shook his head. "I don't believe I just said that."

"Hearse hoss," Red said. "It's got a ring to it."

"Yes, I'd appreciate it if you'd take care of my mare," Palmer said. "I think you'll find hay in the livery, and perhaps some oats."

"And where will you be?" Buttons said.

"Right here, waiting for you." Palmer looked stark and grim and bloodless as the storm cartwheeled around him, putting Buttons in mind of a corpse recently dug up by a resurrectionist.

The horses were grateful to get out of the storm and gave Buttons and Red no trouble as they were led to stalls and rubbed down with sacking before Buttons forked them hay and gave each a scoop of oats.

Buttons had been silent, deep in thought as he worked with the team, until he said, "Red, what do you make of that reverend feller?"

"He's a strange one."

"You mean three pickles short of a full barrel?"

Red nodded. "Something like that."

"He said that there's profit in the dead man. Did you hear him say that?"

"More or less."

"Do you believe him?"

"Enough to listen to what he has to say."

"Here," Buttons said, turning his head to look behind him. "He ain't a ghost, is he?"

"A what?"

"A ghost, a spook, a revenant . . . whatever the hell you want to call it."

Red smiled. "No, I think he's just a downright peculiar feller. Man must be crazy to live in a ghost town."

Buttons pointed a finger. "See, you said it, Red. You said *ghost.*"

"I was speaking about the town, not the preacher. Let's go hear what he has to say."

CHAPTER TWO

The Reverend Solomon Palmer led Red Ryan and Buttons Muldoon to a cabin behind a tumbledown rod and gun store that still bore a weathered sign above its door. The thunderstorm had passed but had left a steady rain in its wake, and when Red and Buttons stepped inside, their slickers streamed water onto the dirt floor.

Palmer lit a smoking oil lamp, and a mustard-yellow glow filled the cabin. Red noticed that a well-used Winchester stood in a gun rack, and hanging beside it, a holstered Colt exhibited even more wear. He decided right there and then that there was more to the Reverend Palmer than met the eye. The man might be a parson now, but that hadn't always been the case . . . unless the firearms belonged to someone else.

A log fire burned in a stone fireplace flanked by two rockers. A small dining table with a pair of wooden chairs completed the furnishings. Above the mantel hung a portrait of a stern-looking man in the uniform of a Confederate brigadier general. The old soldier had bushy gray eyebrows and a beard that spread over his chest, and he bore a passing resemblance to Palmer. The cabin had an adjoining room, but the door was closed. The place smelled of pipe smoke and vaguely of blended bourbon but had no odor of sanctity that Red associated with the quarters of the clergy.

"Help yourself to coffee," Palmer said, nodding to the pot on the fire. "Cups on the shelf." The man removed his top hat, revealing thinning black hair. He set the hat down on the table. "Are you sharp set?"

"We could eat," Buttons said, a man who could always eat.

"Soup in the pot, bowls on the shelf, spoons on the table," Palmer said. "Eat and drink and then we'll talk about Morgan Ford."

The coffee was hot, black, and bitter, but Red found the soup surprisingly good. "Good soup," he said after he'd finished his bowl.

"I spent some time as a trail cook for old Charlie Goodnight," Palmer said. "I learned how to make bacon and beans and beef soup, because it was one of Charlie's favorites."

A cook could acquire a Colt and a Winchester, but Red figured he'd never use them the way Palmer's had been used. He still put a question mark against the reverend's name.

Buttons burped more or less politely and then said, "Tell us about the dead man in the box."

"Brother Morgan Ford came to Cottondale ten years ago, hoping to outrun a reputation as a gunman, and in that quest, he succeeded," Palmer said. "He built the saloon, but when the town died, Morgan took sick and died with it. Him and me, we were the only two left. I remained to take care of him in his last weeks, as was my Christian duty."

"How come the town died?" Red said. "Looks like it was a nice enough place with a church an' all."

"At one time it was," Palmer said. "But then the farmers who wanted to grow cotton here discovered that the cost of irrigating the land ate up any profits. One by one, defeated by the desert, they pulled stakes and left until only Morgan and me remained. Three days ago the heart trouble finally took him and he gasped his last."

"And lost me a fare," Buttons said.

"You still have a fare, Mr. Muldoon," Palmer said. "When Morgan lay dying he told me to contact his only living relative, a niece by the name of Luna Talbot, and ask her if she would bury him. Needless to say, I was surprised that Brother Ford had a niece, but using El Paso as my mailing address, since mail is no longer delivered to Cottondale, I wrote to her and she replied and said yes. She wants his body and will pay to have it sent to her. Apparently, Mrs. Talbot has a successful ranch due south of us on this side of the Rio Bravo. In every way, she seems to be an admirable young lady."

"And you want us to take the body to her? Is that it, Reverend?" Buttons said.

"Yes, I do. That is why you're here. I contacted the Abe Patterson company in San Angelo and made all the arrangements."

Buttons shook his head. "Nobody made arrangements with me that involved picking up a dead man. The Abe Patterson and Son Stage and Express Company doesn't carry corpses, and if it ain't there already, I plan to write that down in the rule book."

"Five hundred dollars, Mr. Muldoon," Palmer said.

"Huh?" Buttons said.

"Five hundred dollars, Mr. Muldoon." A heavy cloudburst rattled on the cabin's tin roof, adding to the reverend's suspenseful pause. "That is the amount of money the grieving Mrs. Luna Talbot is willing to pay for the safe delivery of her loved one."

"I reckon that from here it's around two hundred miles to the ranch you're talking about," Buttons said. "That's a fifty-dollar fare."

"And indeed, you are correct, Mr. Muldoon. The Patterson stage company gets fifty and you keep the rest." The reverend smiled slightly. "Because of the unique nature of the . . . ah . . . delivery, Mrs. Talbot is prepared to be generous."

"Red, what do you reckon?" Buttons said.

Before Red could answer, Palmer said, "I have a sufficient length of good hemp rope to lash the coffin to the top of the stage. We can make it secure so that Brother Morgan can take his final journey in peace."

"Without falling off, you mean?" Red asked.

"Precisely," Palmer said.

Buttons and Red exchanged a glance, and finally Buttons nodded. "Get the rope, Reverend."

CHAPTER THREE

"Damn, but Brother Morgan must've been a heavy man," Buttons Muldoon said, breathing hard as he looked up at the coffin lashed to the top of the Concord. "Coffin weighed a ton if it weighed an ounce."

As always, the Reverend Solomon Palmer was unheeding of the rain that pounded on him. "No, he wasn't. His illness had faded him to a nubbin. It's the coffin that's heavy. It came from El Paso and is crafted from the best walnut available with real silver furniture. Of course, it's lead lined to help preserve our departed brother until he reaches his loved ones."

"He might have been more considerate of the rannies that had to lift it," Buttons said.

"Lead was his dying request," Palmer said. "Brother Morgan wanted to look as fresh as possible when he reached the Talbot ranch."

"Well, he's got me all tuckered out," Red Ryan said. "I got to get some shut-eye."

"Me too," Buttons said.

The Reverend Palmer's hospitality did not extend

to a bed for the night. "Your best bet is the saloon. It's still got a good roof."

"And a hard floor," Buttons said.

"I'm sure you'll be snug enough," Palmer said. "When will you leave in the morning, Mr. Muldoon?"

"At first light." Buttons looked up at the black sky. "Come rain or shine."

"Crackerjack!" Palmer said. "Well, gentlemen, I'll see you in the morning." He turned and left, walking toward his cabin, followed by Buttons's baleful gaze.

"Red, I don't trust that feller. Do you?"

"He has a Colt and a Winchester. Hard to trust a preacher who's armed to the teeth."

"Red, so are we," Buttons said. "Armed to the teeth, I mean."

"Yeah, but we're honest men."

"Are we?" Buttons said.

"Hell yeah," Red said. "Most of the time."

Red Ryan figured he'd had enough rest and rose to his feet. Lulled by the patter of rain on the roof, he'd slept a couple of hours until Buttons's snores, loud as a ripsaw running through knotty pine, woke him. He hadn't a chance in hell of getting back to sleep.

He picked up his plug hat from the floor, settled it on his head, and stepped through darkness to the saloon door that he opened wide, breathing in the storm-washed night air. The rain had petered out and a gibbous moon rode high in the sky. Somewhere close, a pair of hunting coyotes talked to the stars. Red built a cigarette and walked onto the boardwalk. The street was a sluggish river of brown mud that oozed through a town of black shadows, silent as the grave.

He lit his cigarette, walked along the boardwalk a ways, and then returned to the saloon door and Buttons Muldoon's snores. He flicked his glowing butt into the street and reached for the makings again. His hand never reached the pocket of his buckskin shirt . . . halted in the air by the double blast of a shotgun that shattered the quiet into a thousand slivers of sound.

"What the hell?" Buttons yelled.

"Scattergun," Red replied.

Boots thudded on the saloon floor and Buttons joined Red on the boardwalk. "Where?"

"Sounded like it came from the reverend's place."

"Is he shooting at coyotes?"

"I guess not, since he doesn't have a shotgun. Unless he has one stashed away somewhere."

"Well, I guess we should go find out," Buttons shook his head. "Damn it, I'm tired, Red. I haven't slept a wink. Not a wink."

"Me neither."

Red Ryan noticed two things when he reached Solomon Palmer's cabin. The first was that the door was wide open and hadn't been forced and the second was the preacher's body sprawled on the floor under the gun rack. His Colt and Winchester were gone.

"He died trying to reach his gun when he was shot," Buttons said. "Looks like two barrels of buckshot in the back cut his suspenders right quick."

"Seems like." After a few moments of thought, Red said. "I think the reverend knew his killer and opened the door for him. Then something passed between them that scared Palmer and he attempted to get his gun. Then *bang! bang!* and he bought the farm."

Instinctively Buttons dropped his hand to his holstered Colt. "Hell, Red, the killer could still be around here."

"I doubt it. I reckon he stashed his horse close, walked up on the cabin, knocked on the door, and Palmer let him inside. After he killed the preacher, he left by the way he came and lit a shuck."

"I'll take a look around anyway," Buttons said.

After a few moments, Red heard Buttons yell, "I am a legal representative of the Abe Patterson and Son Stage and Express Company. I order you to show yourself."

A couple of minutes passed, and then Buttons stepped back inside. He shook his head. "There's nobody out there."

"Doesn't surprise me. This was a quick, efficient job. I'd say the killer is pretty good at what he does. Buttons, stay where you are. Now look over there by the fireplace."

"I'm looking."

"What do you see on the floor?"

"Somebody's muddy footprints."

"They're the killer's tracks," Red said. "Look at Palmer's feet. He'd taken off his shoes after he came in the cabin. It seems the killer stepped to the fire to warm himself and then said something that scared the reverend."

"And as you said, Palmer was trying for his gun when he was shot," Buttons said.

"That's how it shapes up." Red stared hard at the prints. "Small feet, small man." Then, after a pause for thought, "Unless Palmer was killed by a woman."

"Nah, a woman couldn't do that—shotgun a man in the back," Buttons said. "It ain't in their nature."

"Some women could."

Buttons smiled. "Yeah, a woman like Hannah Huckabee could, and no mistake."

"The question is why?" Red said. "I mean, why gun down a preacher?"

"A preacher with a Winchester and a Colt is a mighty strange kind of sin buster. You said so yourself, Red."

"Yeah, I did, didn't I? All right, let's look around. See if we can find anything that might tell us more about Palmer."

The search of the cabin proved fruitless, except for a silver pocket watch, a Barlow folding knife, and a wallet with forty-five dollars in notes and a *carte de visite* of a half-naked woman named Roxie taken in Austin's Rendezvous Gentlemen's Club.

"A shapely lady is Roxie, ain't she?" Buttons said, studying the photo.

"She sure is." Red shook his head and looked at the body on the floor. "Solomon Palmer, Buttons is right. You were a mighty peculiar breed of sin buster."

CHAPTER FOUR

More sleep was out of the question, so Buttons Muldoon ripped up floorboards and lit a fire in the saloon stove for coffee. A coffee-drinking man, he kept a sooty pot and a supply of Arbuckle for himself and passengers. Just after first light he hitched up the team and set Palmer's mare loose, telling her to run with the mustangs. "Now what do we do with the reverend's body?"

Red said. "I guess we should bury him."

"It's the decent thing to do, huh?" Buttons said.

"Seems like. Us being decent-minded folks and all."

"Speak for yourself," Buttons said. "I'm keeping that picture of Roxie." He sighed. "I saw shovels in the livery. But we'll drive over there. I ain't walking through a foot of mud."

Under a flaming sky, Red threw a couple of shovels on top of the stage and then climbed into his accustomed place in the driver's box. Buttons gathered up the reins and glanced behind him. His eyes bugged. "What the hell?"

Red turned and saw what Buttons saw—a column

of fire and smoke rising into the air in the direction of the Palmer cabin.

"Has the preacher come back to life and set his place on fire?" Buttons said.

"I doubt it," Red said. "More like somebody is covering his tracks by destroying the evidence. Let's drive up there and take a look-see."

Buttons had a difficult time turning the team in the muddy street. When they finally got close to the Palmer place, the cabin was ablaze and a nearby store was also on fire. Despite the recent rain, like most Western towns Cottondale was tinder dry and the conflagration was spreading fast. It had already started fires in buildings across the street.

"No need for a burying," Buttons said.

"Seems like," Red said. "Now get the hell out of here before we burn up with the whole damned town."

Buttons saw the danger and didn't need to use his whip to get the team moving. The closeness of the fires, burning smell, and the red-hot cinders cartwheeling through the air had the horses spooked, and the stage rocked along the street. Great globs of mud flew from the wheels, the coffin bouncing as though Brother Morgan was doing his best to get out. Black smoke shot through with streaks of scarlet hung in the air like a stranded thundercloud as Buttons drove the big Concord through a roaring tunnel of fire and finally reached the town limits. Suddenly he was in the clear, racing across a sandy flat scattered with soap weed, prickly pear, and mesquite. He reined the team back to a walk and then turned, heading south. Red looked to his right and saw that half the town was ablaze, and the remaining half would surely follow.

"Red, is the box still secure?" Buttons said.

Red tested the coffin ropes and said, "Yeah, it's still tight."

"I'll be glad when we deliver the damn thing." Buttons said. "Him jumping around up there makes me think of death and judgment day." He glanced over his shoulder. "Ain't much left of Cottondale."

Red nodded. "And I guess there ain't much left of the Reverend Palmer."

The afternoon came with an oppressive heat, the sun like a ball of flame in the blue sky. The air was still, without the slightest hint of a breeze, and the day lay heavily on Red and Buttons, the ornate coffin a constant and baleful presence. Around them, the land was dry and stony. Here and there were patches of short, sparse grass and stands of creosote bush, scrub brush, mesquite, and cactus. In the distance, purple mountains that neither Buttons nor Red could name looked cool. A parched-mouthed man might fancy that hidden among their craggy peaks were hanging valleys where, with a soft *plop!* lime-green frogs dived through ferns into ice-cold pools.

But Buttons and Red were far from the mountains.

That part of Texas was a vast, inhospitable wilderness, dry as a bone, that travelers crossed only by necessity on their way to somewhere else. As the sun dropped in the sky, Buttons took a three-mile detour to the west and found to his relief that Bill Stanton's station still stood, apparently unharmed by the recent Apache troubles.

"Strange cargo, Buttons," Stanton said as he stood in front of his cabin, watching the stage drive in. Then, "Howdy, Red."

Buttons nodded as he applied the brake. "The first time and the last, Bill. The man in the box went by the name of Morgan Ford and we're taking him to his loved ones for burial down the Brazos way."

"Well, at least he won't eat much," Stanton said, smiling. "Got a nice team for you, Buttons, four of them grays. Good horses, grays, if you can stand the smell."

"Grays don't bother me none," Buttons said. "They still smell better than people."

"Ain't that the truth," Stanton said. "Killed me a hog recent, so I got a nice pork stew in the pot and biscuits to go along with it. You staying the night?"

"Nope, gonna eat and run, Bill. The sooner me and Red get rid of the damned coffin, the better."

"Well, change the team and come inside. The grub will be waiting," Stanton said. He was a tall, thin man with a sparse black beard and sad, hound-dog eyes. "How's ol' Abe Patterson?"

"Prospering, the last I seen him," Buttons said.

"He still living with that high-yeller gal?"

"Sophie?"

"Is that her name?"

"Yeah, Sophie. They seem happy enough."

"Glad to hear it. Red, come inside. You look all tuckered out."

Red nodded. "I guess so. I haven't been sleeping well real recent."

Stanton hesitated. "Before we go inside, there's one thing you and Buttons should know. I got Charlie Brownlow in there. You gents got a problem with that?"

"You mean the Nacogdoches gunslinger they all talk about?" Buttons said. "I heard he never goes west of the Colorado."

"Well, a hemp posse will chase a man west of hell if it's determined enough, and Charlie says that posse was determined enough," Stanton said. "It seems he shot a rancher's son down Caldwell way and the boy's old man took it hard. Charlie had a clear-cut choice . . . get hung or cross the Colorado. He chose to cross the Colorado."

"So how come Brownlow is here, Bill?" Red asked him.

"Me and Charlie go back a ways, to a time when I was studying on taking up the bank-robbing profession. Later, we wrote back and forth, and I told him I'd given up on the outlaw impulse and was running this here stage station. Well, a week ago he showed up on my doorstep and he's been here since."

"They say Brownlow's killed thirty men," Buttons said.

"That's what they say," Stanton said. "Charlie may stay east of the Colorado, but he gets around."

"He won't have any trouble from us. What a man does for a living is his business."

"Wise words, Red," Stanton said. "Now, are we gonna stay out here jawing, or will you come inside?"

"I reckon I'll make a trial of that stew. I'm coming inside."

"Leave the scattergun with the stage, Red," Stanton said. "It could signal that a man has less than peaceful intentions."

"I'll take it. Red, you go ahead and eat. I'll change the team and then join you." As Red climbed down from the driver's perch, Buttons said, "That Brownlow feller may have killed thirty men, but don't let him give you any sass or backtalk, you hear?"

Red said, "Sure thing. I'll keep that in mind."

CHAPTER FIVE

The interior of the Stanton cabin had a hard-packed dirt floor and was roomy enough to accommodate a long table and benches where stage passengers could eat their hurried meals, a fireplace where a stewpot and a coffeepot simmered, and a curtained-off area in one corner with a hand-printed sign tacked to the wall that read LADIES ONLY. The place smelled of cooking meat, coffee, and the ever-present aroma of leather, horses, gun oil, and man sweat.

A tall man, dressed in the frock coat and brocade vest of the frontier gambler, sat in the rocker by the fire, a holstered Colt and cartridge belt draped over his left shoulder.

When Red Ryan stepped inside, the man rose, pointedly buckled his gun belt around his hips, and stood with his elbow on the mantel, the hard planes of his face composed but his intense black eyes watchful.

Red was prepared to be sociable. Rightly figuring that the tall man was Charlie Brownlow, he nodded and said, "Howdy."

Brownlow's gaze moved from the scuffed toes of

the intruder's boots to the crown of his plug hat, lingered a moment on his holstered revolver, and then summed Red up, dismissing him with a contemptuous grimace that could have been a smile.

Bill Stanton had been around gunmen before, and he headed off any possibility of trouble with a smile and a friendly, "Sit yourself down, Red. Stew's coming right up. I got buttermilk. You like buttermilk?"

"Coffee will do just fine." Red sat at the table. Then, the devil in him, he said to Brownlow, "A fair piece off your home range, ain't you, Charlie?"

Brownlow's face froze in an expression of disbelief. It was an affront to his touchy, gunman's pride that this nobody, a shotgun guard for a pissant stage line, would address him directly and use his given name in such a familiar fashion. When he found his voice, he said, "What's it to you?"

Red smiled. "Nothing, Charlie. You mean nothing to me. I'm just making conversation, is all, you being such a friendly feller."

"Mister, I ain't your friend," Brownlow said. "So shut your trap."

"Anything you say, Charlie." Red looked down at the bowl of stew Stanton placed in front of him. "Ah, that smells good, Bill. Glad there's something smells nice in here."

Charlie Brownlow was on the prod that night at Stanton's Station, and there are some, including a few historians, who say he would have pushed Red Ryan into a draw . . . but the cards didn't fall that way. At least, not then. From outside, Buttons Muldoon said something, his voice raised in surprise. A young female answered, and Buttons laughed and hollered, "Well, don't that beat all!"

A moment later he walked inside with a pretty woman in tow.

"Red!" he yelled. "You'll never guess who this is. Not in a million years you won't."

Red stopped chewing and said, "No, I don't suppose I will."

"Damn it all, Red, it's Roxie!" Buttons reached into his shirt pocket and produced the carte de visite. "Lookee. She was younger then, but it's her."

"She's wearing a heap more clothes, but that's her all right," Red said, nodding.

"That was me when I was eighteen," the woman said. "It's me no longer. The name's Leah Leighton."

Red said. "Right glad to make your acquaintance, ma'am. It's a small world, isn't it?"

Then, from Charlie Brownlow came, "Hey, driving man. Let me see that picture."

Buttons hesitated, but Red said, "Let Charlie see it, Buttons. He's downright testy this evening and needs some cheering up."

But Buttons shook his head. "No, this ain't for the likes of you, Charlie." He handed the photograph to the girl. "Here, you keep it."

Leah smiled her thanks and slipped Roxie into the pocket of her ankle-length duster. Under the coat, she wore canvas pants that had been tailored to fit her long, slim legs and black vest over a white, collarless shirt. Spurred boots and a flat-brimmed hat with a low crown completed her outfit, and around her hips hung a cartridge belt with a blue Colt in the cross-draw holster.

Red thought the girl had been alluring as Roxy, but despite the masculine duds, he figured she looked even prettier as the grown woman Leah Leighton.

Brownlow was seething. Buttons Muldoon's snub had irritated him, and he stood by the fireplace and glowered, his hand very close to his gun.

Bill Stanton felt the tension in the air as he stepped to the table where Leah sat. "Young lady, we cater to the stagecoach trade, but you can eat here for two bits." He smiled. "I won't ask why you're in this wild country without a male chaperon."

"Please don't," Leah said. "What do you have to eat?"

"Pork stew and buttermilk to drink, if you like buttermilk."

"Any bread?" Leah said.

"Sure. A loaf of sourdough fresh baked just three days ago."

"Do you have butter?"

"Yes, I have salted butter. It ain't fresh from the churn, but it's still good."

"Bread, butter, and coffee, then. Two bits' worth."

Stanton seemed disappointed. "No pork stew?"

"No pork stew," Leah said. "It sounds disgusting."

"It isn't so bad, once you get used to it." Red placed his spoon on his empty plate.

Then it happened . . . Charlie Brownlow decided to bring things to a head. It was time the uppity shotgun man was taken down a peg or three.

"The lady doesn't want to hear your opinion, on pork stew or anything else," he said. "So, until you pull out of here, keep your trap shut like I already told you."

A redheaded man will only take so much, and Brownlow had crossed the line.

"You making war talk, Charlie?" Red's green eyes suddenly turned cold.

"Not just talking . . . but I aim to back up my words real soon."

If a pin had dropped in the room, everyone would have heard it.

Leah Leighton broke the silence. She rose and said, "Let him be, Charlie. He's ferrying the dead."

Red didn't move. "Ma'am, keep out of this. This is between me and Charlie."

"Listen to the man, lady," Brownlow said. Then, his face twisted into a leer. "Later, when he's dead, I'll deal with you."

"Drop it, Charlie," Buttons said. "We want no trouble."

"Too bad, because you got it," Brownlow said, pushing it again, the words of a born killer supremely confident in his gun skills.

"Mister, I told you these men are ferrying the dead. Let them be."

"Missy, sit down and shut your mouth," Brownlow said. "I'll tell you when to open it."

"Do you really want to kill a man so badly?" Leah said.

"Sure, I do. It's been a while and a killing keeps a man sharp, gives him snap, know what I mean?"

Stanton said, his voice sounding hollow, "Sit down and have a drink, Charlie. Red Ryan is a good man and he has friends here."

"Then his friends can die with him," Brownlow said. His eyes glittered, no longer quite sane.

"They're ferrymen," Leah said. "I won't let you harm them." Her next words dropped into the quiet like pieces of marble falling on glass. "I don't want to kill you, Charlie, so don't push it any further."

The gunman could have reacted in many ways, ut he chose to brush the woman's warning aside as thing of little merit . . . and drew down on Red.

Brownlow was fast. He cleared leather, but his gun asn't yet level when Leah Leighton's bullet slammed ıto him, a center chest hit that staggered him. His ıce a mask of fury and disbelief, he turned on Leah nd tried to get his work in, but the girl saw the anger and fired twice, handling her revolver with mazing speed and dexterity. Two shots, two hits, one o the chest, the other to the belly. A man can't take hat amount of lead and still stand. Brownlow's gun lropped from his hand, and he went to his knees, his yes on Leah as he tried to accept that he was dying ike a dog on the dirt floor of a cabin on the edge of ıowhere . . . at the hands of a woman. The truth hit ıim like a fist in the gut just a second before the dark-ıess closed in on him. He groaned and then fell on ıis face, as dead as he was ever going to be.

Red had drawn, but Brownlow was dead and the langer was past. Red dropped his Colt into the hol-ster and watched Leah reload her revolver. "Lady, somebody taught you the draw and shoot. He taught you real good."

"*She* taught me real good, not *he*," Leah said. She looked at Brownlow's sprawled body, scarlet blood pooling under his chest. "He was notified. He was warned to leave the ferrymen be." She reached into her pants pocket and then laid two silver dollars on the table. "Bury him decent, stage station man."

Bill Stanton was incredulous. "Lady you . . . you killed Charlie Brownlow. Hell, even Dallas Stouden-mire walked mighty quiet around him."

Leah nodded. "Strange you should say that. I kne
Dallas, knew him well. He was a two-gun man, and
remember how fast he was, but he didn't come clo
to me. One time, back in the summer of 'eighty i
El Paso, a couple of years before he was killed, he to
me that women can't shoot a Colt .45. That we don
have the wrists for it. I bet him fifty dollars that
could outshoot him, and he lost the bet." She smile
"As far as I recall, I heard that Charlie Brownlow w
a bully and a braggart, and he wasn't the shooti
Dallas Stoudenmire was back then . . . or I am now.

Stanton shook his head. "Lady, I ain't fool enoug
to argue with you. Buttons, will you help me carr
Charlie to the woodshed? It ain't decent, him lyin
here."

"And when you come back, I still want my coffe
and bread and butter," Leah said. "Two bits' worth.

After Buttons and Stanton carried the body out
side, the woman sat at the table again.

Red leaned back in his chair. "You may have save
my life tonight."

"Think nothing of it," Leah said. "Charlie had the
drop on you. I had to kill him, ferryman. I had no
choice."

"However it happened, I'm beholden to you.
Where are you headed?"

"South."

The clipped tone of Leah's voice discouraged
other questions, but Red ignored it. "Ma'am, since
Mr. Muldoon and me are traveling south, you're
welcome to ride on the Patterson stage."

"I ride alone," the woman said. "But thank you for the offer. You are most kind."

It was strange, Red decided . . . exchanging pleasantries with a beautiful woman who'd just killed one of the most dangerous gunmen on the frontier. Stranger still, Leah Leighton seemed relaxed, at ease with herself, and the implication was obvious . . . that she'd killed a man before. Other Western women carried guns and had gained a measure of infamy. He brought to mind Calamity Jane Canary and Belle Starr, but they were not known as shootists. He did recall a time when a drunk teamster by the name of Tobey Williams tried to cut a whore in a Fort Worth cathouse. The woman, called either Nancy Morrison or Mulligan, drew a .32 caliber Remington-Elliot pepperbox and emptied all four barrels into Tobey, who was dead by the time he hit the floor. Longhair Jim Courtright, who was the city sheriff at the time, said he could have covered the four bullet holes in Tobey's chest with a playing card and hailed Nancy as "Some kind of a *pistolero*."

Maybe that was it. Leah Leighton said she'd been taught to shoot by a woman. She may have learned her gun handling at the Rendezvous Gentleman's Club. Stranger things had happened.

Bill Stanton served Leah Leighton her bread and butter on a blue plate and her coffee in a china cup. He also offered the sanctuary of the ladies' corner where she could sleep that night, should she feel fatigued.

Leah ate the bread and butter, drank the coffee,

and refused Stanton's offer of accommodation "Thank you, kindly, but I'm riding on."

"In the dark?" Stanton said.

"I think I can find my way due south. The stars are out."

"The offer of riding in the Patterson stage still stands," Red said.

"For twenty dollars," Buttons added.

"As my guest." Red angled his driver an irritated look.

Leah smiled. "Thank you, but no. I'd rather ride. Oh, look!" She rose from the table, picked up a little calico cat that was crossing the floor, and hugged it to her breast.

For its part, the cat seemed glad of the attention and purred.

"What's her name, Mr. Stanton?" Leah said.

The man shrugged. "She doesn't have a name. She comes and goes, and I feed her sometimes."

"Then since you're such a pretty kitty and so sweet, I hereby name you Precious." Leah said. She kissed the cat on the top of its head. "But I have to leave you. Where I'm going there already is a kitty, a cookhouse kitty, but he's mean and growly and you wouldn't like it there." She returned the calico to the floor and turned to Stanton. "How much do I owe you for the grub and the hay and oats for my horse?"

Stanton smiled. "Nothing, not a red cent, dear lady. It's on the house."

Buttons and Red stared at the station agent in amazement. He'd never, in all the time they'd known him, given anybody anything on the house, not even a cup of coffee.

"Then again, thank you for your kindness," Leah said. "I'm sorry about what happened here tonight, Mr. Stanton, but Charlie Brownlow called it."

"That's what I'll tell the Hudspeth County sheriff," Stanton said. "And the Texas Rangers." He nodded his head and repeated what the woman had just said. "Charlie Brownlow called it."

Leah Leighton smiled. "Good. Now I must be on my way." She stepped closer to Red. "Her name is Luna Talbot, Mr. Ryan."

Red frowned his puzzlement. "Who?"

"The woman who taught me to shoot. Her name is Luna Talbot and I'm not a patch on her with a Colt's gun."

"Wait up there, missy," Buttons said. "That's who we're taking the dead man to. She's his niece."

"That's right, ferryman," Leah said. "You're Charon, and you'll take Morgan Ford across the River Styx."

"Huh?" Buttons said, confused. "Hell no, I'm not. I'm Patrick Muldoon and I'm taking him to the Brazos."

Leah laid her slender hand on Buttons's shoulder and said, "The Brazos will be just fine." She stepped to the door to leave, but Red's voice stopped her.

"Miss Leighton, earlier tonight were you in Cottondale during the thunderstorm?"

Leah's back stiffened and she turned slowly. "Some questions are best not asked."

Before Red could speak again, she opened the door and walked outside into the silence of the moon-dappled night.

CHAPTER SIX

The stage's sidelamps glowed amber in the gloom as Buttons Muldoon urged the team across the rocky, cactus-strewn flat. To the west, lost in darkness, rose the rugged Finlay peaks, where the Old Ones, the ancient and long-forgotten Indians who once lived there, had left their mysterious mark on the sandstone cliff faces. The moon was still high over the mountains, and it silvered the coats of the coyotes in the draws as they paused in their hunt to stare at the coach as it rumbled by, pluming dust.

"So . . . what do you think, Red?" Buttons said.

"About what?"

"About Leah Leighton. You think she done for the Reverend Solomon Palmer?"

Red Ryan took time to light the cigarette he'd been holding between his lips for the past few minutes and then said through a cloud of blue smoke, "I don't think Palmer was a reverend, and yeah, I'm sure she shot him."

"Murdered him, more like," Buttons said. "The question is, why?"

Red said. "Maybe Palmer was headed for his gun and Leah had no choice but to trigger him. I mean, that's possible, ain't it?"

"It's possible, but what could lay between them that would lead to a killing?" Buttons said.

Red shook his head. "I have no idea. I can't even make a guess."

"Me neither," Buttons said, his eyes probing the gloom ahead. "It's a great mystery."

Red smiled and rapped on the coffin behind him. "I bet he knows the answer."

"Yeah, I'd say he does, but he ain't talking."

At first light, Buttons rested the team and then broke out the grub sack. He and Red shared stale sourdough bread and cold bacon and then each took a swig of whiskey as a morning heart-starter.

Buttons used his gloved hand to wipe crumbs off his mustache and his hand froze in place when he saw the riders coming in from the east, three men on tall horses. He looked at Red, a question on his face.

"Yeah, I see them. Looks like they mean business."

"What kind of business?"

"They'll let us know, I'm sure.

Buttons closed his mouth and then opened it again. "Rangers maybe? They might be Rangers."

"Could be." Red placed the shotgun across his thighs. "I guess we'll find out soon enough."

A minute later the riders proved they were not Rangers. A bullet shot from a rifle spanged off the wrought-iron armrest of the driver's-seat, and a second split the air inches from Red's nose.

He jerked back in alarm. Damn, those boys were good!

Buttons had that same thought and said urgently, "Let them come, Red. We got nothing they want."

"Except our scalps."

CHAPTER SEVEN

Even if they used the shotgun and then went to their revolvers, it was a fight they couldn't win without taking lead themselves. Red knew it and so did Buttons. The best course was to be downright sociable and see what happened.

They let the riders come in at a walk, three men on blood horses dressed in the rough garb of the frontier. Their oiled rifles glinted in the sun. As they came closer Red saw that their saddles, boots, spurs, and gun leather were of the highest quality, probably Texas-made. As a rule, outlaws threw away their ill-gotten gains on whiskey, whores, and gambling, but they didn't stint when it came to spending considerable amounts of money on the tools of their trade—horses and firearms. The three hard-faced men who spread out as they approached the stage were no exception.

When they were within talking distance, Buttons, mighty affable when he had to be, said, "Howdy, boys. Shaping up to be a hot one today, huh?"

A rider with thick, black eyebrows and a huge

cavalry mustache grinned . . . no, he didn't . . . he snarled, showing teeth. "You, shotgun messenger, toss that Greener away and then sit on your hands."

"Red, oblige the man," Buttons said. "He asked you real nice."

"Listen to your driver, feller," Big Mustache said. "I see you even think about making a play, I'll shoot you right offen your perch."

"That's telling him, Hank," said another man, a towhead with crafty eyes.

Two rifles were trained on Red and he knew he faced a stacked deck. He dropped the scattergun over the side and said, "Abe Patterson ain't paying me enough."

"I call that being right sensible," said the man called Hank. "Now both of you unbuckle the belt guns and toss them. Real slow now, like molasses drippin' in January."

Buttons and Red did as they were told.

A breeze came up, bringing with it the mummy-dust smell of the warming desert.

"I hate to let you boys down," Buttons said, "but we ain't carrying money. All we got is a stiff in a box, a gent by the name of Morgan Ford."

"That's who we want," Hank said. "Now untie the coffin and ease it down."

Red said, "Hell, mister, what kind of road agent are you? There's no profit in a dead man."

"There's profit in that one," Hank said. "Now get him down from there."

"Hank, lookee," the towhead said, surprise spiking his voice.

Hank turned his head, following the other outlaw's eyes. Red did the same and saw what the road agents saw. Leah Leighton was riding toward the stage, her horse at a walk. She'd tipped her hat to the back of her head, held by a string around her neck, and her hair was unbound, cascading in glossy waves over her shoulders. Her top shirt buttons were undone, revealing the generous swell of her breasts, and her lips were parted in a come-and-take-me smile.

Hank grinned. "Boys, looks like we're gonna have us some fun today."

"Better we shoot them two on the stage afore the hootenanny starts," the towhead said.

"Yeah, sure Bob, after they get the coffin down," Hank said. Then, his grin widening, "Save our energy for better things."

"You two, untie that box and ease it down here," the towhead said.

"Go to hell." Red was poised, ready to jump from the stage and grab for his shotgun and die in one hell-firing moment of glory rather than get slaughtered like a sheep.

The third outlaw, who was yet to speak, raised his voice in sudden alarm. "No, Hank, leave her be!" he yelled. "She's poison. She's one of them Talbot ranch hellcats. I seen them hang a man for rustling one time, and they're all poison!"

To everyone's surprise, the good and the bad, the man swung his horse away from the stage and headed east at a dead run, trailing a ribbon of dust.

"What the hell?" Hank yelled, startled.

With less than fifty yards to cover, Leah Leighton's

paint quarter horse was suddenly coming on at the gallop. Colt in hand, the woman let out a high-pitched shriek, half war cry, half banshee wail, and cut loose . . . and at once men's lives were measured in seconds.

Hank took a bullet while he was still trying to sort out what the hell was happening. Hit in the chest, he swayed in the saddle and attempted to bring his unhandy rifle to bear. Leah shot him again as she barreled past, then her eyes instantly shifted focus to the shocked towhead. The man recovered and triggered his Winchester, but he fired too hastily and too high. The bullet cracked air inches above Leah's head. A split second later, the towhead's eyes crossed as though he tried to see the chunk of .45 lead that had entered the bridge of his nose and shattered into his braincase. Bob Roper was a rapist and murderer, and his dying scream echoed all the way to the portals of hell.

When the first shot was fired, Red had jumped from the stage and dived for his shotgun. By the time he got to his feet, the gunplay was over and Leah Leighton was in hot pursuit of the outlaw who'd fled.

"Red, over here," Buttons Muldoon called out. "This feller is breathing his last, but he's still alive."

Red joined the driver and looked down at Hank, who was coughing blood and dying hard, fright in his eyes.

"As a representative of the Abe Patterson and Son Stage and Express Company, I advise you that you'd best make peace with your God, mister," Red said.

"You took a bullet over a corpse in a coffin, and sure as hell that can't make your dying any easier."

The man struggled to speak, and then managed a smile, blood staining his teeth. "Lucky cuss," he said. And then his labored breathing stopped, and his open eyes stared into eternity.

Buttons shook his head. "I reckon that's the kind of luck a man can do without."

CHAPTER EIGHT

The Patterson stage was fifteen miles north of the Rio Bravo, following the southwest course of the Arroyo Diablo, when Buttons drew Red's attention to the dust cloud ahead of them.

"We're getting close to the Talbot ranch," Red said. "Could be cattle."

Buttons nodded. "Yeah, it could be, but keep the Greener close." He studied the land around him, a desert wilderness of rolling hills that supported wild oak mottes, scrub brush, cactus, and patches of prairie grass. "No sign of the Leighton gal, so we're on our own."

"I wonder if she caught that feller she was chasing."

"I bet she did, and I reckon by this time he's as dead as mutton in a stew," Buttons said.

"She saved our lives. Thinking back on it, I could have gunned one of those road agents, maybe the two of them, but—"

"Red, we were both dead men from the git-go," Buttons interrupted. "Sure, we could have rolled the dice and made a play, but them boys had us in their sights." He looked up at the blue arch of the sky.

"Yup, the gal saved our bacon and there's no buts or maybes about the thing."

"She could shoot, couldn't she?"

"And ride like a Comanche."

"Quite a woman, Red said."

"I reckon it would take quite a man to tame her," Buttons said.

Red smiled, shaking his head. "You'll find no takers in this direction."

"Too big a job for you, huh?"

"A dangerous job, I'd say. Would you like to argue with her about who dries the dishes?"

"Not me," Buttons said. "I value my skin too much." He looked ahead of him. "One, two, three . . . it looks to me like we're about to meet another . . . I'd say five wildcats."

"This has been a mighty strange trip."

"And getting stranger. Like a sidesaddle on a sow."

Ahead of the stage five riders had drawn rein, waiting. The women wore split riding skirts, boots, shirts, and wide-brimmed hats. Two carried sawn-off shotguns, the other three held Winchesters. All of them wore belt revolvers.

Buttons, ever the gallant cavalier, drove within five yards of the women, halted the team, and then stood in the box. He swept off his hat, bowed, then straightened. Smiling his most winning smile, he said, "I sure didn't expect to meet so many lovely prairie roses in this neck of the woods. Did you, Mr. Ryan?"

Red shook his head. "No, I sure didn't. As a representative of the Abe Patterson and Son Stage and Express Company, I can only say that in all my travels I've never seen the like."

That was a small lie.

Three of the younger ladies were indeed pretty, but the faces of the two oldest showed the ravages of time and hard living. Red had seen features like that before, mostly on prairie women worn out from years of backbreaking work and childbearing. But these women had not been farmers' wives. They looked like whores who had graduated from saloons and dance halls and ended up in hog ranches when they lost their looks. After the hog ranch, a fallen woman could fall no further. But someone had redeemed these women, cared for them, and given them a purpose in life. What that purpose might be, he had no idea . . . but he would find out soon enough.

The oldest woman, tall, thin with a lined face but no gray in her auburn hair, looked hard at Red. "So, you like what you see, huh, shotgun man?"

Red nodded and smiled, putting on his best bib and tucker. "Most assuredly, dear lady," he said. "As my colleague says, prairie roses, each and every one of you."

"Don't get any ideas, big boy. When you arrive at the Talbot ranch, see you keep it in your pants," the woman said. "And that also applies to you, Sailor."

"Ma'am, I'm not a sailor, though I wear a sailor's coat," Buttons said. "My name is Patrick Muldoon. You can call me Buttons. Most folks do."

"I'm not most folks," the woman said. She carried a Winchester, held upright on her right thigh and carried a bone-handled Colt high on her waist, horseman style. "Follow us. We'll reach the ranch in an hour, and supper will be ready." Her eyes moved to the coffin. "Is the stiff in there?"

"As far as we know," Buttons said. "We didn't look real recent. In fact, we didn't look at all."

"Did you bring the right one?" the woman said. "His name is, or was—"

"Morgan Ford," Red said.

"Huzzah for the shotgun man," the woman said. "He ain't as dumb as he looks."

"Ford was Luna Talbot's uncle." Red said, taking no offense.

"Yeah, he was something like that," the woman said. Then, after a pause, "My name is Corrine Walker. I'm one of Miss Talbot's hands."

"Right pleased to make your acquaintance, Miss Walker," Buttons said. "Ain't we, Red?"

"Overjoyed, I'd say."

"Yeah, you look it," Corrine said. "Now, sailor man, gee-up those nags and follow us."

Corrine Walker rode point while the others split into pairs and flanked the stage. Red tried smiling at them, especially the pretty ones, but they didn't smile back. In fact they ignored him, their whole attention fixed on the trail in front of and behind them.

"Right personable gals," Buttons said.

"And that's your idea of a good joke, right?"

"Yeah, it's a joke, but I'm wondering about something that's got me buffaloed," Buttons said.

Red looked at him. "Let me hear it."

"What the hell have we gotten ourselves into? That's what I've been wondering on."

"And it's got you buffaloed, right?"

"Damn right."

"Buttons, I don't know what we've gotten into, but I got a feeling that it isn't going to end well."

Buttons turned his shocked face to Red. "You really feel that? I mean, deep down inside feel that?"

"I sure do. And it's mighty troublesome."

CHAPTER NINE

The Talbot ranch looked like any other in Texas at the time, a low, one-story ranch house showing three windows to the front and a porch hung with several earthenware ollas, a barn, corrals, blacksmith's forge, bunkhouse, and a scattering of outbuildings. What made it different was that there was not a male face in sight. Even the cook who stepped out of the kitchen and threw away a basin of dishwater was a woman. She glared at the Patterson stage as it rolled past, but Red figured that cattle country cooks were an irascible breed, and he paid the woman no mind.

Buttons halted the team outside the ranch house, and within a few moments a crowd gathered, a dozen women dressed in range clothes with a few feminine touches like earrings and bracelets . . . and one of them was Leah Leighton, who spoke for the rest.

"Driver, stay where you're at until you're told to light and set," she said. "That goes for you as well, shotgun man."

"Real nice to see you again, ma'am." Red was prepared to be sociable. "Last I saw, you were flapping your chaps for the Pecos."

The woman's smile was slight. "I didn't need to ride that far. I'm a fair rifle shot."

As was his habit, Buttons cut right to the chase. "Hey, lady, how come all I see is females? Are there no grown men on this ranch?"

"Now and again a man rides by, and if he behaves himself we feed him and send him on his way," Leah said. "But only women work the Talbot."

"How come?" Buttons said.

"Maybe you'll find out, driving man. Maybe you won't." Leah turned and said, "Lucy, Alma and you, too, Eliza, get the coffin off the stage. Driver and shotgun man, you stay right where you're at."

"We'll help," Red said. "The box is heavy."

"No, you won't. The hands can manage it," Leah said.

Buttons smiled. "Red, leave it to the cowgirls."

Leah frowned. "Mister, we're punchers, drovers, hands, waddies, or whatever the hell you want to call us, but what we're not is *cowgirls.* Do I make myself clear?"

"Cow-women?" Buttons said. "Maybe so, huh?"

"Close, but no cigar," Leah said. "While you're here, to make yourself understood you can call us by our names."

"That suits me . . . Leah." Red said.

The segundo nodded. "Now I know why so many shotgun guards get plugged. Big mouths." One of the younger woman giggled, and Leah snapped, "Alma, get that damned coffin down like I told you."

"Where do you want it, boss?" Alma said.

"Take it into the toolshed for now. Mrs. Talbot will deal with it later."

After the women, with considerable effort, manhandled the coffin from the stage and carried it to the shed, Leah told Buttons and Red to climb down.

Both men were puzzled. A toolshed was a mighty unfriendly place to put a loved one.

"Miss Leah, I'd be obliged if I could feed my horses and let them rest for a spell," Buttons said. "Then we'll pick up our five hundred dollars and be on our way. The Patterson stage is always in the highest demand. Ol' Abe Patterson said that, and he's got it wrote down somewhere."

"You won't find passengers in this part of Texas, driving man," Leah said. "We're in the middle of a desert. Takes fifteen acres of range to support a single Hereford cow and a calf, and that's why everybody you meet is passing through. Nobody travels to or from Hudspeth County. Well, nobody honest, that is."

"And that's why we'll head north to El Paso," Buttons said. "The town has a Texas and Pacific railroad station and a Patterson stage depot. Bound to be plenty of folks looking to travel from there."

"Whatever you say," Leah said. "All right. You can put your team in the barn. Oats and hay are scarce, so go easy on both. Once you got your horses settled, wash up at the bunkhouse and then come see Mrs. Talbot about your money."

"I'd be right partial to some supper besides," Buttons said. "I'm feeling mighty gant."

"Luna Talbot won't send a guest away hungry," Leah said.

"We're guests?" Red asked.

"Yes, of a sort," Leah said. "At least, you're not enemies."

"And if we were, enemies?"

"You'd both be dead by now."

* * *

West Texas was a pitiless, sunburned land that waged all-out war on women. But Luna Talbot was winning the battle. She looked to be in her mid-thirties, a tall, beautiful woman who transformed a riding skirt, plain white shirt, and boots into regalia worthy of a queen. She wore no jewelry except for the wide, hammered silver bracelet she wore on her left wrist and a plain gold wedding band.

Red and Buttons paused in their ablutions and watched her as she stood in front of the house talking to Leah Leighton. The segundo asked a question, listened intently to the answer, and then nodded and left in the direction of the toolshed.

Luna watched her go, then turned and walked with a purposeful stride to Buttons and Red. She smiled. "I had the roller towel replaced in your honor." The woman stuck out a hand. "Luna Talbot. Welcome to my ranch."

Red and Buttons each shook the woman's hand, the first time either of them had clasped hands with a female, the dictate of Victorian etiquette then being that a man didn't touch a woman's body part unless he was married to her. Of course, in a brothel, that rule fell by the wayside. With that in mind, Red was at once suspicious about the real purpose of the Talbot ranch.

His misgivings were dispelled when Luna said, "A word of warning, gentlemen. No matter what they were in the past, my hands are ladies, and I expect them to be treated as such. No improper touching, please. No cursing, swearing, or suggestive language in their presence." She smiled, withdrawing the sting. "Not that I would expect that kind of behavior from men who work for the Patterson stage line."

"Madam," Buttons said, puffing up a little, "you are so right. Representatives of the Abe Patterson and Son Stage and Express Company are always polite and considerate around women. It's wrote down in the rule book."

"I'm so glad to hear it," Luna Talbot said. "Now, I'm sure Cook is putting supper on the table, and I believe we're having braised steak, potatoes and gravy, with apple pie for dessert." The woman's smile was dazzling. "After dinner we'll have coffee. I'll pay you what I owe, and after that I'm hanging a man. You have no need to attend."

CHAPTER TEN

The cook was surly, but the meal was excellent, though Red found he didn't have much of an appetite. Luna Talbot's almost casual mention of a hanging was weighing on him. As far as eating was concerned, Buttons took up the slack, but even he seemed several tones quieter than usual.

During supper, between silences, Luna talked about range conditions, how she'd sold the last of her longhorns and invested in Herefords, and how cattle prices had been disastrously low for the past three out of four years.

Never the soul of tact, Buttons stopped chewing long enough to mention the dead Morgan Ford and asked the woman when she planned to bury him. Then, smiling, "Or do you aim to keep him in the toolshed?"

"Soon," Luna said. "I'll lay poor Uncle Morgan to rest soon." After a pause for thought, she added, "Did you first meet my segundo in Cottondale?"

Red answered. "Leah Leighton, you mean? No, not in Cottondale. We met her later."

"Ah, yes, that would be when she saved you from road agents," Luna said.

Red said, bristling. "We could've handled that scrape ourselves. We were ready to open the ball."

Luna smiled. "Open the ball, huh? How interesting . . . that's not what Leah says."

Irritated, Red continued, "And talking about Leah, a man named Solomon Palmer got shot in Cottondale while we were there. He was posing as a preacher and told us he'd cared for Morgan when the man lay dying."

"Yes, I paid him for that and for making the arrangements to transport Uncle Morgan's body," Luna said.

Red used his fork to toy with the beef on his plate and then said without looking up, "Did Leah plug him?"

"Plug whom?" the woman said. Her beautiful face was defensive.

"Palmer, that's whom. He took a couple of barrels of buckshot in the back."

Luna Talbot fought a small battle with herself and then sighed. "Palmer tried to blackmail me. He planned to hold my uncle's body for ransom and tried to recruit Leah in his plan. When she refused, he went for his gun and she shot him."

"And then she set Palmer and the whole damn town on fire," Buttons said. "Why did she do that, I wonder?"

Luna shrugged. "It was a ghost town. It won't be missed, and neither will Solomon Palmer. Besides all that, some things are better kept from the law."

"Like evidence," Red said

Luna smiled. "Now you're being picky, Mr. Shotgun

Man. Leah was involved in a justified shooting, and I don't think a jury would see it any other way."

"Why was the little gal there in the first place?" Buttons said. "Good beef, by the way."

"Thank you. My cook, her name is Bessie Foley, was once a top chef in New Orleans," Luna said. "As for Leah, she was in Cottondale to make sure that Solomon Palmer did as he was paid to do—find a suitable coffin for Uncle Morgan and put him on the stage. But, as I already told you, he had other plans. Ah, here is Bessie with the pie. I guarantee that it's the best you've ever tasted."

And it was. And after it was eaten, Luna Talbot went to hang a man.

Red and Buttons left the house and stood out front in the waning day. From horizon to horizon the sky was a uniform crimson, like a roof of fire over the world. Singly and in pairs, the women drifted toward the barn, walking in a strange, glowing light. No one talked. The only sound was the dry whisper of the desert wind.

"Red, you think she'll go through with it, her being such a nice lady an' all?" Buttons said.

"I don't think Luna Talbot is such a nice lady. She said she'll hang a man, and I reckon she will." Red drew deep on his cigarette and slowly exhaled blue smoke. "What's in the coffin, Buttons? A stiff . . . or something else?"

"It was heavy," Buttons said. "It can only be Uncle Morgan."

"Maybe he's got pockets in his shroud."

"Holding what?" Buttons said.

"Hell if I know," Red said. "You want to go watch a hanging?"

"Last one we saw put me off hangings forever. I never did get over it."

Red said. "That was Big Bill Yearly's necktie party up Abilene way," he said. "As I recollect, we were there for the free beer."

"And do you recollect that the damn noose took his head clean off? It was a sight no Christian man should see."

"I reckon Bill dressed out at around three hundred pounds, and there was the root of the trouble. They should've used a thicker rope or a shorter fall."

"Big Bill was a nuisance right up to the very end, wasn't he?" Buttons said.

Red nodded. "Yeah, that's why they hung him, for being such a damned nuisance, getting drunk all the time."

"And for stealing chickens," Buttons said. "He did a lot of that, as I recall."

"I wonder what this one is being stretched for."

Buttons took in a deep breath, let it out in a rush, and then said, "I guess we should go find out, huh? It's kinda like a civic duty, ain't it?"

Red shrugged. "You could say that, but if you'd rather sit this one out, I'll understand."

"Nah, I'll go," Buttons said. "Anyhow, I don't think Mrs. Talbot will do it. Maybe she just wants to put the fear of God into the feller."

"Could be. I never saw a bunch of women hang a man before. Have you?"

"No, I never have. But one time in a Fort Worth cathouse I seen four whores beat a pimp to a bloody pulp, but he was a pissant pimp and they was big, healthy whores."

"Not the same as a hanging, is it?" Red's eyes were drawn to a small, flat-roofed outbuilding where Leah Leighton and two other women, all three with shotguns, prodded a man out of the doorway. "Buttons, let's go see what's happening."

Red's plug hat sat square on his head, making dark shadows of his eyes, and his holstered Colt hung on his hip. A tall, significant man, he walked with the easy confidence gun skill brings.

Leah greeted him with neither enthusiasm nor hostility. "This is no place for you, shotgun man."

"I came to see your prisoner," Red said. "Nine times out of ten when I see a man who's about to be hung, he's a friend of mine."

"Well, is he?" Leah said.

The condemned man was stocky, of medium height with the arrogant look of the bully about him. His hands and feet were shackled with clanking irons that forced him to walk with small, mincing steps. His face was bruised, one eye closed shut, his bottom lip split.

Red shook his head. "No, I don't know him."

"No surprise there," Leah said. "This animal has no friends."

He managed a thin smile. "You know that for sure, huh?"

"Damn right I do," Leah said. "His name is Barnaby Leighton, and a nightmare ago he was my husband, or what passed for one. Now, give us the road."

Red's face registered shocked surprise as the man said, "Help me, mister. These bitches are set on hanging me."

Leah and the others brushed past, and the man turned his head to Red and yelled, "Help me, damnit! Help me."

Red didn't speak. Leah Leighton was about to hang her husband, and there was nothing to say and nothing he could do about it, short of drawing down on the woman and ordering her to stop.

Button Muldoon's thin whisper in his ear predicted the likely result of that play. "Red, back away or you'll get your fool head blown off."

"He's nothing to me, but she's got to have a mighty good reason for hanging a man. Because he's her husband ain't one of them."

"I reckon many a woman would hang her husband if she could," Buttons said. "Sometimes just being his wife is reason enough."

"Strange talk coming from a confirmed bachelor." Red kept his eyes on the solemn procession making its way toward the barn where lamps glowed orange in the strange amber light.

"Women confide in a stage driver," Buttons said. "They tell him their darkest secrets. Why, I've given marriage advice to farm wives, army wives, miner wives, merchant wives, railroader wives . . . all kinds of wives. What I mean is, after hearing all that wife talk, you can bet that I believe Leah Leighton has a mighty good reason to hang her husband."

Red's aborning smile faded instantly as a terrified shriek from the barn shattered the hush of the evening. "Seems like ol' Barnaby didn't think they'd really hang him. Now he knows different."

"We should stop right here where we're at," Buttons said. "We don't need to watch it."

"That's fine by me." Red looked around and smiled. "Where's the free beer?"

Barnaby shrieked yet another plea for mercy. He choked a little, as though the rope was now around his neck.

Buttons, the bloody decapitation of Bill Yearly vivid in his memory, scowled and yelled in the direction of the barn. "Goddamn it, if you're gonna do it, then do it. Hang the sidewinder and get it over with."

"Steady, old fellow. We've got no hand in this."

All things considered, Barnaby Leighton did not die well.

Between cursing threats directed at his wife, he screamed and begged and screamed again. A long minute ticked past. And then another. The man's rants choked off, leaving a sudden silence as fragile as spun glass.

A horse snorted and kicked in its stall,

And Buttons Muldoon's stored-up breath hissed out of him. "A helluva way to kill a man. Hanging from a barn rafter ain't a quick death."

Red nodded. "Seems like." His hands shook as he built and lit a cigarette. Around him the scarlet sky faded, and the day shaded into darkness and a lantern bobbed in the gloom like a firefly as a woman strode purposely toward him and Buttons.

Luna Talbot stood directly in front of Buttons and said, "He's dead. The world is rid of his vile shadow."

"We heard," Buttons said.

"Barnabas Leighton lived like a pig . . . and he died like a pig," the woman said.

"Bad luck to speak ill of the dead, Mrs. Talbot," Buttons said.

"There's no other way to speak of him," Luna said. "Come into the house. I need a drink. You too, shotgun man."

"I think me and Red should be on our way," Buttons said. "Got a long road ahead of us to El Paso."

"In this country, in the dark, you'll have a busted axle before you travel a mile. No, you can stay the night," Luna said. "There's a room in the bunkhouse we keep for male visitors that's comfortable enough. It has a good roof. You can bed down there."

Buttons looked doubtful and turned to Red.

"The lady has a point. Buttons, you know the country to the north of here. It's a hard way and rocky. As she says, we could bust an axle or break a wheel or lame a horse. Best we leave at first light."

"Make up your minds, gentlemen," Luna said. "I've invited you in for a drink. I won't ask a second time."

"All right. I guess I could use a whiskey," Buttons said. "Or two."

"Mr. Muldoon . . . that is your name, right?" Luna said.

"Man and boy," Buttons said.

"Then believe me when I tell you that Barnabas Leighton needed hanging," the woman said. "Some men don't deserve to live, and he was one of them."

"Tell me about it," Buttons said. "I heard him die . . . and I'd like to know the why of the thing."

"Come inside," Luna said. "I'll tell you about Barnabas . . . if you can handle it."

CHAPTER ELEVEN

Luna Talbot sat in lamplight, and Red Ryan again wondered at her striking beauty, her abundant auburn hair, dark eyes and wide, expressive mouth. She was mysterious, a woman with a story to tell . . . and, as she'd so recently proved, quite ruthless. He imagined that it would be easy to fall in love with her, but difficult to keep her.

And that night Luna did have a story to tell . . . but it was the story of Leah Leighton, not her own.

"Barnabas Leighton swept Leah off her feet with his honeyed words and his free-spending ways," she said. "She was an orphan and had lived with two foster families in Kansas, one that abused her and treated her as a slave, the other, a preacher and his constantly ailing wife. They had pretty much ignored her except to feed her a diet of prune juice and scripture. She saw Barnabas as her salvation and married him shortly after she turned fourteen."

"Young," Button said, "for marriage and birthin' babies."

"Yes, too young," Luna said. "But Leah couldn't

give Barnabas a baby and he hated her for it. Made him feel less of a man, I guess. After they were married two years, he decided to try his hand at farming, grow wheat or corn or whatever, but when he failed at that, he started to drink heavily and began to beat her." Whiskey glowed amber in the crystal glass in Luna's hand. "Pretty soon it became a daily occurrence."

"I don't hold with that, a man beating his wife," Buttons said. "Red, you recollect Jim Poor that time?"

"Buttons, you pounded Jim Poor because he beat a *dog*."

"Yeah, but a man who beats a dog will beat a woman," Buttons said. "That's a law of human nature and it's wrote down somewhere." He said to Luna, "So, what happened next?"

"Luna ran away. I mean, she ran across the Kansas prairie for several days, saw Indians a time or two, she says, and then when she'd no run left in her, more dead than alive, she was rescued by a couple of punchers and was nursed back to health at their ranch. Leah says the spread was the Lazy-J and she'll never forget their kindness."

"And then she came here," Buttons said.

"Not quite," Luna said. "Barnabas was hunting her, and Leah wanted to stay a step ahead of him and ended up selling it at the Gentlemen's Club cathouse in Austin. Yes, Mr. Muldoon, she became a whore. Does that offend you?"

Buttons smiled. "The only thing that offends me is a wheeler hoss that won't pull his weight. How about you Red?"

"I've known a lot of whores and liked all of them

just fine," Red said. "Well, except maybe the El Paso whores. They're a tough bunch, always on the prod, and they're mighty fond of derringers."

"And it was then that Leah ended up here, huh?" Buttons said.

"Bessie Foley brought her here," Luna said.

"Your cook?"

"Yes. Bessie killed a Cajun man in New Orleans. Shot him six times with a pepperbox revolver for cheating on her. She was sentenced to twenty years of penal servitude at a female prison farm in a Louisiana swamp, served three years, and then escaped. She ended up in Austin, cooking for the gents that used the Gentlemen's Club."

"How did Bessie hear about you?" Buttons said.

"We had a girl here, a reformed soiled dove, who called herself Ora Blake. Ora tried hard but couldn't take to ranch life and went back to her old ways. She met Bessie in Austin and told her about the Talbot ranch."

"And Bessie told Leah," Buttons said. "Small world, ain't it?"

"Yes, small world. Leah and Bessie talked it over and made the decision to come here."

"And Barnabas Leighton found out and followed them to your spread, so you strung him up," Red said.

"Yes. He tried to force Leah to leave with him, and he could have talked, stated his case, told her he'd changed, but he didn't. He made the mistake of pulling a gun," Luna said. "I shot it out of his hand. I don't know if you noticed, but Barnabas was missing his right thumb and trigger finger. A poorly aimed .45 bullet will do that."

"I didn't notice, but I know what a bullet can do," Red said.

"The shooting was two weeks ago. Better for him if Barnabas had bled to death instead of dying yellow like the woman-beating coward he was."

Red picked up the decanter, poured himself more whiskey, and said, "Why do women like Leah and Bessie come to your ranch, Luna?" He smiled. "Is it for the grub, or do they just like cattle?"

"I provide a refuge," Luna said. "If a woman is in despair and has nowhere else to turn, I want her to turn to me and the Talbot ranch. Here she can learn the cattle business, earn her thirty a month, and once again hold her head high. The women who come here are broken and I help mend them. I said *help*, mind you. Each woman must do most of the mending herself."

"And you teach her how to use a gun," Red said.

"We live on the frontier, Mr. Ryan, where gun skills are a necessity. All the hands on the Talbot can shoot, and they ride for the brand."

Red didn't know it then, but future violent events would prove that statement wrong. All but one of the Talbot women rode for the brand . . . her loyalties lay elsewhere.

Buttons said, "How did you get started in the refuge business, Mrs. Talbot, if you don't mind me asking?"

"I have things to do tonight, Mr. Muldoon, so I'll make my answer short," Luna said. "My husband was a deputy for Judge Isaac Parker's court until he was murdered in the Indian Territory by a half-breed scoundrel called John Long. That was four years ago. Peter Talbot was a good man and a fine husband, and we had six wonderful years together before he died. I was suddenly a widow with few living relatives, forced to live on my husband's meager savings. I can't say I lived, but I survived, hungry most of the time, in Fort Smith for six months and then my uncle—"

"Morgan Ford," Buttons said.

"Yes, he heard of my plight and loaned me enough money that I could buy this place." Luna said. "Then, it was a run-down spread held together by string and baling wire, and I got it cheap. The first two years were hard, but I made a go of it and then had the idea of hiring women who were in the same dire straits as I'd been." The woman smiled and rose from her chair. "Now, I really must go. Please excuse me, gentlemen."

As he and Red got to their feet, Buttons said, "Whatever happened to that John Long ranny?"

"One of Judge Parker's deputies told me Long died of consumption six months after he killed my husband," Luna said. "He'd been arrested and convicted but passed away the day before he was due to meet the hangman."

"Well, that's just too bad," Buttons said. "He cheated justice."

"Perhaps his consumption was God's justice," Luna said. "I like to think that was the case."

"Amen," Buttons said with unusual piety.

Red said nothing, his eyes fixed on the window.

Outside, dozens of candles glowed in the darkness, their flames guttering in the wind.

CHAPTER TWELVE

After Luna Talbot left, Red followed her outside. He walked onto the porch as the woman joined the dozen others who stood in the yard, candles in their hands. Morgan Ford's coffin lay on the ground among them, then, at a motion from Luna, six of the women picked it up by the handles and walked slowly toward the barn. The others followed in slow and solemn procession. No one spoke.

"Notice something, Buttons?" Red asked when the driver stepped beside him.

"Yeah, it's a burying."

"Look at the coffin lid."

Buttons peered into the gloom and shook his head. "Too dark. I can't see it."

"They opened the coffin. And didn't put the lid back on properly. It's about an inch open on one side. Strange that, don't you think?"

"So, Luna Talbot wanted to take a last look at the face of her loved one," Buttons said. "Some folks do that, but I don't know why.'

"Or besides Uncle Morgan, there was something in the coffin she wanted."

"Treasure? Money?" Buttons said.

"Maybe both."

"The coffin was heavy."

"Not that heavy."

"Paper money don't weigh much," Buttons said. "Hey, look. They're dragging something out of the barn. What the hell is that? Can you see?"

"Nope, but I'll guess it's Barnabas Leighton. Plant one stiff, you might as well plant the other at the same time. Get it done with."

"What do you think, Red, should we mosey on over there, pay our respects?" Buttons said.

"No, I don't think we'd be welcome. And if what Luna Talbot took from the coffin is as valuable as I think it is, we might even get shot."

"Well, she gave us our five hundred, so we're out of here at first light," Buttons said. "We'll have a story to tell about the West Texas ranch where only women ride for the brand." He grinned. "Lady cowpokes . . . wranglerettes . . . buckerooettes . . . don't that beat all?"

"Yeah, some lovely ladies who do their own share of killing and hanging. I reckon the Talbot ranch is one tough outfit."

Lanterns burned in one of the many box canyons of the steep and rocky Quitman Mountains and drew Crystal Casey like a moth to the flame. Twenty-three years old that summer, she was a former San Francisco whore who'd been taken in by Luna Talbot and made a competent rider. But despite that kindness, her loyalties lay elsewhere . . . with the man she'd met in a Barbary Coast brothel and who'd recently reentered her life—Johnny Teague.

Gunman, killer, and outlaw, Teague had come down from the New Mexico Territory and entered Texas like a blight. He and his gang had robbed, plundered, and killed their way across the state, and the Rangers had branded them "the most vicious band of desperados in the history of wrongdoing on the frontier."

But the night Crystal Casey rode into his camp in the canyon, Teague had even bigger fish to fry . . . that is, after he'd killed a man. Unlike many gang bosses, Teague always made it clear to newcomers that anyone could shuck the iron and challenge him for leadership. Over the course of two years of banditry, two gunmen threw down the glove and Teague killed them both. But on the night in question came the most serious challenger yet.

"Pure pizen on the draw and shoot, quick as the snap of a bullwhip," was how, in 1936, retired Teague gang member Dave Quarrels described Sabine River Sam Canning to the Ohio newspaperman A. B. Boyd. Canning, who'd run with Wes Hardin for a spell and had been top gun in the Colfax County War up in the New Mexico Territory, had killed seven men, and Johnny Teague was aware of his reputation.

Nobody considered Canning a bargain, and Teague would take no chances with him.

Crystal Casey dismounted and yelled, "Johnny, I have news," as she ran toward him.

Standing tall and grim in the flickering firelight, Teague didn't turn in the girl's direction. "Not now."

He motioned to the man facing him and smiled. "When he's dead, you can tell me all about it."

"But Johnny—"

"Later, Crystal," Teague said. "I got something to do here first."

"Better listen to the little lady, Johnny," Canning said, small, wiry with dead gray eyes. "Just step aside, and you won't get hurt. Them's words of wisdom."

"The day I step aside for a tramp like you, Sammy, will be the day I hang up my guns and retire," Teague said.

"Big talk, Johnny," Canning said. In the fire glow his thin, black mustache made him look like a limelit stage villain in a bad melodrama. "But the time for talking is done. I'm taking over. We need some new leadership around here."

"It's your prerogative at any time, Sammy," Teague said. "That's how it's always been and always will be. Now, shuck the iron and get to your work."

Dave Quarrels would later say that Sam Canning's face changed the instant his hand dropped for his holstered Colt. "He knew even before he grabbed his gun that he was beat, that Johnny Teague was too fast for him and that he was a dead man. I seen John Wesley Hardin on the draw and shoot. I seen Wild Bill Longley on the draw and shoot and I still say that Johnny Teague was the fastest gun that ever was. Yes sir, fast as chain lighting was Johnny."

But the fight was not quite as the then eighty-six-year-old Quarrels remembered it.

Teague opened the ball all right and made his play just a fraction of a second ahead of Canning. Playing catch-up, Canning went for his gun and cleared leather. But Teague held on to his edge and fired first. His bullet was low and to the left, entering Canning's body just under his right rib cage, exiting in the lower back, staggering the little gunman. Canning knew it was a killing wound but stayed in the fight. He fired back, missed, and took a second hit dead center in the chest. Canning shot again, and Teague winced as the bullet burned across the meat of his left shoulder. His teeth clenched in anger and determination, Teague rapidly got his work in, three shots, all hits, that triggered his Colt dry. But Canning was shot to doll rags. Wounded twice in the chest, side, and twice in the belly, the gunman dropped to his knees, stared into Teague's eyes for a moment, and then fell flat on his face, dead a split second after his bloody mouth bit on dirt.

After the roaring racket of the gunfire, the ensuing silence was as quiet as the nave of a midnight cathedral.

Then from behind a drift of gun smoke, Teague said as he thumbed cartridges into his Colt, "Boys, too much ambition is a dangerous thing. Sammy learned that lesson the hard way."

Crystal ran to Teague and threw herself at him and said, "Johnny, are you hurt? Your arm is bleeding."

"I'm fine. It's only a scratch, so don't fuss at me, woman." He holstered his gun. "So what was in the coffin, apart from the stiff? Was it what I expected?"

The girl smiled. "Yes, it was in his hand, rolled tight and sticking up so Luna would see it."

"Are you sure it was the map?"

"Yes, I'm sure. What else could it be? I saw her take the paper and look at it and then shove it between her tits."

"Woman hides a thing there, it means it's important." He frowned in thought for a while and then said, "It's got to be the map to the Lucky Cuss mine. Got to be."

A man with a hard, serious face stepped over Sam Canning's body into the firelight and said, "Is this why you led us into these godforsaken badlands, Johnny? For a map to a gold mine?"

"Not just any map, Tom," Teague said. "The Lucky Cuss will make us all rich." He smiled. "Sam too, if he'd lived long enough."

Tom Racker was fifty years old, a close, personal friend of the dour Frank James and as bad as they come. A hired killer who used a gun, knife, poison, arson or whatever came to hand to get the job done, he'd murdered fourteen men and two women, and none of them disturbed his sleep of nights, or so he claimed.

"Johnny, you know how many treasure maps I've seen in my time?" Racker said. "Dozens, I tell ya, and not one of them played out. It's easy to draw up a map to a lost gold mine and sell it to some rube for fifty dollars. Hell, I've seen it done. In Dodge, a feller by the name of Wyatt Earp drew up a map to a silver mine in the New Mexico Territory and then pissed on it and let it dry in the sun to age. He sold it to a railroad brakeman for a hundred dollars and then skipped town. I seen that with my own eyes. How do you know your map is any different?"

Teague's gaze swept over the nine men facing him, all of them hardened killers, all of them figuring that what Racker had said made sense. And Johnny figured right along with them that his killing of Canning had not set well with most of them and he had some fast talking to do or face a mutiny. Bad grub, no whiskey, and the hostile desert around them made men's tempers short, and they were quick to anger.

Teague said, "Boys, I can't say the map to the Lucky Cuss is sure enough genuine, but it came from a ranny by the name of Morgan Ford who lived in a town called Cottondale, up El Paso way. Ford claimed he struck it rich and after that never worked a day in his life."

"Who says, Johnny?" Racker said.

"A feller called Solomon Palmer says. He once did a job for me in El Paso and later he told me that he was headed back to Cottondale on account of how he'd recently been hired by Ford's niece to look after the old man and box him when he turned up his toes. Palmer had passed himself off to Luna Talbot as a preacher, so she trusted him."

A tall, loose-geared man wearing a black-and-white cow skin vest spoke up. "I recollect Palmer from El Paso. He's a small-time cardsharp and goldbrick artist and a damned liar. I wouldn't believe a word he says."

"Luke, I know what Palmer is. That's why I hired him," Teague said.

"Hired him for what?" Racker said.

Teague smiled. "As a lookout."

"A lookout?" Racker said. "Looking out for what?"

"Looking out for the husband of a married lady I was sparking. Her husband was the town blacksmith and he could tie a bowknot in an iron horseshoe. A bad man to catch me in the sack with his wife."

Men laughed, the tension eased a little, and Teague took advantage. "Listen up, boys. There were a lot of folks in El Paso who'd lived in Cottondale, and there was plenty of talk about the Lucky Cuss and how Morgan Ford would disappear into the Cornudas Mountains for weeks at a time and return with a poke of gold big enough to keep him in whiskey and whores for a year."

Racker said, "So at death's door Ford made a map to his mine . . ."

"And now it's between Mrs. Talbot's tits," Crystal said, a not-very-intelligent girl trying to be helpful. "Since he'd no other kin, he wanted his niece to have it."

Racker ignored that and said, "How do we get the map, Johnny?"

Teague turned to Crystal Casey. "How many hell-cats does Luna Talbot have at her ranch?"

"Twenty, Johnny. Twenty-one if you include Mrs. Talbot."

"I include her. I hear she's the worst of them."

"She's very strict," Crystal said.

"And good with a gun," Teague said.

"Very good. She was taught to shoot by her husband. He was a lawman."

"Yeah, Pete Talbot. I've heard of him." Teague turned his attention back to Tom Racker. "We could ride into the ranch and grab the map from between the Talbot woman's tits, but we'd leave too many men dead on the ground and I don't want that."

"Then how do we play it?" Racker was irritated. "I've had about enough of kicking my heels around this place."

Teague smiled. "Patience, Tom. Luna Talbot has the map, and my guess is she'll use it right away. Crystal, the ranch has had a few bad years and she needs the money. Ain't that so?"

"Yes, Johnny. I heard Leah Leighton, the segundo, say things were tight."

Teague nodded. "Hear that, Tom. Things are tight. If she wants to stay in business, I reckon Luna Talbot will go after the gold pretty damn quick."

"And where does that leave us?" Racker said.

"For the time being, right here. Crystal will keep us informed. When Luna Talbot goes prospecting, we'll be right behind her."

"Anywhere you look, there's miles of open country," Racker said. "She'd spot us for sure."

Teague smiled. "That's why I keep a breed on the payroll. Ain't that right, Sanchez?"

"I can follow her without being seen," Juan Sanchez said. The spawn of a Mexican bandit father and a Chiricahua woman, Sanchez had lived and raided with Apaches. His horse's bridle was braided with forty scalp locks, most black but a few of them blond or red. He dressed flashily, like a vaquero and, unusual at that time in the West, wore two guns and was quick and deadly on the draw and shoot.

"You heard Sanchez, Tom. He can scout for us," Teague said. "The varmint is half bronco Apache."

"I know what he is," Racker said. "Johnny, I don't want bad blood between us, but you got three days. After that, if the Talbot woman doesn't leave her ranch, I'm pulling out of this hellhole and others will come with me."

"Aha," Teague said.

"Aha," Racker said. "What the hell does that mean?"

"It means I guarantee we'll be gone from here

before your three days are up. Crystal, get back to the ranch and keep your ears to the ground. I want to know what's happening, so don't let me down."

The girl nodded. "I won't, Johnny. Now I must get back before I'm missed."

After the girl galloped into the night, Teague said to Racker, "We're all gonna be rich men, Tom."

"You got three days to prove your claim, Johnny."

CHAPTER THIRTEEN

Buttons Muldoon had already turned in, but Red Ryan wasn't yet ready for sleep and stood outside the door of their room at the east wing of the bunkhouse. The moon rode high, silvering the night, and out in the badlands hungry coyotes yammered. He built another cigarette, thumbed a match into flame and then let it drop to the ground as the plodding sound of a tired horse reached him out of the darkness.

His eyes already accustomed to the gloom, Red stepped into shadow and saw a woman ride to the barn, dismount, and lead her paint horse inside. She emerged a few minutes later, looked around, and then ran across the yard to the bunkhouse. He heard a door quietly open and close . . . and then silence.

He frowned in thought. Why was the young woman riding so late? Had she met a lover out there in the desert? That was highly unlikely. There were few men around that part of Texas. Few anybody. Perhaps her horse could tell him something. Red crossed to the barn and stepped inside. The lathered paint stood in a stall nearest the door. He'd come a fair way at a run and judging by the blood on his flanks, the woman had put the spurs to him. Red shook his head.

He searched around, found a piece of sacking and a brush, and worked on the pony for a solid twenty minutes before he was satisfied. A further search revealed a bag of oats, and he gave the animal a generous scoop.

Red patted the paint's neck and said, "That's the best I can do for you, little feller. Eat, and then sleep well."

He was about to step out of the stall when the four clicks of a cocking Colt froze him in place.

"Step out of the shadow where I can see you." Luna Talbot's voice. "I can drill you from here any time of the day."

"Don't shoot. It's me. Red Ryan."

"What the hell are you doing here this late, shotgun man?" the woman said.

"I was taking care of an abused horse," he said. "One of your ladies doesn't know how to care for her mount after she's ridden him into the ground. You ought to have taught her better, Mrs. Talbot." He heard Luna lower the Colt's hammer and then slide it back into the holster.

She stepped to the stall and ran her hand over the paint's back and shoulder. "He's still hot. How long has he been here?"

"About twenty minutes or so. He'll be all right. I brushed him down real good."

"Who rode in on him?" Luna said.

"I don't know who it was. A woman. One of your'n, I guess. Unsaddled the paint and then she fogged it for the bunkhouse."

"Crystal Casey rides this horse," Luna said. "Was it her you saw?"

"I don't know who I saw. Just a woman running in the dark."

"It had to be Crystal."

"Seems like."

"She had visited someone."

"Seems like," he said again.

"Who?"

"Beats me."

Luna bit her bottom lip, deep in thought, and then said, "Red, can I trust you?"

"Hell, no."

"Is Muldoon to be trusted?"

"Hell, no."

"No matter. I have to put my trust in someone. I think the word has gotten around."

"What word?" Red said.

"I can't tell you . . . not now. Maybe later after I talk with Crystal."

"It's something to do with the coffin from Cottondale, isn't it?"

"It's everything to do with the coffin from Cottondale," Luna said.

Red smiled. "All right, so there was money in it, and outlaws can smell greenbacks from two hundred miles away."

"Not money . . . something else, something even more valuable," Luna said.

"Now I'm interested. Suppose I tell you I can be trusted to keep my mouth shut? Is that enough?"

"Enough for the present. All right. I want to talk with you and Buttons Muldoon," Luna said. "Tomorrow morning after breakfast."

"Then make it early," he said. "We're pulling out at first light, headed up Fort Concho way."

"I'll tell Bessie to have breakfast ready early," Luna said.

"Yeah, and tell her it was Buttons Muldoon's idea, not mine."

The woman smiled, stepped to the door, and then looked back. "Red, thank you kindly for taking care of the paint."

"Glad I could help. He couldn't do it for himself." He watched Luna walk into the moonlight, a fine-looking woman becoming one with the night.

CHAPTER FOURTEEN

The same moonlight that tangled in Luna Talbot's hair lay lightly on the steep slopes of the Cornudas Mountains sixty miles to the north as Jacob Brook led his burro into a valley between two peaks that lay just south of the New Mexico Territory border.

A talking man with no one to talk to, Brook, as was his habit, addressed the burro. "We'll camp for the night among them rocks over there, Thomas Aquinas, and bile us up some coffee. How does that set with ye?"

The burro, an animal with a philosophical turn of mind, hence the grand name that Brook had given him, said nothing, stoically carrying his burden of hard rock mining tools and a few meager supplies without complaint.

"Glad you agree," the old man said. "High time we rested our old bones and got some shut-eye."

Jacob Brook was eighty years old, but he figured he might be a year or two younger, or older, he didn't rightly know. He'd fought in the War Between the States in the 4th Mounted Volunteers, 1st Regiment, Sibley's Brigade, was wounded in the Red River

Campaign and thereafter walked with a limp. He'd been prospecting since the war ended but he'd never hit pay dirt. He hoped all that was about to change. The West was a gossip mill, and there were vague rumors that a man called Matthew or Mitchell Ford had lived like a king in Cottondale after striking it rich in the Cornudas. Well, Cottondale was a ghost town, and folks said Ford was dead and had taken the secret location of his gold mine to the grave with him. But Jacob Brook figured where there's smoke there's fire, and if the rumors were true, a fortune in gold was his for the taking. He'd never had much, never hoped for much, but a strike after all these years could put him in a rocking chair on the front porch of some big-city hotel with a fat cigar in one hand, a glass of champagne in the other. As he had told Thomas Aquinas so many times, their luck was about to change.

And he was right about that. His luck was about to change, but not for the better . . . for the worse . . . a lot, lot worse.

Brook staked out the burro on a patch of grass, then boiled coffee over a hatful of fire, sat back against a rock, a steaming cup in his hand and his pipe in his mouth. Beside him lay the old .44-40 Henry that he'd carried in the war and that had served him well. When he finished his coffee, he took a Jew's harp from his coat pocket and twanged out a credible version of "Buffalo Gals," much to the irritation of the straitlaced Thomas Aquinas, who deplored music of any kind.

Unfortunately, at that tuneful moment in time, death had begun to stalk Jacob Brook.

The chase closed in moments after the old prospector said, "What will I play next, Thomas? What's your pleasure?"

Brook heard a rustle in the brush behind him but paid it no heed. A night creature, the restless desert breeze, that and nothing more.

Emboldened, death slunk closer.

"How about 'Turkey in the Straw'?" Brook said. "That's always been one of your favorites, huh?"

Small sounds slithered all around him. Breathing. Did he hear breathing?

Something was moving in the night . . . something dark. Something sinister.

There! A flicker of movement. A bent figure, tall, white, running toward him. No, not one. Two . . . three . . . four . . . five . . . more . . .

Alarmed, Brook shoved the harp back in his pocket and reached for the Henry.

He never made it.

They came at Brook from all sides, six or more, half-naked, pale-skinned, and they piled on top of him. Frenzied arms rose and fell, fisted knife blades plunged home time after time, gleaming in the moonlight. The old man screamed as his lifeblood erupted above him in a scarlet fan, staining red his ashen attackers. But a moment later Brook's screams gurgled to a halt and the only sound was the triumphant, wild shrieks of his killers. Thomas Aquinas died a martyr's death. Quickly, the burro was knifed to death, butchered, and his meat wrapped in his skin and carried away. Silence once again fell on the

Cornudas, but for the discordant twang of the mouth harp that one of the savages had found in Brook's pocket. That too faded into distance and the indifferent moon and the stars shone in their sky . . . as though nothing at all had happened.

CHAPTER FIFTEEN

The stars were still bright in the sky when Bessie Foley rudely woke Red Ryan and Buttons Muldoon. Buttons, a notoriously sound sleeper, came in for some extra attention by being tipped out of his cot, blankets and all, and thudded onto the hard timber floor.

Bessie, large, threatening and stern, waited until Buttons had finished turning the air blue with his cusses and then she said, "Both of you, faces and hands washed and hair combed before you join Mrs. Talbot for breakfast." Then, ominously, "You've got ten minutes."

Buttons scowling, said, "Woman, be damned to ye fer turning a Christian man out of his bed in the middle of the night."

"It's five-thirty, mister," Bessie said. "Half the day is gone. And now you have nine minutes." She stared hard at Red who was blinking like a startled owl. "Hot-cakes, bacon, scrambled eggs, and coffee. Come and get it or I'll throw it out."

Red nodded at her. "We'll be there."

Buttons grumbled but washed up and wetted down

his unruly hair before parting it in the middle and laying it flat as an ironing board on either side. "How do I look? Will her highness approve?"

Red smiled. "Buttons, you're a sight for sore eyes."

"Damn right I am. As good-looking a driver as ever set foot on a Concord stage," Buttons said. "Now lead the way, Red. And your hair isn't combed right."

As it happened, breakfast was delayed for five minutes as an openly defiant Crystal Casey was given a horse, a three-day supply of grub, and twenty dollars, and told to leave and never set foot on the Talbot ranch again.

Red and Buttons stood on the porch in front of the house and heard Luna say, more in sadness than anger, "You lied to me, Crystal. You didn't go out for just a moonlit ride. You met someone. Why? And who was it?"

The insolent sneer on the girl's face made her look ugly. "You'll find out soon enough, Mrs. High-and-mighty Talbot."

Leah Leighton wore her gun and a furious expression. "Woman, answer the boss's question or I'll shoot you right off that horse."

"You go to hell!" Crystal yelled. She rammed her spurs into the pony's ribs and took off at a fast run.

Leah immediately shucked her Colt, but Luna said, "No, let her go. Whatever mischief took place out there in the range can't be undone by a killing."

Leah looked disappointed as she holstered her gun.

Luna Talbot said to Red and Buttons, "Breakfast, gentlemen? Miss Leighton will join us."

Despite its unpromising beginning, breakfast was

a pleasant affair. Luna talked about her childhood, growing up poor on the west bank of the Brazos with her ferryman father, her mother having died when she was three. Leah Leighton talked cattle and the rumor that the army would soon require an additional twenty thousand head of beef to feed the Indian reservations and its own soldiers through winter, and that could only drive up demand and prices. Then came some woman talk to which Buttons contributed, mentioning how small the hats and how huge the bustles he'd seen being worn by the New Orleans belles during his recent visit to that city. Luna and Leah were suitably scandalized, or pretended to be, but no one mentioned Crystal Foley until breakfast was over, and then only indirectly.

"I have something to tell you gentlemen, and then a proposition to make," Luna said. "I hope you will hear me out."

"As long as it doesn't contravene the rules of the Abe Patterson and Son Stage and Express Company. I am set on that condition."

Luna smiled. "Mr. Ryan, where on earth did you learn a word like *contravene*?"

"It's wrote down a few times in the Patterson rule book," he said. "That, and some other big lawyer words."

Leah said she had to rouse the hands and left.

After she was gone, Luna said, "I'm offering you a fare. Does that contravene the rules?"

Buttons said, "No it doesn't. Passengers are always welcome. Now state your intentions, Mrs. Talbot."

"My intention is that you take me to the Cornudas Mountains."

"And back again?" Buttons said.

"Of course."

"Why?" Red said.

Luna sat back as Bessie refilled her coffee and when the woman left she said, "You've been wondering what was in the coffin you brought here."

"Besides the dear departed, yes. We've been puzzling over it."

"We figured it was treasure," Buttons said. "Gold coins and the like."

"No, it's not treasure or gold coins. It's a map," Luna said.

"A map? A map to where?" Red said.

"To the Lucky Cuss gold mine," Luna said.

That last rang a bell with Red, and he said to Buttons, "Here, remember that road agent Leah Leighton shot? The one they called Hank?"

Buttons nodded. "I recollect." He smiled. "How can I forget?"

"His dying words were 'Lucky cuss,' and I remember thinking that it was a strange thing to say because a man with a bullet in his brisket ain't lucky. Damn it, he was talking about the mine. He wanted the map from the coffin, and that's why he held us up."

"I think Solomon Palmer did too much talking in El Paso," Luna said. "Now it seems that every outlaw in Texas knows about the Lucky Cuss."

"And maybe a whole heap of tin pans," Buttons said. "Pretty soon you might find yourself in the middle of a gold rush, Mrs. Talbot."

"And that's why we need to talk. I want to find out if there really is a gold mine, and I want you to take me there. Riding north with half a dozen of my hands would attract too much unwelcome attention.

In the coach, I'm just a rancher headed to El Paso on business."

"It will cost you four hundred dollars for the round trip," Buttons said. "You have that kind of money?"

"I can do better than that," Luna said. "How does ten percent of every ounce of gold we dig out of the mountain sound to you?"

Red Ryan shook his head. "Buttons and me, we're headed for the Patterson stage depot in El Paso and then to San Angelo, up Fort Concho way. We're a driver and shotgun guard, not miners."

Luna smiled. "Silly, you won't have to dig out the gold yourself. I'll hire men to do that. All you have to do is sit back and let the money roll in. Red, think about it. If the mine pans out, you'll be rich or close to it."

"We can take you to the mountains for two hundred dollars, and then we part company. That's the best I have to offer."

"Twenty percent," Buttons said.

Red stared at him in disbelief. "Buttons . . ."

"And we'll take you there and back."

Gold fever. Buttons Muldoon had caught the disease. Red could see the symptoms of it . . . the glitter in his driver's eyes and the flushed skin, the beads of sweat on his forehead.

Luna didn't hesitate. "Done and done."

"And if there's no mine?" Red said.

"Then all bets are off," the woman said. "You drive me back to the Talbot and then go merrily on your way to San Angelo or wherever with no hard feelings."

"Buttons, I don't like it," Red said. "We're already overdue at the El Paso depot."

But the driver would have none of it. "Red, we can

split twenty percent of a gold mine and retire. Maybe settle down in some big city. Live the good life."

"I hate big cities, and we're too young to retire," Red said.

"But not too young to get rich," Buttons said. He was breathing hard, tasting gold.

"Any age is a good age to get rich," Luna said.

"You've got yourself a deal, lady," Buttons said. "When do you want to leave?"

"Now. We leave now. I'm leaving Leah Leighton in charge."

"I'll hitch up the team," Buttons said.

"I got a feeling about this arrangement." Red rose from the table.

"What kind of feeling?" Buttons said.

"That it ain't going to end well."

CHAPTER SIXTEEN

Papa Mace Rathmore was worried, and he voiced his concern to his eldest surviving son. "Damn your eyes, Elijah, the outsider we killed was a prospector. If he knew that there's gold in the Cornudas, others might. They could descend on us like a plague of locusts, and we can't kill them all."

Tall, pale, and emaciated like all his kin, Elijah said, "Papa, the gold is almost gone. We can move away from this place where the Kanes prey on us and shoot us for sport. We could live in the forest."

"Forest? What forest?" Papa Mace said.

"We'll find one," Elijah said. "Head north to where the bears live."

"Are you afraid of the Kanes?"

"Yes."

Papa Mace sighed. "The quartz vein continues into the rock. We must dig deeper."

"But how long will that take?" Elijah wore an old army greatcoat that made him look skinnier. His thin-stranded black beard was matted from that morning's burro meat soup, and his eyebrows met above his eagle beak of a nose.

"Not long. Just until we uncover more of the quartz seam. Put your brothers to work, and their lazy wives if need be."

"And the slaves?"

"Not the slaves. The gold must be found by our blood. The slaves can continue to crush the ore. Use the whip on them if they don't work hard enough."

"We have a new repeating rifle, a Henry," Elijah said.

"From the prospector. Yes, I know," Papa Mace said.

"It will help protect us from Ben Kane and his cowboys," Elijah said.

"We must catch another cowboy and send Kane his skin like we did before," Papa Mace said. "They didn't hunt us for a long time after that."

"Ben Kane is an evil man," Elijah said.

"We steal his cattle to feed ourselves." Papa Mace shrugged. "He hates us for that."

Thirty-seven people crowded into a narrow arroyo that morning—Papa Mace and his brood, his seven sons and their wives and twelve children, and ten captive Mexican males held as slaves. The Mace clan was an unwashed, underfed bunch and none of the sons had inherited their sire's smarts. They dressed in whatever rags they could steal, adding animal skins in cold weather. Papa Mace, a conman, robber, dark-alley killer, and sometimes fire-and-brimstone preacher, had been thrown out of a dozen towns, twice on a rail wearing a coat of tar and feathers. He was hardly an imposing figure. He stood only five feet, four inches tall but weighed close to four hundred pounds, and his great belly hung between his knees like a sack of grain. Run out of the New Mexico Territory, he'd assured his tribe that Texas was the promised land . . . but he'd led them into an annex of hell.

Deprivation coupled with their low intelligence had made the thieving Mace clan brutish, violent, and deadly. Only the meager amounts of gold from the abandoned mine they'd found kept them alive. Grim old rancher Ben Kane and his Rafter-K riders hated them with a passion.

The news that the mine's gold-bearing quartz vein had lost itself in solid rock was a blow to Papa Mace. For the past three years his sons had sold enough gold in Forlorn Hope, a struggling settlement at the northern edge of the Chihuahuan Desert, to buy meager supplies, though Papa Mace made sure his whiskey and cigars were always a priority.

His brood would have to dig out the quartz vein, hard work that his sons shunned, but there was no other way. The gold must be mined by those of his own blood. God had told Papa Mace that . . . or had it been the devil? Either way he didn't much care, so long as the precious metal was found, and his family continued to prosper.

"I don't like this, Jake," Rafter-K cowboy Milton Barnett said. "We don't know these mountains."

"No, but we know the folks who live in them," Jake Wise said.

"The boss won't like it." Barnett swallowed hard, his nervous gaze fixed on the Cornudas. "I mean, Mr. Kane ain't one fer harming woman and children."

"Even if they are a bunch of animals?" Wise said.

"Even so," Barnett said. He tipped his hat back on his head, letting the breeze cool his sweating forehead. "I mean, killing young 'uns . . ."

Wise said, "We ain't gonna kill no young 'uns, just their daddies. And old Ben ain't gonna find out, because we ain't gonna tell him. You seen what that Rathmore trash done to Jesse Holt."

"I know," Barnett said. "I seen it, all right."

"Then let me hear you tell it," Wise said. "Say it, Milt. Let me hear you say what they done to Jesse."

"They skun him."

Wise nodded. "That's right. They skun him alive. Real white folks don't do that. See, the Rathmores ain't real white folks. Like I said, they ain't human. They're animals."

Jake Wise was big and blond and pale-eyed. Big defined him. Big shoulders, big chest, big hands, a big yellow mustache under a big beak of a nose, big in the confidence that many eighteen-year-olds possess, especially those who walked tall around men and slept with grown women.

By contrast, Milton Barnett was small and dark and slim and quick and nervous. But he was good with a gun and had killed a man in El Paso.

Wise said, "Anyways, we ain't gonna kill anybody. Just shake up them Rathmores a tad, booger them real good. See the smoke rising from the arroyo over yonder? That means there's a nest of them in there. We gallop past and shoot into the arroyo, make them remember the Rafter-K. That's all we're gonna do today, Milt. Just shake 'em up."

The morning sun was well risen in a turquoise

sky and the shadows on the mountain slopes had lowered. The day promised to be a hot one. The frail breeze had dropped and the smoke from the arroyo rose straight as a string.

Wise gathered his pony's reins and said to Barnett, "You ready to give her a whirl?"

"One pass and then we're outta here," Barnett said. "Enough to let them know that the Rafter-K is thinking about them. That's all, Jake. You hear me?"

"I hear you," Wise said. "Now let's grab us some fun."

The two young cowboys rode down a sandy slope cluttered with cactus, mostly claret cup and cholla. A lot of fat, black flies were buzzing in the air.

Wise waved a hand in front of his face. "What the hell?"

"Something dead," Barnett said. "Smell it?"

"Coyote, maybe," Wise said.

"Or a jackrabbit," Barnett said.

"It stinks, whatever it is," Wise said. "I'm taking a look." He kneed his horse into a canter.

A few moments later he and Barnett rode up on a patch of grass growing between some sizable rocks where a moving mass of flies covered a stinking gut pile and a few feet away sprawled the naked, mangled body of a . . . man or woman. At first glance it was hard to tell.

"It's a man," Wise said, leaning from the saddle for a closer look. "It's got a beard under all that blood."

"Hell," Barnett said. "He was took by wild animals. Wolves maybe. I think it was wolves."

"No, looks more like knife wounds," Wise said. "A whole heap of knife wounds."

"The Rathmores?"

"Who else? Damned white trash. They murdered him . . ."

"And his animal. Burro's head lying over there by the rock," Barnett said.

Jake Wise straightened in the saddle and stared at the smoke rising from the arroyo. He shook his head and then slid his Winchester from the boot under his knee. He racked a round into the chamber and said, "Well, let's go bag us a few Rathmores."

"No, Jake. I got a bad feeling," Barnett said. "I don't like this."

Wise scowled. "What kind of bad feeling?"

"Real bad. Like they know we're coming and they're laying for us. It's so bad, I feel like puking."

"Then you stay here and puke out your yellow," Wise said. "I'll do the shooting for both of us."

Whooping, the young man set spurs to his horse and galloped in the direction of the arroyo.

With bleak eyes, Barnett watched him go, the smell of death everywhere around him. "You big, dumb ape," he yelled after Wise. "What do I tell Ben Kane if you get killed? What do I tell him?"

Wise didn't hear. He made a galloping pass across the mouth of the arroyo, his Winchester hammering. The hooves of his horse drummed and kicked up small explosions of dust, and then he was beyond the arroyo. He turned, battled his rearing mount for a few moments, and charged again. He grinned, having himself a time.

Milton Barnett shook his head and watched Jake Wise die.

Later, he couldn't rightly recollect how many rifle

bullets hit Wise that day. A lot. They kind of pinned him in the saddle for a spell, jerked him around like a ragdoll, and then slowly . . . ever so slowly . . . the big man bent over and slid to the ground. His horse trotted away a few yards and stopped, its head hanging.

A bullet whispered past Barnett's ear as several men ran toward him, stopping every now and then to shoulder their rifles and fire. He'd been right. The Rathmores had seen him and Wise coming and had lain in ambush around the arroyo. Jake had ignored his friend's premonition and had paid for it with his life.

Barnett fired once, a miss, swung his horse around, and lit a shuck at the gallop. He glimpsed behind him and saw men, woman, and children swarm over Wise, their knives rising and falling, and he hoped to God that the big man was already dead when the blades went in.

Barnett's mind reeled as he put a heap of git between him and the Rathmore savages. Would he be blamed for the death of Jake Wise? The big man was an arrogant piece of dirt and he'd thrown his life away, figuring he was bulletproof. He'd been a fool, riding straight into an ambush like that. But Jake was a top hand and Ben Kane set store by him. He could hear the old man now . . . *"You damned yellow-bellied coward. You should've gone to Jake's aid when you saw him fall from his horse."*

Damn, it was so unfair.

Barnett's anger at Wise soured inside him like acid and turned into a burning hatred. He knew what he'd tell Kane. He'd tell him that it was high time the Rathmores were wiped out—seed, breed, and generation, man, woman and child—so their shadows, wherever they fell, no longer defiled the earth.

Jake hadn't died in vain. Yeah, that's what he'd tell him.

CHAPTER SEVENTEEN

"I tell you this for a natural fact," Bill Stanton said. "There ain't no gold in the Cornudas and there never has been."

"I guess Mrs. Talbot has to find that out for herself." Red Ryan toyed with the beef and beans on his plate. "Damn, Bill, this meat is tough."

"Longhorn," Luna Talbot said. "Hereford beef is much more tender." She looked up from her plate at the stage station manager. "Maybe there's gold in the Cornudas, maybe there isn't. But if there is, I'll find it."

"Then good luck, lady," Stanton said. "You're gonna need it."

Buttons Muldoon walked into the cabin. "You got some good-looking horses in the corral, Bill," he said. "Makes a change. I'm glad to get shot of them grays. I used to cotton to them but not any longer. They don't pull their weight, and that's a natural fact."

"I ride a gray."

This from a man who sat by the fire, his open hands extended to the flames.

"No offense," Buttons said.

"None taken," the man said. He rose to his feet, a tall, handsome figure wearing a caped gray cloak. Under the cloak his frock coat bulged on both sides of his chest, and Red pegged him for a two-gun man wearing shoulder holsters, a gambler by the look of him and a successful one at that.

The man stepped across the room and stopped at the table. "Forgive my forwardness, ma'am," he said with a slight bow, "but I saw you when you first walked inside and was anxious to make your acquaintance."

Luna laid her fork on her plate and smiled. "You are very gallant, sir. Luna Talbot is my name. And yours?"

"Arman Broussard, formerly of New Orleans town." the man smiled, showing good teeth. "But now a poor wanderer in the desert. A wanderer in darkness, I must say, that is until I saw you, dear lady. As your name suggests, you carry your own moonlight."

"Vous êtes aimable, monsieur," Luna said.

Broussard smiled. *"Je ne parle que la vérité."*

Buttons, never the soul of discretion, frowned and said, "Hey, are you on the scout, mister? And what's all that fancy talk?"

"The fancy talk is French, and if you mean am I running from the law, then the answer is yes," Broussard said. "I killed a man in New Orleans, a rich man's son, so there was no justice for me. I escaped and fled into Texas. That was three months ago, and I've been on the run from the rich man's bounty hunters ever since."

"When you killed the man, was it a fair fight?" Buttons said.

"He drew on me, but was too slow." Broussard

shrugged, a very Cajun gesture. "A sore loser should not take a hand in a poker game."

"Tell the Rangers that you killed a man in fair fight in New Orleans and they'll let you go with a warning to behave yourself in Texas," Buttons said.

"Ah, is that the case?" the gambler said. "Then I may take your advice." He said to Luna, "I see you've finished dinner, ma'am. Again, please pardon my boldness, but would you care to take a stroll with me before retiring?"

Red didn't let Luna answer. "Mrs. Talbot is a fare-paying passenger of the Abe Patterson and Son Stage and Express Company of which I am a representative," he said. "Since I am responsible for her safety, I cannot allow her to walk out with a stranger."

"Mrs. Talbot . . . please accept my apology," Broussard said. He seemed flustered. "I had no idea that you were a married woman."

Luna smiled. "I am a widow, Mr. Broussard. And I'd love to walk out with you and get some fresh air." She rose and placed her hand on Red's shoulder. "I'm sure Mr. Broussard is a gentleman and that I'll be quite safe."

The gambler gave a little bow. "My arm, Mrs. Talbot?"

"Of course." Luna took Broussard's arm, and after a detour to the apple barrel, they walked out of the cabin.

"Buttons, I don't like this," Red said after they were gone.

"They won't walk far in the dark," Buttons said. "And Mrs. Talbot can take care of herself."

In that assessment Buttons was right . . . and wrong.

* * *

Arman Broussard and Luna Talbot strolled along a path beaten hard by the passage of feet going to and from the barn and corrals. The moon cast a mother-of-pearl light on the station's outbuildings and the desert beyond and picked out the date 1881 on a fencepost that stood upright and alone to the left of the track. The post marked the spot where an Apache war chief named Iron Vest had fallen to Bill Stanton's rifle during the last Chiricahua outbreak. Stanton had planned to carve the Indian's name on the post but had never gotten around to it. The evening of the burning day was cool, still, and hushed.

Broussard's slightly accented voice sounded as loud and hollow as the beat of a muffled drum. "I'd like to check on my horse and give him this." He held a bright green apple in his hand. "He's mighty partial to sour apples."

"Have you always favored grays, Mr. Broussard?" Luna said, not out of any real sense of curiosity but making conversation in a night grown too silent.

"No, I can't say I have," Broussard said. "I won him in a poker game. He's a good horse, a lot of Thoroughbred in him, and he's as game as they come . . . fought off a cougar one time, and he has the scars to prove it."

Luna smiled. "Poor horse."

"Poor cougar. It took quite a beating." Broussard stopped and said, "I heard Stanton say you're looking for gold."

"I am, and he thinks it's a fool's errand."

"It seems that everyone in the West is hunting gold of some kind . . . happiness being the mother lode."

"Are you happy, Mr. Broussard?"

The man smiled. "I've never been happy. You?"

Luna nodded. "I was happy once, at least for a while."

"When you were married?"

"Yes. But it didn't last long. My husband was killed."

"I'm sorry to hear that," Broussard said.

"I thought I'd never get over Peter's death, but I have. Well, mostly I have. Starting my ranch helped."

"You have a ranch?"

"Yes, south of here on the Brazos. Cattle prices have been low this last couple of years, and money's been tight."

"And that's why you're gold prospecting."

"Not prospecting. I'm looking for a gold mine."

"Then I hope you find it," Broussard said. He saw Luna shiver, swept off his cloak, and placed it around her shoulders. "It's warmer in the barn. He smiled. "You can give Ace his apple."

"Ace is a good name for a horse." Luna drew the cloak closer around her shoulders.

"Good name for a gambler's horse, I guess," Broussard said. "But he was already called Ace when I won him. Ah, here's the barn and here's the apple. I'll light the oil lamp."

The big gray responded to Broussard's low whistle and Luna fed him the apple. Ace was still munching when Luna instinctively glanced over her shoulders and then whispered tightly, using Broussard's given name for the first time, "Arman . . ."

The gambler turned and saw what Luna had seen. Three hard-faced men stood in the livery doorway. They were unshaven and dusty, as though they'd just come off a long trail, and each was armed with a rifle and a holstered belt gun.

One of the three, a short, stocky man wearing a shabby ditto suit and bowler hat, said, "Well, howdy, gambling man. It's good to see you at last. It's been a long trail."

"Bounty hunters," Broussard said, contempt in his voice. "Are you three tramps the best Gaspard Trahan could find?"

The smile slipped from the stocky man's face. "We're enough, Broussard. Now it seems like you got a decision to make."

"And what might that be?" Broussard was tense, ready. Beside him Luna Talbot stood in shocked silence.

"Well," the stocky man said, "you can come with us since Mr. Trahan is very anxious to meet you. Really looking forward to it, you might say."

One of the other bounty hunters giggled.

"And if I don't?" Broussard said.

"Well, fact is we got ourselves a real big tin bucket with a tight lid and a sack of salt," the stocky man said.

"What's that for?" Luna said.

"Good question, lady," the stocky man said, his eyes ugly. "If it's how things turn out, we'll take your gambling man's head back to New Orleans pickled in brine."

"I wouldn't like that," Broussard said.

The stocky man smiled. "I know. So as I said, you got a decision to make."

"And so have you," the gambler said. "You can walk away from this."

"Like hell we will," the stocky man said.

"Then I've made up my mind." Broussard went for his guns, his arms crossing over his chest.

Mistakes were made, and excuses for those mistakes are in order . . .

Three men, rifles in their hands, were caught flat-footed. Not one of them figured Arman Broussard would be crazy enough to make a play against that much artillery.

None of the bounty hunters had ever seen Broussard on the draw and shoot and were unaware of his reputation as a skilled gunman.

All three of the bounty hunters were tired after riding long, difficult trails from New Orleans, and their normally sharp reflexes had slowed from fatigue.

The youngest of the three, a man named Crawford, or some say Cranston, had gained minor notoriety when he outdrew and killed bank robber Ncd Brown in Galveston in the summer of 1880, but he was a pistolcro and the Winchester was not his weapon of choice.

Taken together, the bounty hunters were ill prepared for Broussard's flashing speed and uncanny accuracy. The man was hell on wheels with the Colt gun.

Broussard cut loose with both hands, and his first two shots dropped the stocky bounty hunter and the man beside him. As he fell, the stocky man got off a shot, but it went high and wide and did no execution. Crawford panicked. He fired, missed, racked a round into the chamber, and then was hit under the chin by a horribly mangled bullet that bounced off the Winchester's receiver. With his eyes popping out of his head, Crawford staggered back, scarlet blood running down his throat and chest, and the rifle dropped from his hands. Broussard shot him twice more and the youngster fell, dead when he hit the ground.

"What the hell happened here?" Bill Stanton, holding a shotgun, ran into the barn through a drift of gun smoke. Behind him, guns in hand, so did Red Ryan and Buttons Muldoon.

"These men planned to kill Mr. Broussard," Luna said, rushing the words. "They were aiming to cut off his head and pickle it in brine and take it to New Orleans."

Red said, "That was downright unsociable of them. Mrs. Talbot, as a fare-paying passenger of the Abe Patterson and Son Stage and express Company, it's my duty to ask you if you've been harmed in any way."

"I am just fine," Luna said. "Mr. Broussard was defending himself."

"Made a thorough job of it, didn't he?" Stanton said.

"They were notified," Broussard said. "They could have walked away."

Stanton swung the scattergun on the gambler. "Mister, you give those pistols to Mrs. Talbot until I've figured out the right and the wrong of this thing."

Broussard hesitated, and Red said, "Better do like the man says. That there Greener is both wife and child to him."

"I'd be obliged if he'd point his family in another direction," Broussard said. "Make me feel like it's my own idea."

Stanton lowered the shotgun. "All right, now pass them irons."

Broussard gave Luna his Colts and then said, "Now what?"

"Now I do some studying on why there are three

dead men in my barn," Stanton said. "It's late, and I suggest we all get some shut-eye. Broussard, I'll talk to you in the morning. Mrs. Talbot, behind the curtain in the cabin there's a cot with a good feather mattress. You'll be comfortable enough in there."

Luna nodded. "Yes, I do feel tired." Then to Broussard, "No one can blame you for defending yourself. I certainly don't."

The gambler said, "I appreciate that, Mrs. Talbot. Now, I suggest you retire and sweet dreams."

"'Sweet dreams.' You ever said that to a woman, Red?" Buttons whispered as he squirmed around and pulled and kicked at his blanket, trying to make himself comfortable on the cabin floor.

Red drew on his cigarette, and a point of crimson light glowed in the darkness. "Can't say as I ever have. Of course, I've never slept with a regular woman, like a schoolteacher or some such. Maybe I'd say 'sweet dreams' to a schoolteacher."

"I wouldn't," Buttons said. He'd settled down and was lying on his back, his open eyes staring into gloom. "Sweet dreams. Hell, I'd never say that to any woman."

"Well, it could be that Broussard is a gentleman and we ain't. Gentlemen know the right things to say to a woman. They got all kinds of good manners."

"Could be that's why Mrs. Talbot is smitten by him," Buttons said.

"Shh . . . keep your voice down. She might hear us," Red whispered. "What do you mean, smitten?"

"She's got his brand on her heart. Mark my words, that's a natural fact," Buttons said.

"Quick, wasn't it?"

"Doesn't take long to fall in love with a person," Buttons said. "I reckon he's going to be with us all the way to the Cornudas." He sighed. "Somebody else to share our gold."

"Buttons, I think I liked you a lot better before you got rich."

Behind the curtain, Luna Talbot heard . . . and smiled.

CHAPTER EIGHTEEN

Ben Kane was angry, a scorching hatred that scalded his belly and brain like acid and for which there was only one cure. "We'll wipe them out," he said. "Kill them all lest some escape and their vile contagion spread to other places."

"Boss, it's got to look good to the Rangers," Ansley Dryden, Kane's foreman said. "We're talking about a lot of people here."

"You going soft on me, Anse?" Kane was looking for a fight, looking for somebody to blame for the presence of the Rathmores on range he considered his own.

Dryden shook his head. "Mr. Kane, that's a helluva thing to say to me. I've done my share of killing for you in the past. I've shot and hung near two score men in my time—rustlers, nesters, and Indians—but we got to step careful. That's all I'm saying."

"Damn it, Anse, don't give me problems. Give me answers," Kane said.

Kane, Dryden, and Milton Barnett sat in the old rancher's parlor, part of the sprawling stone house that had replaced the Rafter-K's original two-room log cabin. Along with the two cowboys, Kane had included his personal bodyguard and sometime adviser, the Austin gunman Dave Sloan, a sour, taciturn man who was slowly wasting away from consumption and was as dangerous and unpredictable as a rabid wolf.

"What about you, Milt?" Kane said. "You saw the Rathmores up close when Jake Wise was murdered, or so you say. How do we destroy the nesters and square it with the Rangers?"

"Kill 'em all and then bring a mountain down on them," Barnett said.

"Bring a mountain down on them," Dryden repeated, scorn in his words. He'd set store by Wise, a top hand. "You're one crazy peckerwood."

"Wait, Anse. Maybe he's crazy, maybe he isn't," Kane said. "Bring down a mountain . . . how?"

Barnett swallowed hard, then said, "Well, not a whole mountain. We drive them Rathmores into an arroyo carrying their dead and then bring the walls down on top of them with giant powder. Hell, the Rangers will never find them. Nobody will ever find them."

"We could set it up beforehand," Kane said. "Have the barrels placed so they're ready to blow the minute the Rathmores are in the arroyo. Anse, what do you reckon?"

"It could work," the foreman said. "Take some planning, but it could work. Destroy the evidence under tons of rubble."

"White people lying in unmarked graves, now

there's a disturbing thought," Kane said. "But who cares? The Rathmores aren't really white. They're scum."

"Unmarked graves is all they deserve," Barnett said. "They'd no need to kill Jake. Bushwhacked us and never gave us a chance."

"Milt, you're a smooth talker, but I'm not sure about you," Kane said.

"Because of what happened to Jake?"

"Jake's in his own unmarked grave by now," Kane said. "That grieves me."

Barnett shook his head. "Boss, it wasn't my fault. There was nothing I could do. Jake went down with the first volley and then they came after me. There was a lot of them Rathmores. Too many for one man to handle."

"Anse, take this man out and give him a job to do," Kane said. "And study on that gunpowder idea. It has to work and it has to work soon, savvy?"

The big foreman nodded. "I'm on it, boss."

As Dryden and Barnett stepped to the door, Kane said to Dave Sloan, "Dave, you stay here. We need to talk."

After the punchers left, Kane said, "How are you feeling?"

"Coughing up my lungs and slowly dying a little more each day," Sloan said. "When it gets real bad, I'll blow my brains out."

"I hope that day doesn't come any time soon." Kane was a hard man forged on the anvil of a merciless land and the hammer of a lifetime of violence but trying his best to be compassionate.

Sloan shrugged, unwilling to accept sympathy from anyone. "What do you want to talk about, Mr. Kane?"

"I want to talk about killing." Kane smiled an evil old man smile. "On a grand scale."

"How many of them Rathmores?" Sloan said.

"Forty . . . no more than fifty."

"Including children?"

"Of course. The Rathmore trash breed like rabbits."

"Pulling the trigger on young'uns gives me pause," Sloan said.

"Nits make lice, Dave," Kane said. "Tom Quick the mountain man said that when he was taken to task for killing Indian brats. Ol' Tom knew what the hell he was talking about."

Sloan was silent for a moment, thinking, and then he said, "All right. Let's say ten fighting men at most. Mr. Kane, you've got enough gun hands to take care of them, especially if we hit them when they least expect it."

"At night?"

"You read my mind."

Kane said, "Huzzah, for the man from Austin! Kill the men and then drive the women and children into the arroyo and blow them to hell, huh?"

"No. Kill the men and bring the arroyo down on top of their bodies. The women and children can leave."

"Damn it all, man. First chance they get, they'll tell the Rangers," Kane said. "We kill every last one of them, Dave. I ain't gonna argue with you on that point. I want the whole Rathmore clan dead. They've been a thorn in my side for the last three years."

Sloan was about to object, but the door slammed

open, and Ansley Dryden rushed inside, his face like thunder. "Boss, you'd better come see this. Jake Wise ain't in his grave. He's come home . . . at least, some of him."

Kane rose to his feet, his eyes wild. "They skun him?"

He read the answer to that question on his foreman's face and ran outside.

The bloody skin of Wise's upper body hung on a T-shaped frame that was tied upright to the saddle of his horse. A dozen punchers surrounded the grisly trophy, staring at it in horror.

"Boss, the horse come home by itself," a young hand with a sparse beard said to Kane. "It brung Jake's skin back."

"Damn you, I can see what the horse brung back," Kane said. "You men, don't just stand there gaping. Bury that obscenity." Then, loud enough so that everybody heard it plain, "The God-cursed Rathmores will pay for this. They'll pay in blood."

A murmur of approval ran through the punchers as a young man with unruly black hair said, "When do we ride, boss?"

"Real soon, Curley. I'll give the word when the time comes. In the meantime, load up your guns and be ready."

"Damn right," Curley said, and another puncher grinned and slapped him on the back. Encouraged, the youngster said, "After what they done to Jake, I reckon them Rathmores ain't even human."

"No, they ain't human. They're animals, Curley," the backslapper said. "They done the same thing to

Jim Shaw, but that was afore your time. Jim was one of the nicest fellers you could ever hope to meet."

He wasn't. Jim Shaw was mean, nasty, and downright dangerous in drink, but the passage of time had conferred martyrdom on a man that until the day he died nobody had cared to remember.

Ben Kane bought into that sentiment. "I done right by ol' Jim. I hung three of them Rathmores from the same cottonwood, and I'll do right by Jake. We'll come down on those savages like the wrath of God."

That last brought a cheer.

Sensing the mood of his men, Kane declared a day off for every hand. "Plenty of whiskey for every man jack of you."

Dave Sloan had earlier given him an additional piece of advice that Kane would not soon forget. "Keep them boys drunk between now and the attack on the Rathmores," he'd said. "A likkered-up man kills easier."

CHAPTER NINETEEN

"Three bounty hunters came after him and he killed them in self-defense." Red Ryan stood by the stage and handed up his shotgun to Buttons Muldoon. "Can't blame a man for that."

"Dead or alive," Bill Stanton said. "That's what they told him. Mrs. Talbot said they planned to take his head back to Louisiana in a pickle jar. She told me that."

"Well then there you go," Buttons said. "As clear a case of self-defense as ever there was."

"When a Ranger comes by, I'll tell him," Stanton said. "Do my duty, like."

"Sounds about right." Red climbed to his perch beside the driver.

Buttons handed him the shotgun. Luna Talbot was already aboard, and Arman Broussard was saddling his horse and hadn't showed yet.

"He told me to keep the dead man's horses and traps," Stanton said. "Said he didn't want to profit from the deaths of three men, even bounty hunters. Well, the horses ain't worth much, three hammer-headed mustangs that don't go any more than eight hundred pounds. But it was white of him nonetheless. Ah, here he comes."

Broussard rode up on the coach, touched his hat to Luna, and then said to Buttons, "I'll tag on behind you."

"And eat dust from here to the Cornudas." Buttons said, shaking his head. "Ride on ahead of us and keep your eyes skinned for road agents."

Broussard smiled. "Whatever you say. You're the boss." He urged his gray forward, waved to Stanton, and rode fifty yards in front of the stage before he drew rein.

"See you on the return trip, Bill," Buttons said. "You take care."

"Yeah, you too, Buttons, and you, Red, take care."

Red nodded and settled back in his seat as Buttons slapped the team into motion. Drivers never showboated leaving a stage station. Usually there was no one around to watch.

The Patterson stage had entered the grassland and yucca country of the Chihuahuan Desert when Red Ryan got a familiar feeling at the back of his neck that told him he was being watched by someone on his back trail. He mentioned it to Buttons Muldoon.

"Damn it, Red, I wondered why your head was on a swivel this past ten minutes," Buttons said. "You see anything?"

"Yeah, I thought I caught a glimpse of dust. It was there and then gone."

"Wolves in this country," Buttons said. "But they don't usually hunt at this time of the day. Could be a deer."

"Or a rider."

Buttons turned, and his eyes scanned the rolling terrain behind him. After a while he said, "I don't see anything. Red, the desert loves to play tricks on a man."

"Seems like. Damn it, I had a feeling we were being watched, but it's gone now."

"It was a deer, Red. Deer watch what men are doing, and maybe they never saw a coach and horses before. They stared and stared and made you feel it at the back of your neck."

"Yeah, that's probably it." But Red picked up the Greener and placed it across his thighs. He was sure he'd seen dust.

Juan Sanchez reined in his pinto mare and drank sparingly from his canteen. The breed wiped his mouth with the back of his hand and watched the receding dust cloud kicked up by the stage. It was headed for the Cornudas. Had to be. Where else would there be a gold mine? To his northeast rose the steep, rocky hills of the Sierra Tinaja Pinta, but once when he was on the scout he'd camped there for several days and there was no sign of gold workings.

The stage, with Luna Talbot and the treasure map inside, was headed for the Cornudas all right . . . and that's what he would tell Johnny Teague.

Sanchez had no liking for Teague, but the man paid him a top share of the loot whenever they made a score and usually footed the bill for women and whiskey when they hit a town. Tom Racker and the others had given Johnny three days to come up with a plan, so it was high time he headed back and told him what was happening.

But that could wait.

It should be noted here that Juan Sanchez harbored more than his share of the savage Apache hatred for Mexicans and white Americans and he was as dangerous and avaricious as a lobo wolf. He was a violent, mindless criminal in the worst sense of the word and he possessed no sense of empathy for other human beings.

When he saw the two travelers in the distance he watched them with menacing black eyes as a predator would study its prey.

In the lead, riding a burro, was a plump man with a full beard, the flat-brimmed hat on his head pulled low over his eyes. He led a pack burro, heavily laden. Trailing a few yards behind, a woman sat a third donkey. She held a small yellow parasol directly above her head and wore a dress of the same color that was hiked up for riding, revealing an expanse of white thigh.

Sanchez was not a smiling man, but his thick lips pulled back from his teeth in a feral grimace as he came to a decision. Johnny Teague could wait a little longer. Sanchez had other fish to fry. Two of them.

He urged his horse into a canter as he rode toward the man and woman at an oblique angle, so as to cut them off. The man saw him pretty soon and turned a startled face to the newcomer. When he was a few feet from the bearded man, the breed drew rein.

"And good morning to you, sir," the man said, smiling. He looked to be about fifty. "I take it you are a fellow traveler."

"You could call me that," Sanchez said. "Then again, you could call me plenty of other t'ings."

The fat man smiled again. His beard was so thick and black his mouth was almost hidden behind it. "Then let's get off to a sociable start, shall we? I am the Reverend William T. Loveshade and yonder on the burro is Mrs. Loveshade, my new bride."

The breed's gaze moved to the woman, not a grown woman, but a girl of around fourteen or so. She was slim and not pretty, but not ugly, either. A "plain Jane" described her. But she looked clean, judging by her hair and naked leg, and she showed no fear. In fact, she smiled at Sanchez as though she was mighty glad to see him.

He turned his attention back to the reverend. "Fat man like you shouldn't be riding a burro. Break its back, is what you'll do."

"'And when the ass fell down under Balaam and Balaam's anger was kindled he smote the ass with a staff.' Numbers: 27," Loveshade said. "When it comes to lazy burros, I follow Balaam's example and spare not the rod. Now, will you give me the road? I know that to the west there are many people in need of soul-saving. Fire and brimstone is what I give the sinner. Yea, verily, I put the fear of the living God into them, man or woman, as I did with my own dear bride."

It is said of Juan Sanchez, one of the most savage outlaws to ever plague the West, that he never mistreated an animal and that for no apparent reason horses and dogs were drawn to him. He once adopted a little tabby cat that he carried around for years before it drowned in the Great Indianola Hurricane of 1875 while Sanchez was in the local jail.

Sanchez swung out of the saddle and grabbed the burro's reins when Loveshade tried to ride away. "Git off that animal. Stand on your own two feet."

The reverend's face flushed, and he said, "Have a care. You're dealing with a man of the cloth. I will not be handled in this way."

The breed ignored that, pulled Loveshade off the burro and then said, "I want your wallet, watch, and the ring you're wearing. *Rapido*!"

"And if I don't?" the fat man said, defiance in his brown eyes.

"Then I'll shoot you in the belly and leave you for the wolves," Sanchez said. "Come dark they'll find you and you'll still be alive. A bad t'ing for you, I think." He thumbed back the hammer of his drawn Colt. "Make your decision."

Loveshade saw the writing on the wall and quickly produced his wallet and silver watch.

"And the ring," Sanchez said.

"It's my wedding ring," Loveshade said. "I bought it for my lady wife."

"He's a liar," the woman said. "He found it in the street outside the post office in Buffalo Gap."

"The ring," Sanchez said to Loveshade.

The preacher tugged at it. "I can't get it off."

"Well, that's all right," Sanchez said. "I'll shoot your finger off."

"No, no, I got it. Here, take it. I got it," Loveshade said.

The breed took the ring and then said to the woman, "Get off the burro." Then to the reverend, "Strip the burros. And remove the pack."

"Why?" Loveshade said.

"Because I'll shoot you if you don't," Sanchez said.

The reverend immediately saw the logic of that statement, stripped the burros, and removed the pack from the smallest donkey. Sanchez yipped and hazed the three burros, waving his arms. For a moment the animals stood stock still, perplexed over what the yelling human wanted them to do. Then it dawned on them that they were being set free. The last Sanchez and the others saw of them, they were kicking their heels in a southerly direction and were soon lost behind a dust cloud.

"Here, that won't do," said the Reverend William T. Loveshade. "I need an animal to carry my water and supplies."

"You have a broader back than the donkey had," Sanchez said. "Carry your own supplies."

"But it could be many miles to a settlement," Loveshade said. "I can't carry that much of a load."

"I reckon that's what the burro thought," Sanchez said.

The reverend was a man much given to sweat, and his light gray coat was stained black at the armpits and back. He turned to his wife and said, "Daphne, pick up the pack. You're younger than me."

"You go to hell," Mrs. Loveshade said.

The preacher looked like he'd been slapped. "*An excellent wife is the crown of her husband, but she who brings shame is like rottenness in his bones.* Proverbs 12:4. Daphne, you have shamed me before this highwayman. Now make amends and pick up the pack."

With what could have been a stillborn smile tugging at the corners of his mouth, Sanchez said, "Better do as your husband says."

"No, I won't," the girl said. "Mister, you saved me from him and I'm not going anywhere he goes. He weighs close to three hundred pounds and he uses me like a rutting hog."

"Then why the hell did you marry him?" Sanchez said.

"I'm an orphan, and he paid a farmer and his wife two hundred dollars for me," Daphne said. "He told me he'd give me a better life . . . and then led me into this desert."

"Yes, I did, for I'm a good shepherd seeking a flock," Loveshade said. "Now, do as you're told, woman, and pick up the pack."

"No," the girl said, stiff-backed and defiant.

"Then, verily, I will not spare the rod," Loveshade said. He unbuckled the thick leather belt he wore around his waist and advanced on his wife.

"I wouldn't do that if I was you," Sanchez said. To Daphne he said, "Get over here. You're coming with me."

The girl smiled. She had bad skin and was small and thin, as though she'd missed a lot of meals in her young life. She hurried to Sanchez, a gaunt carpetbag in one hand, yellow parasol in the other.

"You damned brigand, this is an outrage," Loveshade said, his bearded face black with anger. "By God, sir, I'll see you hanged."

Sanchez swung into the saddle and then pulled the girl up behind him. He leaned from the saddle and said, "Mister, I've killed men for less than that, but shooting a preacher might be bad luck, I think." He touched his hat. "*Vaya con Dios.*"

"Damn you. What about my pack?" Loveshade yelled as Sanchez and his bride rode away.

The breed turned his head toward the girl. "Well, señora, what about your husband's pack?"

"He can shove his pack up his ass," Mrs. Daphne Loveshade said, from under the meager shade of her parasol.

CHAPTER TWENTY

Buttons Muldoon leaned over in his seat and called into the coach, "Cornudas Mountains in view, Mrs. Talbot. And a pretty sight they are too."

Luna Talbot looked out the window and then said, "Will we reach them before nightfall, Mr. Muldoon?"

"Unlikely," Buttons said. "Looks like the shadows are halfway up the mountain slopes already."

"Where is Mr. Broussard?"

"He rode ahead on a scout."

"Does he think we're in any danger?" Luna said.

The stage bumped over some rocky ground and Buttons raised his voice a little to be heard. "No danger. Red did see dust behind us, but he reckons it was only a pronghorn. Don't worry, Mrs. Talbot, Broussard is a right careful man." He sat back in the seat and studied Red Ryan for a moment. "Never seen you white-knuckle that Greener afore in open country. You expecting trouble?"

"Nope, I'm not expecting trouble, but I don't want to be fooled is all."

"You sure you ain't got them Irish feelings of your'n

again, seeing things happen that ain't happened yet?" Buttons said.

"My ma was an O'Leary, and she had the gift of second sight," Red said. "She called it the *dara sealladh,* and she often saw the coming of sudden death to her kinfolk and even strangers."

"Hell, Red, don't say stuff like that," Buttons said. "Do you have the dara see . . . sela . . ."

"No, not like my ma had."

"Well thank God for that," Buttons said. "For a moment there you had me all affrighted thinking about sudden death and us feeding the buzzards."

"Where the hell is Broussard?" Red's voice was so edged that Buttons stared at him in surprise.

And then in equal bewilderment he stared at his guard's continuing death grip on the scattergun. "Red, I'm sure he'll be back directly."

"I hope so. Hey, it looks like thunderheads moving in over the mountains. Black sky over there."

"Nah, it's just passing clouds," Buttons said. "I reckon we're in for a spell of dry weather. We passed a flock of quail out in the open, and that's always a sign of no rain."

Red said, "I didn't see any quail."

"Well, sure enough, they were there," Buttons said, blinking.

Arman Broussard avoided the worst of the downpour by sheltering under a rock overhang in a shallow arroyo overgrown by brush and cholla. He saw no alternative but to wait out the storm, especially since out in the desert a mounted man would represent a tall target for a stray lightning bolt. Above him, the sullen sky looked like curled sheets of lead. He lit a cigar and waited. Nearby his horse grazed on bunchgrass and didn't seem to mind the thunder and relentless rain.

The storm passed quickly, but by that time the sun had fled the sky and the day was shading into evening. Broussard led his horse to the mouth of the arroyo and in the murky distance to the south he saw two bobbing lights, the sidelamps of the Patterson stage. The gambler decided to wait where he was until the stage arrived . . . a decision he'd later regret.

"Wherever we find graze for the horses is where we'll camp," Buttons Muldoon said. "Plenty of trees growing around there, so we'll do all right for firewood."

Red said "Strange we've seen no sign of Broussard."

"He probably waited out the storm someplace." Like Red, Buttons wore his slicker, and again like Red, a slightly worried expression. "Bill Stanton says there are a couple of underground springs in the Cornudas. Be good to camp near one of those."

"Seems like." Red's eyes restlessly searched the distance ahead.

And that worried Buttons even more. "Hell, Red, are you seeing things again?"

"Before the rain started, I thought I saw smoke."

Buttons groaned. "First dust, now smoke. Red, there ain't nobody in them mountains. Trust me. People don't live there, and I doubt the Apaches ever did."

"Well, I thought I—" Red shook his head. "You're right. It couldn't have been smoke."

"Damn right, I'm right. And I'd appreciate it if you quit choking that Greener. You're putting the fear of God into me again."

"I still got a strange feeling though, Buttons." Red removed his plug hat and shook rainwater from the brim. "Like there's somebody watching me, studying my every move."

"A bad-intentioned somebody?" Buttons said. "Like road agent somebody?"

"Maybe." Red replaced his hat and smiled. "Or the ghost of some old miner."

Buttons let out with an exasperated snort, leaned over, and yelled into the stage window, "You hear that, Mrs. Talbot?"

"Hear what?" the woman said.

"Red's hair is standing on end. All of a sudden, he's sceered of ghosts and ha'nts an' the like."

There was a pause, then Luna said, "I feel the same way, Mr. Muldoon. It's as though there are eyes on me."

"Because it's getting dark," Buttons said. "Lots of folks see scary things in the dark, usually wolves and bears an' the like."

"Yes, that must be the reason," Luna said. "Because it's getting dark."

Arman Broussard watched the stage roll closer, coming on slowly, the tired horses at a walk. He threw away the dead stub of cigar and prepared to mount, figuring he'd ride out to meet the others. He never made it. Hearing a sound behind him, the shuffle of feet, the gambler spun around, his hand instinctively reaching for the gun under his coat. Before he could draw, something hard slammed into the back of his skull, and suddenly he was falling headlong into a black abyss that had no beginning and no end.

CHAPTER TWENTY-ONE

An arc-shaped clearing surrounded by high rock walls promised grass for the horses, and Buttons Muldoon reined the team to a halt. "Take a look, Red. They don't need much feed, just enough."

Red nodded and climbed down from the seat. Buttons was wary enough that he passed his guard the Greener. "Take care." He glanced at the sky. "The moon is coming up. Give you some light over there."

"Not much. It's as black as the bottom of a dry well." Clutching the scattergun, Red walked into darkness.

Luna Talbot exited the stage and looked up at Buttons. "Why have we stopped here, Mr. Muldoon?"

"I think there's grass over there, ma'am. If there is, I'll let the team graze and we'll set up camp. It's rocky, uneven ground and I don't want to bring the stage any closer. I could lose an axle quicker 'n scat."

"Where is Mr. Broussard, I wonder?" Luna had taken her gun rig from her carpetbag and had slung the holstered revolver over her shoulder. The ivory handle of the Colt was white in the gloom.

Buttons didn't comment but thought she was a

careful woman. He also noticed that she was prettier than a woman had a right to be after spending most of the day in a hot, dusty stage. "I reckon Broussard can take care of himself, but he should be here. He must've seen us coming."

"Yes, it's a worrisome thing," Luna said, frowning.

"Yes, ma'am," Buttons said. "It sure is." But he wasn't worried. Not really.

"I'm thirsty," the woman said.

Buttons handed down a canteen, holding it by the canvas strap. "Take a stingy drink, Mrs. Talbot. If we don't find a spring, that's our coffee water, and I'm a coffee-drinking man." He smiled. "Why, here's a little story. I recollect the time back in the winter of 'seventy-eight when I was driving for the old Anderson and Lawson company. Me and a guard by the name of Lonesome Charlie Wagner got snowed in for a two-month at a settler's cabin up in the Kansas Flint Hills country. Well, me, Charlie, and the settler ran out of conversation after the first week, coffee after the second, and I thought I was like to die."

"I'll only have a little," Luna said, smiling. She took a few sips and handed the canteen back to Buttons.

He laid the canteen beside him on the seat and said, "Lonesome Charlie came to a bad end, got hung for a mule thief in El Paso. I don't know what happened to the settler. I guess he's still sod-busting. Anyhoo, talking about coffee, I recollect another time back in—"

A shotgun blasted apart the night quiet, roared again, and then came a scream.

Buttons jumped down from his seat and, Colt in hand, hit the ground running. "Stay there," he yelled over his shoulder to Luna Talbot before he vanished into darkness.

The woman drew her gun and stood with her back to the stage, her eyes probing the gloom. The team was restive, and the leaders tossed their heads, their harnesses chiming. Out in the desert scared coyotes no longer talked to the rising moon.

A long minute ticked past . . . then another . . . and another.

Luna felt the rapid thump-thump of her heart, and she found the night air hard to breathe. The stillness was profound, the deathlike silence ominous and threatening, full of malice. Her thumb lay on the Colt's beautifully curved hammer and she shivered as the desert rapidly cooled. Finally, she called out, "Red . . . Mr. Muldoon . . . are you there?"

The moon was well above the horizon, and a wan white light stained the outcrops of rock on the slopes of the peak nearest to her. As though she'd just remembered, Luna took a cartridge from her belt and slipped it into the empty chamber that had been under the hammer. It was a test, that was all . . . a test to see if her hands shook. She was pleased that she hadn't fumbled . . . hadn't trembled. Good. She was tense, but not scared. Not scared of the dark or the hush . . . just . . . cautious.

"Is anyone there?" Luna called. "Mr. Ryan? Mr. Muldoon?"

Nothing. Behind her the horses stirred, jostled, pawed the ground.

"Oh, hell," the woman said aloud, taking comfort in the sound of her own voice. "I'm not standing around here all night."

She stepped out in the direction taken by Red

Ryan and Buttons Muldoon. What had happened to them? Standing somewhere jawing to each other probably. Women were always accused of talking too much, but men were just as bad.

The darkness enveloped her, and she stared down at the rocky ground as she stepped, careful not to put a foot wrong and stumble. After twenty or thirty yards—she'd later say that she couldn't remember how far she'd walked—Luna stopped and called out, "Red? Red Ryan, are you there?"

Then footsteps behind her. Luna turned, smiling, expecting Buttons or Red. She saw neither . . . only the hate-twisted face of Elijah Rathmore. The man jumped on her, and his weight forced her to the ground. Her Colt flared in the darkness as she managed to get off a shot. But then she was overwhelmed by other members of the clan, men punching her, women clawing her. Luna was forced onto her belly, and rough hands bound a rope around her ankles and she was dragged behind the Rathmores. At least six of them, men and women, had a hand on the rope.

"Let me go, you damned animals," Luna yelled. Her back and hips bumped across the rocky ground and her canvas skirt rode up over her thighs. A younger man with a slack mouth bent over her, leered, and then backhanded her hard across the face. The blow hit her on the right side of her jaw and knocked her into unconsciousness.

By the time they dragged the senseless woman into the arroyo, the Rathmore males were already arguing about who would have her first.

CHAPTER TWENTY-TWO

"I send you on a scout and you come back with a woman," Johnny Teague said. He was highly amused. "Sanchez, where in hell did you find a woman in this wilderness? Even a downright homely one like her?"

Sanchez shrugged. "She was traveling with her husband, a preacher, and wanted to come with me. She doesn't like her husband much, I think."

"Have you done her yet?" Teague said.

"No."

Teague ran unenthusiastic eyes over the disheveled, sunburned Daphne Loveshade. "Yeah, well, there's no rush, is there?" Then, "Here, you didn't gun her old man, did you?"

"No."

"*Bueno.* Killing a preacher is bad luck."

Tom Racker, looking mean, said, "Sanchez, did you do what the boss told you to do, huh?"

"Yes. The stage with the Talbot woman is headed for the Cornudas Mountains," the breed said.

"That would make sense," Teague said. "I've always figured there was gold in them mountains." He smiled.

"Along with plenty of others who figured the same thing."

"And that's why there's a map," Crystal Casey said.

"We only got the breed's word for it," Racker said, on the prod. "For all he knows they could've headed into the New Mexico Territory. He should've stuck on their trail for a while longer instead of picking up a woman."

"Racker, you doubt my word?" Sanchez said, speaking low, slow, and tight.

Racker heard the tone, saw the devil in the breed's eyes, and decided he wanted no part of him that morning . . . or any other morning come to that. "I was just saying—"

"Saying what, Racker?" Sanchez said, pushing it.

"Saying that they could be headed anywhere north of here."

"Sanchez claims the stage was bound for the Cornudas," Teague said. "I don't see any reason to doubt him. I'm willing to bet the farm that the Lucky Cuss gold mine is somewhere among them peaks."

"Then I say we saddle up and get 'er done," Racker said. "I've had enough of this damned desert to last me a lifetime."

"Suits me, Tom," Teague said. "But have a cup of coffee first. You ain't had any yet, and it's making you downright unsociable. You, too, Sanchez, and the woman looks like she could use a cup."

"What about the woman?" Racker said.

"We'll take her with us. She can ride Sam Canning's horse. Sam don't need it no more."

As the Teague gunmen stood around smoking and drinking coffee, Crystal Casey revealed that impulsive compassion that some whores possess. She put her arms around Daphne Loveshade's shoulders, found a place for her to sit, and gave her coffee. Within five minutes the two were conversing like old friends, and an eavesdropper might even have heard Crystal talking about the ups and downs of the oldest profession and advising Daphne to consider it as a future career path. The girl seemed more than interested, her face alight as the possibilities of such a glamorous life overwhelmed her.

Johnny Teague and his nine gunmen and two women broke camp before noon and headed north, leading a mustang packhorse. Since he considered Daphne Loveshade a new pet that had to be protected at all cost, Juan Sanchez rode between the women. He had no sexual intentions toward the girl, mainly because he considered the dogs and cats he'd owned at one time or another all a sight prettier than she was.

Daphne was blissfully unaware of the gunman's attitude toward her, but if she'd known, it might have put a damper on the newly minted vocation that called her to the whoring profession.

Teague and the others rode under a blue sky and a hot sun.

There was little talk among the men, and for some reason Tom Racker was still brooding, nursing his ill temper of the morning. There was little reason to believe that Racker sensed something amiss, that his bad luck was about to turn blacker.

Former gang member Dave Quarrels always insisted that the gunman knew death was stalking him. "Later that day,

I reckon he went into the gunfight with Arch Storm and them knowing he was a dead man," Quarrels said during his 1936 interview with newsman A. B. Boyd. "Hell, after that battle even Johnny Teague was never the same again. That's my opinion and you can take it to the bank." Asked by Boyd if he thought the Lucky Cuss mine was jinxed, Quarrels said, "Of course it was hexed. You know all the bad things that happened in them mountains because I told you about it yestidy. But the fight with Arch Storm and them other three was before all that. Now, you tell me this . . . if'n that wasn't an ill-starred mine then why did Arch catch up with us while we were on our way there? Huh? I'll tell you why. Because the Lucky Cuss brought nothing but death and destruction to everybody who was ever associated with it, an' that's a natural fact. It was cursed . . . cursed by God and the devil, an' there's the truth of it."

Quarrels had maintained that the Teague/Storm gunfight erupted because Arch had wanted to avenge the death of his brother, killed by Johnny Teague in a Dallas poolroom. But that was hogwash. Arch Storm once did have a brother, but he'd died of scarlet fever when he was seven. No, the one and only reason for the gunfight was that Arch had wanted the women.

Arch Storm was forty-seven years old that summer. He'd been a buffalo hunter and an army scout and made a precarious living as a wolfer. With him were Noble Hunt, Jud Epps, and Benson Egan. Like Storm, the three had been buffalo hunters. Epps had been a New Mexico Territory lawman for a spell, and Hunt had just spent two years in Huntsville for rape.

All four were big men who affected wolf skin capes,

fur hats, and miners' boots, and collectively they smelled like a gut wagon. Epps had a slight reputation as a pistolero. The others favored the .44-40 Winchester, with which they were extremely skilled.

Taken together, they were men to be reckoned with.

Johnny Teague was the first to spot the freight wagon that had halted on the trail, a couple of mounted men flanking it. As Teague and his boys rode closer, two men jumped down from the wagon and stood watching them, rifles across their chests. Always on the lookout for a fast profit, Teague correctly pegged the men as wolfers and doubted that they carried much money, but the two draft animals and the horses ridden by two of the men were worth something.

The stink of the pelts in the wagon and the stench of the wolfers themselves became unpleasantly apparent as Teague and his gunmen drew rein at a distance of five yards.

"Howdy, boys," Teague said, smiling. "Where you headed?"

"Go to hell," Arch Storm said. "I ain't in the mood for pleasantries. I'll cut to the chase . . . how much do you want for the women? We got a cold winter coming up, and we need female company."

The two mounted men swung out of their saddles and joined Storm and Epps in front of the wagon.

"Ah, that depends on how much you're willing to pay," Teague said. His eyes flicked over the horses and was disappointed. About thirty dollars at a knacker's yard for all three.

"If she isn't diseased, fifty dollars for the blondie,"

Storm said. "Twenty for the other one. She ain't worth much."

Teague grinned. "Hell, man, just looking at you, I know you don't have that kind of money."

"Try me. Do we have a deal?" Storm said.

"No deal." Teague decided to play with the wolfer. "The blonde's name is Crystal Casey. She ain't diseased and she's worth an even two hunnerd. The other one, well, I'll take a hunnerd for her." His grin widened. "Come now, let's be thrifty. I'll part with both for two-fifty on the barrelhead. Now, show me some gold. I won't take Yankee scrip from a stranger. Man never knows if it's even genuine."

Storm's bearded face hardened. "You're messing with me. I don't like a man who messes with me."

Supremely confident in his nine gunmen, Teague said, "Who's messing with you? You want the women as winter belly-warmers, you pay the price. Simple as that."

"I said fifty for the blonde, twenty for the other one," Storm said. "You're one deef bullethead, ain't you?"

Teague decided that the game was over. It was time to see if the wolfers were worth robbing. "Let's see your money." He sighed as though the dickering had worn him out.

To Epps, Storm said, "Jud, take seventy dollars from our stash." As Epps reached into his cape, brought out a canvas bag, and began to root for coins like a great, shaggy bear, Storm said, "I'll need to see them gals naked. I ain't buying no pig in a poke."

"Mister, you ain't seeing me naked," Crystal said, her eyes blazing. "And why don't you take a bath now and then?"

"You shut your trap, girlie," Storm said. "We'll take care of you later."

Teague was primed for the draw and the confiscation of the wolfers' bulging money poke, but he didn't start the gunfight . . .

A butterfly did.

"It was one of them yellow, fork-tailed butterflies you get in Texas. You know the kind," Dave Quarrels would later recall. "Damn thing fluttered past one of the wolfers, a man called Joe or maybe it was Jim Epps, I never did find the right of his name, but a few days after the gunfight the Ranger who reported finding the bodies called him Joe Epps, a one-time deputy sheriff out of the New Mexico Territory. Well, anyhoo, that's how it was wrote in the newspaper, so it's probably right. Now, where was I? Oh, yeah, the butterfly. Well sir, Epps took a swat at it . . . and the ball opened.

"That damned crazy lunatic Tom Racker, who was always looking for the trigger, thought Epps was drawing down on him and shucked his own gun. He shot Epps in the belly and then Johnny Teague yelled, 'No, I don't want any gunfighting,' but it was too late. Them wolfers unlimbered their Winchesters and commenced to shooting. Epps meantime, dead on his feet but as game as they come, cut loose on Racker. Hit him, too. Tom took a bullet to the chest and went out of the saddle like he'd been whacked by a twenty-pound sledge. Now the fighting had become general.

"At that time I rode a three-year-old mare, and at that age a horse knows nothing. When the firing started, she gave me no end of trouble. I snapped off a shot but only God knows where it went. Next thing I know, I'm on my back in the dirt, watching the fight from the ground. I seen three of our boys go down, seen the Casey gal get hit by a stray round, and then I seen Steve Curtis get plugged. We called him Dancer Curtis on account of how he loved to shake a hoof and he was mighty good with the iron. Bullet took his jaw clean off. I spied that with my own two eyes and it was no sight for a Christian man. Well, it didn't take but a minute before the wolfers were all shot to pieces, lying in the dirt weltering in their blood. We lost five of our own that day, all good men, true blue you might say, and the Teague gang never recovered from that fight. No sir, it never did.

"The damnedest thing is, the wolfers had but ninety dollars and twenty-seven cents in their poke, so we fought that battle for next to nothing. I still recollect to this day what Johnny Teague said to us after the smoke cleared."

"I'm sorry boys," Johnny Teague said, looking around at the dead. "This was all my fault. I called the play."

"No fault of your'n, Johnny," Dave Quarrels said. "Racker figgered one of them wolfers was drawing down on him."

"Why the hell did he move like that?" Teague said.

"The wolfer?" Quarrels said. "He swatted at a butterfly."

Teague looked stricken. "What are you talking about, Dave?"

"A butterfly flew past him and the wolfer swatted at it. Racker thought the man was going for his gun. I seen it all."

"Nine men," Teague said. "Nine men dead because of a butterfly?"

"A yellow butterfly. Yeah, what you said just about sums it up."

"And what about me, Johnny? What about me, you crazy man?" Crystal Casey stood and glared at Teague, her fists on her hips. The left side of her head was bloody, and Daphne Loveshade dabbed at it with a piece of white cloth she'd torn from her petticoat.

"She was grazed by a bullet," Daphne said. "She'll be all right."

"I lost some curls, Johnny," Crystal said. "I lost a whole handful of curls. I wanted to have my likeness made in El Paso or somewhere. So now what do I do?"

Teague looked at the woman but did not really see her. He walked away, sat, and hugged his knees, his head bent.

Crystal angrily stomped in his direction, but one of the surviving gunmen blocked her path. He shook his head and said, "Not now."

Crystal looked into the man's eyes, got chilled by the green ice she saw, and turned away. "Daphne," she called. "My head's bleeding again."

The green-eyed gunman looked at Teague and felt a tremor of shock run through him. Johnny was bleeding from a neck wound! The word always had been that the bullet hadn't been cast yet that would harm Johnny Teague. Yet one had. And for the gunman, that was a worrisome thing . . . for the first time he realized that his boss was not invincible.

CHAPTER TWENTY-THREE

Red Ryan woke to pain and a steady hammering sound, like metal hitting a stone wall.

"Hell, I figured you was dead for sure," Buttons Muldoon said. "You haven't moved for hours, lying still as a sack of flour. Seen that my ownself and it scared me some."

Red opened his eyes, blinked them into focus, and through the gloom saw Buttons sitting opposite him. The driver's feet were bound, and his hands seemed to be tied behind his back. They were in a cave of some kind. To Red's right, a rocky floor sloped away from him and lost itself in darkness. He could not see an entrance and the only light came from a guttering oil lamp.

"What happened?" He tried to stand and realized he was trussed up like Buttons.

"They jumped you, Red. And then they jumped me."

"Who?"

"I don't know who. A bunch of screaming devils, that's all I remember."

Red tried to piece together the events of the night. He recalled walking into the rocks and then being overpowered by a pack of snarling, half-naked men. He said, "I got a shot off."

"And winged somebody, I reckon," Buttons said. "I heard a yelp, but nobody got plugged real serious. Near as I could tell, that is."

"Have you seen Luna Talbot?" Red asked. His head hurt like an anvil had been dropped on him.

"Last I saw her was when I left her at the stage," Buttons said.

"Damn it, Buttons. Why did you leave her?"

"Because I heard you shooting at something and came after you. I told her to stay right where she was at."

"As representatives of the Abe Patterson and Son Stage and Express Company, we're responsible for Mrs. Talbot's safety," Red said.

"Well, there's not a whole helluva lot we can do about that right now, can we?" Buttons said.

"Who were those guys? I couldn't see much in the dark."

"I have no idea. Wild men, I reckon," Buttons said. "They sure acted like wild men."

Red took a long pause for thought, then said, "We're in a fix, ain't we?"

"Seems like," Buttons said. "They brung us here. I think this is the Lucky Cuss mine. It's the mine shaft, got to be. Can you hear the picks farther down the tunnel?"

"They say raw gold has a smell. Can you smell it?"

"No."

"Neither can I." Red said. Then, "They took our guns."

"No kiddin'," Buttons said. "I never noticed that."

"Jeez, we're in a fix." Red said.

"You've already said that, and your head is bleeding."

"Somebody must have hit me with a rock. I know my lights went out right quick. Where's my hat?"

"I don't know," Buttons said.

"I set store by that hat. It's English wool felt. The best derby money can buy."

"Maybe we'll find it," Buttons said.

"Yeah, maybe," Red said. "Why did they bring us here, you reckon?"

"I don't want to think about that," Buttons said. "Those boys were wild men. That's all I know."

"Cannibals?" Red said.

"I said I don't want to think about it, and neither should you."

But Red did think about it a few minutes later when four men, naked except for loincloths and crude leather sandals, walked into the mine and untied Buttons's feet and then his.

A man with dirty, lank hair to his shoulders and swamp-water eyes prodded Red with the muzzle of his Winchester. "Get up, you."

Red got to his feet and a wave of nausea and dizziness swept over him. When he could finally talk, he said, "Where are you taking me?"

"You'll see." The man with the rifle prodded again. Harder. "Move."

"Move where, you crazy—"

The rifle butt slammed between Red's shoulder blades, revealing the direction.

"That way," the man said. Then to his companions, "Bring the fat one."

It was a measure of Buttons's anxiety that he didn't object to being called fat. Normally he would have protested indignantly, but these were far from normal times. He'd fallen in with savages and his future looked mighty bleak.

Red was pushed and prodded along a tunnel that gradually sloped upward toward the entrance. The lanterns carried by the long-haired men cast grotesque, moving shadows on the rock walls and glittered on a gouged quartz seam that bore evidence of pick-and-hammer work. That this was the Lucky Cuss mine, Red had no doubt . . . but would it prove to be unlucky for him and Buttons?

Blinking against the sudden daylight, Red Ryan was pushed into a narrow arroyo that was nonetheless crowded with people—men, slat-thin and ragged women, and wide-eyed children. They stared at Red and Buttons without curiosity. Mixed in with the throng, a Mexican carried a load of firewood and another stood at a fire and patiently stirred an iron pot that steamed over the flames and smelled of boiling meat. Under a two-man guard, four more Mexicans, picks on their shoulders, shuffled toward the mine entrance.

The place was rank with the stench of so many unwashed people crowded together in a confined space that Red tried to close off his nose as a Winchester prodded him and Buttons toward the deeper part of the arroyo. The canyon walls became narrower, barely allowing the passage of a broad-shouldered man, but after about thirty feet they widened again before opening up into a natural amphitheater of reddish-brown rock about half an acre in extent. Directly facing Red was a shallow alcove where an enormously fat man sat on a natural stone shelf.

Two things troubled Red in that moment. One was that the fat man wore his plug hat. The other, much more disturbing, was the sight of Luna Talbot sitting at the man's feet. A rope was looped around her neck, and the end was grasped in the fat man's chubby fist. Luna's face was badly bruised, and there was fear and anger in her eyes.

"Elijah, are these the new slaves?" the fat man said.

"Sure are, Papa," the man called Elijah said. "They look strong enough, so I'd say they got a six-month of work in them. A year, if'n we don't beat them too much and feed 'em right."

Papa Mace Rathmore waved a negligent hand. "Pah, we can always find slaves." His grin was unpleasant as he yanked on the rope. "Unless they look like this one. Women like this are rare."

"Yeah, she's a looker all right," Elijah said, his slack mouth wet. "After you're finished with her, you gonna share her around, Pa?"

"No, you damned son of a cross-eyed whore," Rathmore said. "Look at them women out there, worn-out harlots every last one of them. I think it's time I took a new bride for myself." He looked down at Luna and leered. "Ain't that right?"

"Go to hell, you fat, smelly hog," Luna said.

That earned her a harsh yank on the rope, and she winced in pain.

"Before long I'll teach you respect, woman," Rathmore said. His mouth twisted like a snarling animal. "I'll beat it into you."

Red Ryan tensed, doing a fast mental calculation.

There was about ten feet of open ground between himself and Rathmore. Even with his hands tied behind his back, he could close the distance in about a second. Then a jump and a boot into the fat man's scowling face.

Buttons read the signs, the sudden tautness of Red's body and his sharp intake of breath, and yelled, "Red, no!"

Too late.

Bent forward because of his bound hands, Red ran at Rathmore and had time to register the look of surprise on the man's face. He leapt into the air and lashed out with his right boot, aiming for Rathmore's head . . . but the fat man was no longer there. Displaying amazing speed and agility, he'd moved to his right, avoiding the kick. Off balance, Red did a half-somersault, landed hard on his back, and his wind erupted out of him.

His hands tied behind his back, nauseous and desperately struggling for breath, Red Ryan was easy prey.

Elijah Rathmore and one of his brothers immediately laid into him with rifle butts. Unable to defend himself, Red kicked out at his attackers as blows thudded into his head and chest. Buttons Muldoon attempted a rescue and got pummeled to the ground by four more Rathmores wielding shovels and wooden clubs. Red struggled to get to his feet, but a rifle butt to the back of his head dropped him and he knew no more.

Papa Mace waddled to his sons and held up a hand. "Stop, you ill-begotten imbeciles," he yelled. "I don't want them dead. I want them as slaves." The blows stopped, and the fat man said, "Take them to the mine."

"Papa, lookee there!" Elijah Rathmore said, pointing to the rock face.

Papa Mace's gaze followed his son's finger and his eyes popped. The woman was climbing, trying to reach the top of the arroyo.

Elijah levered a round, threw his Winchester to his shoulder, and grinned. "I'll bring her down."

"No!" Mace yelled. "You damned whoreson, don't shoot. Get after her."

Elijah threw down his rifle and said, "I'll catch her, Pa." He ran to the wall and began to climb.

"You others, get on top of the arroyo. Bring her back here." Then, his flabby face vicious, Papa Mace said, "Somebody get me my whip. I'll beat the defiance out of that damned tramp."

The long-haired man was gaining on her, scaling the rock face like a grinning mountain goat. Worse, Luna Talbot had twisted her ankle almost as soon as she'd started her climb, and the pain had slowed her considerably.

Elijah Rathmore was close, very close, close enough to be clearly heard. His grin widened, rotten teeth showing behind thick, peeled-back lips. "Ooh, you're gonna get a whippin'. Pa's all riled up."

Papa Mace's angry voice came from the bottom of cliff. "Elijah, fetch her down here," he yelled. "Don't let that woman get away."

Without taking his eyes off Luna, Elijah answered, "I won't, Pa. I got her."

"Get away from me," Luna said. She tossed a loose rock at Elijah's head . . . and missed.

"Got you." Elijah grinned, his clawed, outstretched hands reaching for her.

Samuel Colt saved Luna Talbot that day. Or at least his single-shot Model 3 derringer in .41 rimfire caliber did.

Up until the moment Elijah Rathmore stretched to grab her, Luna had forgotten the little pistol. Without much thought, she'd dropped it into the pocket of her riding skirt before leaving the ranch. It was a recent habit she'd acquired after a visiting Texas Ranger happened to mention the time during a gunfight when a spent percussion cap jammed his revolver and a Remington derringer had saved his life.

Now Luna hoped a Colt derringer would save her own.

One shot. One cartridge. One chance.

She backed away from Elijah and flattened herself against the rock, taking the couple of seconds she needed to draw her gun and thumb back the hammer. Elijah's hands were on her shoulders, dragging her closer to him. Even as she smelled the feral stink of the man's body, she shoved the muzzle of the Colt into his belly and pulled the trigger.

The crash of the shot echoed through the arroyo and drowned out Elijah's hysterical shriek of pain. Luna wrenched out of his grasp and pushed him away. For an instant the man's face registered a wide-eyed mix of shock and terror. Then he was falling, tumbling head over heels, plummeting earthward until his back slammed into the rocky ground and most of his internal organs exploded.

For a moment Papa Mace stood transfixed by the horror he'd just witnessed. He roared his rage and picked up the Winchester Elijah had discarded earlier.

A bullet spanged off rock inches from Luna's head. Then another. She looked down and saw the fat man shooting at her and others running to his assistance. She climbed for her life, the parapet of the rock face still twenty feet above her. The limestone rock smoothed out the higher she climbed, and secure foot- and handholds became fewer. She slowed her climb as bullets smashed splinters around her.

Ten feet to go . . . Luna winced as a rifle ball burned across her right shoulder, immediately drawing blood that stained the torn fabric of her shirt. She climbed on.

Five feet . . . her chest heaved, and her breath came in short gasps.

She slipped on loose rock and clung by her fingers to a narrow rock shelf as she struggled, her legs kicking, to find a foothold. The Rathmores were not marksmen, but bullets peppered the rock, close enough to her head that a jagged fragment of lead drew blood from her cheekbone.

Luna found a toehold, a shallow niche that was secure enough that she could push and pull herself over the top of the escarpment and onto level ground. She rolled away from the edge and then rested a few moments before she stood. Shouts warned her that the Rathmores were on top of the arroyo and closing fast. A talus slope fell away from her at a steep angle for about a hundred yards before it reached the flat, and Luna Talbot flung herself at it. Running, she slipped and fell several times, grazing her hands and knees bloody before she reached the level and stumbled across stony ground into the cover of heavy brush and sage.

Exhausted, Luna threw herself flat and tried to make herself small . . . like a hunted animal.

CHAPTER TWENTY-FOUR

"Ryan, how are you feeling?" Arman Broussard said. "You can't take too many more beatings."

"And that's a natural fact," Buttons Muldoon said, himself sporting a black eye and bruised cheekbone, just visible in the dim lamplight. He sniffed a chunk of the boiled meat his captors had provided, made a face, and set it aside. It smelled like dead horse.

Red said, "I thought they'd never stop hitting me with their damned rifle butts. How long have I been out this time?"

"About three hours. It's dark outside," Broussard said.

"Who are these people?" Red asked. "No, don't answer that. First tell me, where is Luna Talbot?"

"They were shooting at her . . . I remember watching her climb the rocks before I went out like a dead cat," Buttons said.

Red said, "So right now, you don't know if she's dead, alive, or captured?"

"About the size of it," Buttons said. "Broussard here missed all of it, including the kick you aimed at the fat man's head." He smiled. "That was funny."

"To you, maybe," Red said, talking slow, favoring a split lip. "I didn't think it was so funny."

Brossard said, "The fat man's name is Papa Mace Rathmore, and he's the big auger around here. According to what I learned from the Mexicans, Mace led his seven sons with their wives and children into these mountains calling them the promised land. Only it wasn't. The Rathmores found nothing but disease and starvation and constant war with a local rancher . . . but then they discovered the gold mine."

"That's why we're here," Buttons said. "Luna Talbot giving me and Red a share in the mine, an' all."

"A share of nothing is still nothing," Broussard said.

Buttons frowned. "I'm not catching your drift."

"The mine is played out, and there wasn't much gold here to begin with," the gambler said.

"I find that hard to believe," Buttons said. "Feller by the name of Morgan Ford struck it rich and called the mine the Lucky Cuss. He drew a map to the place and left it to Luna Talbot before he died."

"Whoever that man was, I believe he made a fair living mining a single quartz seam, and for the past couple of years the Rathmores have done the same," Broussard said. "But the seam buried itself in solid rock and the Mexicans are now trying to dig it out. The Rathmores put me to work with a pick down there, and the vein is getting narrower. Two or three feet deeper into the rock and I reckon it will be gone. Maybe less than that."

"And that's it?" Buttons said. "All the gold in the Lucky Cuss is in a single, goddamned quartz vein that's about played out?"

"I'm afraid so," Broussard said. "Sure doesn't make

Luna Talbot's map worth much, does it? And there's even more bad news."

"Hell, man, you're just full of calamity, ain't you?" Buttons said, scowling, visions of future riches popping in his head like soap bubbles.

Broussard ignored that last comment and said, "The timbers holding up the roof are old and full of dry rot. It won't take much to bring down the whole shebang and half the mountain with it." He smiled. "A good sneeze might do it."

Buttons was disappointed and determined to be crabby. "Broussard, who the hell are these Mexicans you're always talking about?"

The gambler answered, "They're slaves. Slaves of the mine like me, you, and Red. We're all to be worked to death."

Buttons shut his mouth, sorry he'd asked the question.

Red Ryan, hurting all over, dozed for an hour and was wakened by a rifle muzzle jammed into his ribs.

"On your feet," one of the Rathmore brothers said. Like the others, he was thin and wore only sandals and a skin loincloth, but the Winchester he held was shiny and new.

Red rose to his feet. Buttons and Broussard already stood, guarded by another rifle-toting man with a knife scar on his left cheek.

"Outside," Scarface said. "All of you."

"All three of you," said the Rathmore guarding Red.

"I can count," Scarface said. "I know there's three of them."

"No, you can't count." The man prodded Red. "Go."

Buttons, still in a bad mood, said, "Where are you taking us?"

"Outside," Scarface said again.

"Why?" Buttons said.

"You will honor the dead."

Red Ryan felt a stab of alarm. Was Luna Talbot dead? Had she been shot off the cliff? "Is the woman dead?"

Scarface glared at him in disgust, spat, and then pushed him toward the mine entrance.

A pulsing, single beat on a hand drum and the wailing shrieks of women greeted Red Ryan and the others as they approached the rectangle of flame-streaked darkness that marked the entrance of the Lucky Cuss. Rifle butts herded the three men to the opening, where they were told to stand.

"Bow your heads," Scarface said. "Show your grief."

The funeral procession had stopped, Papa Mace in the lead, Red's hat on his head. He had blackened his face with soot, and around his fat neck he wore a rusty piece of armor, a gorget that had belonged to one of the old Spanish conquistadors that had once visited the mountains in a vain search for gold. As he had Luna Talbot, Mace held another human being by a rope, a terrified Mexican who visibly trembled as Rathmore forced the man to his knees. Behind Papa Mace, seven lamenting women screamed and tore at their hair and cut themselves, blood running down their thin arms in tendrils of scarlet. Behind the women a shrouded corpse lay on a makeshift litter, two silent male pallbearers on each side.

Arman Brossard's Cajun parents would not dig

a hole on Good Friday lest it quickly fill with the Savior's blood, and now the superstitions of his childhood returned to haunt him. "Who lies dead in these mountains?" he said.

"Elijah Rathmore, my brother and the firstborn son of Papa Mace," one of the guards said. "Murdered by the whore you brought among us."

Red felt a surge of hope. "Where is Luna Talbot?"

The question was answered by a backhanded blow across Red's face. During his days as a booth fighter, Red had been hit harder by bigger men, and although he staggered back a step, he remained on his feet.

Scarface had delivered the wallop, and he gave Red the answer to his question. "The witch escaped, but we will find her. And when we do, we'll burn her."

"Silence, Jeremiah," the other guard said. "The time has come for the Mexican to pay the price for Elijah's sins so that our brother may enter paradise."

The wails of the women ceased and a quiet so profound fell in the arroyo that the only sound was the crackle of the fires. A ragged child with huge brown eyes handed Papa Mace a braided leather riding crop about three feet in length with a hammer-shaped ivory handle. As Red and the others watched in horror, the whip rose and fell, slashing across the Mexican's face, shoulders, and outstretched, pleading hands.

The helpless Mexican's screams ringing in his ears, the sight was more than Red Ryan could bear. Stiff and sore from his beating, he nonetheless needed to stop the atrocity . . . and this time his hands were not tied.

Before his guards could react, Red crossed the few yards of space between him and Papa Mace. The fat man looked at him in astonishment, a split second before Red delivered a powerful straight right to his face. Mace Rathmore staggered back, his smashed nose spurting snot and gore, but Red was relentless. His shoulders and arms bulged with a pugilist's muscle, a holdover from his days as a bare-knuckle booth fighter. When he followed up with a looping left, it snapped Mace's head back and set the man up for Red's tremendous right uppercut. Papa Mace fell on his back, and his feet gouged the dirt as he convulsed like a stranded white whale.

The two Rathmore brothers raised their Winchesters, but Buttons and Broussard immediately tackled them, and their shots went wild, whining off the rock walls of the mine. Buttons, stocky and strong, had been in many a fist-and-boot scrap, and he got in a few good licks at both Rathmores before he was overwhelmed by two more brothers and several screeching women. Broussard, a revolver fighter, was not handy with his fists, and he quickly went down, beaten into unconsciousness.

The remaining two Rathmore brothers went for Red, aided by four enraged women who snarled and clawed and bit like panthers. Like Buttons, Red was by nature a brawler, and he took both men to the woodshed, ignoring the women. He made a good accounting of himself before a rifle butt to the back of his head dropped him.

Slipping into unconsciousness, he was aware that the Rathmore brothers were giving him a savage, terrible beating with fists, rocks, and rifle butts, but his feeble attempts to fight back were brushed aside. He finally blacked out and didn't hear Papa Mace yell, "Don't kill him. I want him to burn."

Buttons Muldoon, himself on the ragged edge of oblivion, opened his swollen eyes and saw Red lying still in the dirt. Then from somewhere distant, he heard his dead mother's lilting Irish voice say, "Patrick, your friend is going to die. Bejaysus, he's lost enough blood to paint the back porch."

Buttons tried to say something, reassure his ma that Red would survive, but all he heard was the frail, meaningless croak of his own voice . . . and then the darkness took him.

CHAPTER TWENTY-FIVE

Townes Pierce handed Johnny Teague a cup of coffee and said, "You got to get over it, boss. What's done is done and there's no going back to change it."

Teague said, "Five men, Townes. Five of the best. Tom Racker, Fulton Smith . . . the others. We're done. Finished. The hoedown is over."

The night was dark, silent, brooding, as though the desert was lifeless.

"You got four of us left, boss," Pierce said. "You got me, Dave Quarrels, Slim Porter and the breed. It's enough."

"Enough for what?" Teague said, the black dog of depression ravaging him. "Townes, you got no right to say it's enough."

"Frank and Jesse did some of their best work with four," Pierce said.

"How do you know that?" Teague said.

Pierce lowered his head and didn't answer.

Juan Sanchez had been listening, and he stepped away from the fire. "Johnny, including you, there's five of us, enough to take the gold mine."

"Sure enough," Dave Quarrels said. "Hell, I heard of mines where a feller could just walk into the shaft an' pick nuggets up off the ground. I heard that plenty of times."

Teague raised lusterless eyes to Sanchez. "You still sure the stage with the Talbot woman was headed for the Cornudas?"

"Yeah, damned sure," Sanchez said.

Teague thought that through for a spell and then said, "Well, maybe we'll head out that way."

"We got to do something, boss," Pierce said. "We need to get some money and leave this desert."

"Is there any alternative?" Teague said. "If we don't go for the mine, what else can we do?"

"Nothing," Sanchez said. "Except split up and go our separate ways."

"We could rob a bank," Dave Quarrels said. "Plenty of fat banks in El Paso. I say we rob a bank and then skip over the border into Old Mexico."

"We're already all shot to pieces," Teague said. "You really want to rob a bank in a town with some tough lawmen? Remember what happened to Jesse and Frank and them in Northfield? No, robbing banks is out as far as I'm concerned. At least for the time being."

Quarrels looked contrite. "Well, all right then, maybe a bank in some other town . . . a small town, huh?"

"Dave, don't say the word 'bank' again or I'll shoot you dead," Teague said.

"And if you ain't dead, I'll make sure of it," Sanchez said.

"Well, if somebody makes a decision soon I'll go along with it," Pierce said.

"Me too," Slim Porter said. He was a tall, round-shouldered man with a pleasant, open face. Later Dave Quarrels would say of him that Slim was the best of a bad bunch, fast and deadly with a gun but much given to reading the Bible he kept in his saddlebags. And he'd had a good mother.

Teague stared over his coffee cup into darkness, seeing nothing as a night bird made a trilling sound. The breeze had a cool edge and made the campfire flames dance.

After a while, he looked up at Sanchez and said, "I'm taking your word for it. We'll head for the Cornudas and claim ourselves a gold mine. We ride out at first light."

"Johnny, melancholy comes to a man that sees no future for himself," Sanchez said. "Now you got a future, it's time to throw off the woebegone, I think."

"What's in my future, Sanchez?" Teague said. "You got a crystal ball?"

"Striking it rich, by golly," Quarrels said.

Sanchez nodded. "Like the man says."

"We may have to kill to get it," Teague said.

"We've all killed before," Sanchez said.

Teague smiled. "Gets easier, don't it? You kill a man. Time goes along, and you kill another and pretty soon you don't feel it anymore."

"Yeah, the more you kill, the easier it gets," Sanchez said. "It's a natural law."

"An' it's also a natural fact," Quarrels said, grinning.

* * *

Crystal Casey and Daphne Loveshade had been deep in whispered conversation, and they stepped to where the men were gathered around Johnny Teague.

"Ahem, gentlemen," Crystal said. "Listen up. Daphne has an announcement to make, something she wants to tell us. Speak now, Daphne. Don't be shy."

The girl smiled . . . shyly . . . and said, "As you know, I've left my husband and now wish to make a new life for myself. Since I'm very young and not used to the ways of the world, I've been talking things over with Crystal, and she's given me valuable advice on my future profession."

Five men, all of them hardcases, stared at Daphne in puzzlement, wondering where all this was headed.

"My decision was not an easy one to make, but with Crystal's encouragement I've finally decided on the forthcoming course of my life," the girl said. In the dull, rose glow of the firelight she was thin, painfully shy, and painfully plain.

"So, what's your decision, girlie?" Dave Quarrels said, a known mankiller but the most affable male present. He smiled. "We're all waiting to hear."

"I have decided"—she swallowed hard—"to change my name to Daphne Dumont. That's French, you know."

"Now tell them the most important part," Crystal said. "Speak up, loud and clear."

"Oh yes," Daphne said. "And I've decided to become a prostitute."

Surprised as they were, the laughter of the men was a little slow in coming, but then it arrived with a gale-force gust of guffaws. Johnny Teague forgot his depression and even slapped his thigh in delight.

Tears in his eyes, he gasped his laughter. "Good luck with that, Daphne Dumont. I'm sure . . . oh, God help me . . . I'm sure . . ." He ended in a breathless rush, "I'm sure you'll get plenty of customers."

According to newsman A. B. Boyd, Dave Quarrels told him that he didn't laugh, out of regard for the girl's feelings. In fact, he rolled around on the ground, clutching a knee, tears streaming down his cheeks as his ringing peals of merriment threatened to cut off his breathing. Slim Porter laughed, and even the dour Juan Sanchez managed a grin.

But the newly minted Daphne Dumont was not amused, and neither was Crystal Casey.

"What are you men laughing at?" she said. "Daphne's got the right to be a whore if she wants to. She'll prosper in the profession, I can tell you that."

"Sure, she will," Teague said. "Just so long as a man ain't too fussy."

At that Daphne showed some spunk. Leaning forward, her hands on her hips she said, "Well I can tell you this, Mr. Johnny Teague, you'll never get a taste. And for your information, Preacher Loveshade never complained about our time in bed."

"No, I guess he didn't," Teague said, blinking away tears.

"Then I guess he wasn't fussy," Dave Quarrels said.

"Then I guess I'd make a bad preacher," Porter said.

And the men laughed again.

"Come on over to the fire, Daphne," Crystal said. "We won't get a lick of sense out of those jackasses tonight."

Both women turned on their heels and flounced away.

Fifty miles north of Johnny Teague's camp as the crow flies, Luna Talbot hid in the brush and shivered in the evening cool. Rain clouds covered the moon, and she was grateful for the darkness. The Rathmores made a search after she shot Elijah but finding a slender woman in a wilderness of brush and cactus was like looking for a needle in a haystack, and Papa Mace called off the search when the day shaded into night.

Luna was sure Red Ryan, Buttons Muldoon, and Arman Broussard were already dead, and that grieved her. She'd liked all three of the men, and she admitted to herself that she was attracted to the Cajun gambler and his gentlemanly ways. The woman hugged her knees and planned her next move . . . though the choices were limited. She could head south toward her ranch or . . . or . . . There was no other option. She'd foot it south and the rising sun would give her direction. Luna considered her chances of making it to the ranch, and they were slim. She'd be at least two days on the trail, maybe three, under a burning sun and without water. Walking at night and resting up during the day was a possibility, but the desert was treacherous, more so in the dark, and her chances of survival would not improve any.

Her head on her knees, Luna Talbot came to a decision. She'd start walking south at first light . . .

"And God help me," she whispered.

CHAPTER TWENTY-SIX

"What do you think, Broussard?" Buttons Muldoon said. "I mean, how badly hurt is he?"

"I'm not a doctor," Arman Broussard said.

"Then Red is in a bad way, huh?"

The gambler nodded. "I don't know if he has any broken bones and I don't know if he's got injuries to his insides."

"Hell, man, what do you know?" Buttons said.

"One time in Wichita I saw a puncher who'd been caught in a stampede," Broussard said. "He looked pretty much like your friend does."

"Did the puncher make it?" Buttons said, hope in his eyes.

"No, he died."

The mine shaft was lit by a single oil lamp, and the Mexican who'd been whipped for Elijah's sins was dying. The other slaves clustered around him, their lips moving in prayer. Red Ryan lay near the entrance where he'd been dragged.

Broussard stared at Buttons in the evening gloom, the only sound the whispering of the Mexicans and the constant cough from one of the Rathmore guards. "I've got to get to my gun."

"Easier said than done, my friend," Button said. "Your gun, my gun, Red's gun, they could be stashed anywhere."

"Muldoon, I can't fight them without a Colt in my hand."

"Seen that already. You ain't real handy with your dukes."

"If the good Lord wanted us to fight with our hands, he would've given us claws," Broussard said.

"That's a thought," Buttons placed his palm flat on Red's chest. "He's breathing easier. I'm pretty sure he's breathing easier."

"He's tough," Broussard said. "I think he'll make it. Damn, he looks bad, though, with the shadows gathering on his face."

"I've seen that on the faces of dying men," Buttons said. "But Red isn't a dying man. He's too tough and ornery to die."

"You're right," Broussard said. "He's not dying." Then, after some thought, "I need my pistol. I'm not much of a hand with a rifle."

"Then your education is sadly lacking," Buttons said, his hand still on Red's chest. Red's breathing was shallow but not labored.

Broussard said, "My father taught me to shoot. He was a gambler on the Mississippi riverboats. I'd like to say he was a fine man, but if I did, I'd be a liar."

"Then he taught you how to put a bullet in a man across a card table," Buttons said.

"You hit the nail right on the head," Broussard said. "Draw fast and place your first shot where it counts. That's what he always told me. It was his way."

"Did he kill many men?" Buttons said.

"I don't know, but I guess so. My mother never talked of it. But maybe she knew, because she left him when I was eight, said she didn't want to be wed to a gambling man any longer. He never talked about that, either, only he told me one time that she'd ran off with a steamboat engineer." Broussard smiled. "When I was a boy I wanted to catch up with that engineer and put a bullet in his brisket, but I never did find him or my mother.

"You're right. Ryan is breathing easier and I think the color is coming back to his face."

As though he'd heard, a guard left the entrance and stood over Red. He prodded him with his rifle and Buttons angrily swatted it away.

Like all the Rathmore brothers, the man was tall and thin, but this one had a wispy chin beard. "Will he live?"

"Damn you, yes, he'll live," Buttons said.

"Good," the guard said. "Papa Mace intends to burn him at the stake."

The second brother, who stood just inside the entrance covering Buttons and Broussard with his Winchester, sniggered. And then said, "You and the other slaves will watch."

Broussard, at that point thinking more rationally than the enraged but severely weakened Buttons, said, "When will the burning take place?"

"When he's strong enough to stand," the bearded man said.

The guards walked away to take up their posts at the mine entrance, and Buttons watched them go, hate burning in his eyes. He put his hand on Red's chest again and said, "Don't get better, old fellow. Best you die peacefully. I don't want to see you burn."

Arman Broussard heard sadness and genuine affection in Buttons Muldoon's voice, and he wondered at the bond that could develop between a stagecoach driver and his shotgun messenger. Before tonight, he'd considered a stage a necessary evil, a hot, dusty, and uncomfortable means of getting from one place to another, and he'd paid little attention to the two usually profane men up in the box. Now he was seeing them in a different light. Men capable of grief and feelings like any other . . . like himself.

The truth would hurt, but maybe a lie would do. "Buttons," Broussard said, "Red will be just fine, because we're going to get him out of here."

"Red isn't going anywhere," Buttons said. "He can't even stand. How is he gonna walk?"

"He doesn't have to walk. We'll carry him," Broussard said.

Buttons shook his head. "Think about where you are, Broussard. How are we going to carry Red out of this arroyo surrounded by Rathmores who'd like nothing better than to put bullets in all three of us?"

"I don't know how," the gambler said. "But we'll find a way."

"There's always a way, ain't there?" Buttons said.

"Sure there is," Broussard said.

Buttons said, "Not here. There's no way out of here."

"There's got to be," Broussard said. "We need to come up with a plan, that's all."

Buttons looked at the man and said nothing, but his eyes were dead. Like gray river stones.

* * *

Her name was Clementine, a thin, slack-breasted woman with gray showing in her brown hair. She was the mother of three children and had almost died delivering the last one. Her common-law husband, Asher Rathmore, wanted to force another pregnancy on her. He said Papa Mace needed more babies to increase the numbers of the family, especially now that Elijah had been killed. Asher had beaten her—Clementine's fingers strayed to the bruises on her cheek—and forced himself on her in full view of anyone who cared to look. There was no privacy in the arroyo that was the Rathmore hovel. Asher said things would get better, that Papa Mace was going to lead them to a safer place, with plenty of gold to set them up. Only there wasn't plenty of gold. Clementine had heard from one of the other wives that the quartz vein had been a big disappointment and that most of what the slaves had mined had gone to pay for the supplies they'd bought in the Forlorn Hope settlement. Papa Mace was penniless, and if the gold seam didn't start to produce soon, they'd likely starve.

Clementine made up her mind. She had to leave this terrible place and the vile Asher Rathmore who wanted to make her pregnant again, a man who held her life so lightly, a man she'd grown to hate. She could take her children and run, but if she didn't die in the desert, she'd soon be caught and given a beating. Yet she had hope . . . the three men who'd arrived with the stagecoach. All three seemed tough, though one of them might die soon, either from the licking he'd taken or by fire. The man dressed in a gambler's finery could be her salvation. She'd seen cardsharps before when she'd worked in a Dallas cathouse, elegant, well-mannered men but men best left alone. In a fight, they quickly went to the gun, a bold new breed of shootists the newspapers had taken to calling draw fighters, fast as a lightning strike and just as deadly.

Clementine was sure the Louisiana gambler they called Broussard was such a man.

Asher had taken his revolver. It was a plain blue Colt with a much-worn gutta-percha handle and was wrapped in a blanket along with his watch and gambler's ring. The woman made up her mind. That night she planned to take the slaves their supper, tough boiled meat from one of the stage horses, and something extra . . . the gambler's gun. If he could shoot himself to freedom, Clementine planned to be with him. As she retrieved the Colt from the blanket, she knew the chances of her plan succeeding were slim . . . but a chance that offered little was better than no chance at all.

CHAPTER TWENTY-SEVEN

A woman used to picking up after children, Clementine Rathmore had sewn a large pocket onto the front of her ragged skirt. The blue Colt was in there, but by moving carefully she didn't think it showed, and besides, her pocket usually sagged with the chunks of quartz and interesting rocks the children used as toys. She saw Clara Rathmore standing beside the cooking fire, stirring a steaming, soot-blackened cauldron, and said, "Clara, I'll take the slaves their supper tonight."

Clara, maybe ten years younger than herself, may have been pretty once, but she wasn't any longer. The woman shrugged and said, "Suit yourself, go right ahead," and then, "Why?"

"Just being nice," Clementine said.

"Being nice doesn't abide in this place." Clara frowned. "Here, are you hiding something?"

Clementine felt a pang of alarm. Oh, dear God, did Clara know she had a gun? Was she about to take her play away from her? She blinked and said, "What would I be hiding?"

Clara smiled, a joyless grimace. "That maybe you're sweet on one of the slaves."

Pretending to join in the joke, Clementine said, "Yeah, I am. The one Papa Mace is gonna burn to a few cinders."

It was hard to tell if Clara thought that funny or not. The woman turned on her heel, gave a wave, and walked deeper into the moonlit arroyo. Clementine realized she'd been holding her breath. She sighed and began to ladle the pungent meat into the earthenware bowl she held. Later she'd fill another for the Mexicans.

Fires were burning, casting a scarlet glow on the arroyo walls, and people were scattered about, reclining or engaged in conversation. Nobody paid attention to Clementine as she walked to the mine entrance. But the two guards—a couple of the Rathmore brothers she hated as much as she did her husband—were alert.

"What's in the bowl?" one of them said.

"Horsemeat," Clementine said. "Want some?"

The man shook his head. "No, we'll eat later." He nodded in the direction of the mine shaft. "One of them dying in there, the one with the red hair."

"He won't eat much," the other guard said.

"Good, that means more for the others." Clementine hardened her face. "Keep up their strength for digging."

"Papa Mace had a great vision, did you hear?" said the guard with the stingy beard.

Clementine shook her head. "No, I didn't."

"He said an angel took him into the mine and showed him what lies behind the rock," the man said.

"The quartz vein is five foot thick, stretches for half a mile, and holds so much gold, it glitters like sunlight on snow. That's what Papa Mace said."

"That is wonderful news," Clementine said. "Soon we can all leave this place."

"Leave the mountains?" The guard was genuinely surprised. "No, you stupid woman, we won't ever do that. Papa Mace said we'll use the gold to hire gunmen and then use them to wipe out that devil's spawn Ben Kane. After his ranch and cattle are ours we will live in peace and prosperity forever after."

Clementine was not stupid. She was intelligent enough to realize that if Papa Mace's vision was real, he would keep the gold for himself. His sons trusted him . . . but she did not.

"Ah, now I see the future Papa Mace has planned for us and I'm most happy and grateful," Clementine said. "All praise to our great leader."

"I should think so," the bearded Rathmore said. "Woman, I know you trust Brother Asher, your husband. I know you do because he told me so, and soon you will be with child again. But above all you must trust Papa Mace in all things. Remember that. Now, take the meat inside and feed the dogs."

Clementine smiled and nodded, the very picture of the subservient wife and mother, and carried her reeking bowl into the mine shaft.

Clementine entered the shaft, stopped, and looked around. The Mexicans were gathered around the slave Papa Mace had killed with his whip that day, and the white men sat a distance from them, keeping vigil over the redheaded man from the stage. An oil lamp cast a fitful light, and the only sound was the whispering of the Mexicans praying to their god.

What she had to do had to be done quickly and without anyone noticing, even the slaves. Her heart racing, she took a few deep breaths to steady herself, placed a bowl of meat near the Mexicans, and then stepped to the gambler, his fine clothes stained and torn by his work in the mine.

Clementine stood in front of him, staring into his eyes. "Food," she said, laying down the bowl.

The gambling man looked up at her and said, "Is that what you call it? I have another word for it."

For the benefit of the guards, the woman yelled, "Pig!" and slapped Broussard across the cheek, a blow that made a satisfyingly loud smack.

There's no telling what the gambler would have done next had Clementine not reached into her pocket and dropped his Colt into Broussard's lap. For a moment in time he and the woman froze, fearing discovery, but the instant passed, and the gambler grabbed the revolver and quickly shoved it under his coat.

Raising her voice, Clementine yelled, "And the next time you complain about the food, I'll dump it over your head!"

The guards were still grinning at that when she stepped out of the mine. Scowling, her back stiff, she walked back to the cooking fire. "Time to feed the Mexican slaves more meat," she sang out to no one in particular . . . and no one in particular looked in her direction.

CHAPTER TWENTY-EIGHT

"Use it, Broussard," Buttons Muldoon said. "Get yourself out of here."

"We're all getting out of here," the gambler said. He looked around, then checked the loads in the Colt. "Six, that's perfect. I can make a good accounting of myself."

Buttons shook his head. "Red isn't going anywhere. You're on your own."

"Then leave him," Arman Broussard said. "We can get help and come back for him."

"Get help where?" Buttons said. "There is no help. We're in the middle of a stinking desert."

"Muldoon, Red might never recover. You've got to think of yourself. Stay here and they'll work you to death. You'll leave your bones in this mine."

"I won't leave Red," Buttons said. "He's my shotgun guard, he's my friend, and he's saved my life more times than I can count. If he does die, I want to be around when it happens. Say a prayer for him maybe. Maybe say a lot of prayers."

"You're an honorable man, Muldoon," Broussard said.

"I don't know about that, but I won't desert a friend. Never quit on a friend in his hour of need. I think that's wrote down in the Patterson stage rule book."

"And where does that leave me?" the gambler said. "It leaves me feeling guilty for running out on you."

"Why should it? You ain't my friend or Red's either," Buttons said. "Hell, Broussard, you ain't even a bona fide, fare-paying passenger of the Abe Patterson and Son Stage and Express Company. You got the gun, now look to save yourself. And you'd better git going."

"If I escape and gun some of the Rathmores, they'll kill you for sure."

"Then that's the chance I'll have to take," Buttons said, a stubborn man with no backup in him. "I'll stay right here with Red to the end."

Broussard sat in silence for a while and then said finally, "I have to try it. The woman gave me my opportunity and I must take it."

"Of course, you do." Buttons managed a smile. "And when you reach civilization, send the Rangers, a whole passel of Rangers."

"Buttons . . . I . . . I mean, I wouldn't last long with doing pick-and-shovel work. I've never done a day's hard labor in my life."

A Mexican sniffed his tears and the shifting light from the oil lamp crawled over the wall, back and forth, moving a little at a time. Outside, a woman laughed and a man cursed as though he'd just stubbed his toe.

"Don't justify your actions to me, Broussard. If I was the man with the gun, I'd do the same thing you're doing." Buttons nodded to the far wall. "There's a full canteen over there. Take it."

"Muldoon, no hard feelings?" the gambler said, his face anxious, as though he feared what Buttons's answer would be.

"No hard feelings. Get it done, gambling man, and good luck."

Broussard rose to his feet and the mourning Mexicans turned and stared at him. He put his forefinger to his lips and whispered, "*Silencio.*" He picked up the canteen, put the strap over his shoulder, and then walked on cat feet to the entrance.

Both guards were still there, one of them smoking a pipe, but their Winchesters were propped against the walls and they stared at something happening deeper in the arroyo, giving Broussard the edge he needed.

He chose the pipe smoker to his right, quickly covered the few yards that separated the guard from himself, and slammed his Colt into the man's head. As his companion groaned and dropped, the other guard turned, saw what had happened, and grabbed for his rifle.

"I wouldn't," Broussard said.

The man ignored him and tried to bring the Winchester to bear. Broussard fired, and his bullet crashed dead center into the man's naked chest. It was a killing wound and the bearded guard knew it. He screeched as he staggered back and slammed into the hard rock of the mine shaft wall.

Broussard didn't wait to see the man fall. He ran out of the mine into darkness and headed for the mouth of the arroyo. Footsteps pounded behind him, and the gambler turned and saw the Mexicans hard on his heels, making their own break for freedom.

One of the Rathmore brothers loomed from the darkness in front of Broussard, his arms extended as he yelled at him to stop. Broussard brushed the man aside and the Mexicans trampled over him.

Broussard ran out of the arroyo, then turned his head, expecting a pursuit, but all he saw were the Mexicans, all nine of them following him as hounds chase a fox.

"Get the hell away from me!" the gambler yelled. "*Vete! Vete!*"

Broussard sprinted into brush heavy with greasewood, prickly pear, and sage, and bent low, making himself as small as possible. The Mexicans did the same and he cussed them out in Cajun that they didn't understand. Figuring his contrary state of mind, they kept a distance between themselves and the man with the deadly six-gun.

The darkness closed in around Broussard, and after a few minutes, he straightened up and slowed to a walk. The Mexicans were no longer eating his dust, but still followed, small, thin men dressed in white shirts and pants and rawhide sandals. Broussard couldn't figure out why the little men clung so close to him. He had given them no encouragement and he could only think that they drew some comfort from the gun in his hand. If there was a fight with the Rathmores, the gringo could defend them.

Broussard took a drink from the canteen, let the Mexicans have a swallow, and then said, "Any of you boys speak English?" He got no response and tried, "Habla usted Ingles?" All he got were blank stares and a few grins.

Drawing on the little Spanish he knew, Broussard told the Mexicans he was headed south. They could go in any direction they liked, just so long as it wasn't the direction he was taking.

This declaration was greeted with nods and grins and plenty of "Sí," "Sí," "Sí" . . . but when he started walking again, the Mexicans followed him like a bunch of wiry ducklings trailing their mama.

They walked through the cool night, Broussard intending to bed down during the heat of the day. The wild land around them was dry as a bone and one canteen would not last ten men for very long. It was a worrisome thing.

At first light he stopped walking and looked back at the Cornudas, surprised at how far they'd come. He saw no dust in the distance, no sign of pursuit. Brossard was sure the Rathmores had horses stashed away in one of the canyons near a spring, including the members of Button Muldoon's team that had escaped the cooking pot. Why were they not out hunting him? Then it dawned on Broussard . . . the answer could be *numbers*. Papa Mace had seven sons, and two of them were dead, possibly the best of them. He'd only five fighting men of dubious value. Attacking across open ground into a gun and a man trained to use it could cost him dearly.

That was Broussard's belief . . . but in the end Papa Mace would call the shots.

First light brought the dawning of another scorching day. By noon, heat waves shimmered, and in the distance, dust devils spun like dervishes. The air was thick and hot and hard to breathe. Once the whole region had been the bottom of a vast sea and the ground was hard and gravelly overlying a layer of compacted lime as hard as granite. The Chihuahuan Desert was not land for the plow, nor was it suited for humankind, yet both men and women challenged the wilderness to do its worst and endured.

Over the next three days Broussard and his nine Mexicans would be put to the same test . . . and only the strongest of them would survive.

CHAPTER TWENTY-NINE

Fear drove Papa Mace Rathmore.

Two of his sons were dead and only five remained. It was not enough. The next time Ben Kane and his tough punchers attacked would be the last, because he would kill everyone. In the dim morning light, Mace opened the gold sack that he kept hidden in a niche in the rock, stared hard at his stash of flakes and small nuggets, some of them still embedded in quartz. He hefted the sack. Maybe ten pounds, including some quartz. He did a swift mental calculation. Three thousand dollars, give or take, enough to keep him for a few years in . . . his destination had to be Fort Worth. The place was booming and had plenty of snap. He'd take one of the better-looking women with him, maybe Ella, his son Malachi's wife. She hadn't yet given birth and was still shapely and willing. Later, once he was established, he could pimp her out as added income.

His mind made up, Papa Mace put the sack back into the niche. Time was of the essence. Of the two springs in the Cornudas Mountains, one was close to his compound in the arroyo. The other was near another peak where he kept the horses. He could pick out a couple of good mounts for himself and Ella and then make some excuse to leave. On a scout maybe. He'd think of something that wouldn't arouse suspicion.

Naked except for his loincloth and sandals, his great belly hanging, Papa Mace left what he called his throne room and walked into the compound. It was only an hour after dawn, but the cooking fire was already boiling meat, and the woman and children were up and doing. The morning light sliced into the arroyo but cast deep shadows. The mood among the surviving Rathmores was grim. The women's faces were again blackened in mourning, and the men were still at their guard posts as they'd been all night. Two were on duty in the mine and the other three at the mouth of the arroyo.

As was his due as their savior, the women bowed their heads as Papa Mace walked past, but their eyes were not friendly. There had been too much death, and now all the slaves were gone. Who would dig for the gold that they needed so badly? It was time for Papa to do something . . . something miraculous.

When he stepped into the mine shaft, he was greeted by silence. The *chip-chip-chip* of picks on rock and the constant chatter of the Mexicans was gone. The morning light had not yet reached the entrance. Red Ryan lay in gloom. Buttons Muldoon, his gray face showing strain, sat beside him.

Mace stood over Red, looking down at him, hate in his eyes. "Is he dead yet?"

"Not yet," Buttons said. "He can't stand."

Mace smirked. "Then I can burn him lying down."

"Do that, and I swear I'll kill you," Buttons said.

"Big talk from a man who can barely stand himself," Mace said. "I may burn you both."

Buttons made no answer and Mace said, "How did Broussard get the gun?"

"I don't know."

Mace kicked him in the ribs. "How did Broussard get the gun?"

"I don't know."

Another kick, Mace's horny toes thudding into Button's side, bringing pain.

"How did Broussard get the gun?"

Gasping, Buttons said, "Go to hell."

"Did you have a hand in it?" Papa Mace said, his small, piggy eyes vicious.

"No."

"You're a liar."

"I had no hand in it."

Mace scratched his huge, hairy belly. "Tell me who it was, and you can go free. I'll give you a horse and a canteen, and send you on your way."

"I don't know who it was," Buttons said. That earned him another kick.

But Buttons Muldoon was a fighter and he'd only take so much. Moving with the explosive speed possessed by so many short, stocky men, he reached out, grabbed Mace's leg, and clamped his teeth on the man's shinbone where he knew it would hurt like hell. As Buttons held on, growling like a terrier with a rat, the fat man screamed in pain and then fell, unable to balance on one leg.

But then it was over. The two guards laid into Buttons with their rifle butts as Papa Mace shrieked and stared in horror at the blood welling from his gnawed leg.

Buttons was pounded into insensibility, but his last conscious thought was *Damn, I enjoyed that.*

His mangled leg bandaged, Papa Mace Rathmore attended the burial of two more sons. Once again, the women wailed, but he paid them little heed, preoccupied with his plans for his escape to Fort Worth with Ella, who was not as worn out as the rest of the women. As one of his sons read from the Good Book and droned on about death and redemption, Mace's busy brain turned to other things. Uppermost in his mind were Buttons Muldoon and Red Ryan, who had turned out to be a disappointment. He'd been told by the women that there was barely enough wood to feed the fires, let alone burn two grown men. There had to be another punishment, just as savage, and Mace was suddenly inspired.

He would ignore them . . . tie up his enemies good and tight and just leave them in the mine shaft to die of thirst. Papa Mace wanted to smile but couldn't, not when he was burying whores' whelps. Seven sons and every one of them born of a whore he'd used, abused, and then discarded. It was no wonder he took no pride in them. But enough of that.

He turned his thoughts to the stagecoach men again. He'd once been told by an old prospector that a man without water would start dying after three days and would be dead by seven. The visions in Mace's mind were so exquisite, so tantalizing, that he would gladly postpone his flight with Ella to savor them. He would visit the two vile creatures every day and torment them. He would guzzle water . . . pour it into the ground beyond their reach . . . tease them with cups of water, cold from the spring, slopping over rims that almost touched their cracked, parched lips before being snatched away. Oh, the fun he'd have. He'd listen to their harsh croaks for mercy, their dusty cries for water . . . day after terrible day for seven long days.

Papa Mace gave a start. Everybody was looking at him. Why? Then he realized that the prayers had ended, and they waited on his signal to start the burial. He raised a hand and his surviving sons began to pile rocks on the grave. Ella's face was blacked like the other women, but the glance she gave him was bold, inviting, a look that promised much.

Papa Mace Rathmore was mightily pleased.

CHAPTER THIRTY

Morning came, and Arman Broussard and his Mexicans halted. The coolness of the evening desert had fled, and the hot sun came up like a copper coin in a brassy sky. It was their second day on the trail south. The water in the canteen was almost gone, and strain showed on the faces of the Mexicans who'd been poorly fed and driven hard in the mine from dawn to dusk seven days a week for years.

One of them, an older man named Vincente Fonseca, was in a bad way. He was bone-tired, sagging from weariness, and his eyes were hollow. Before he was taken by the Rathmores he'd had six children, but he didn't know where they were, and he believed his wife had died. When he'd been young and strong Fonseca had been a carpenter, but that was years ago and now his strength was almost gone.

Positioning himself so that his shadow fell on the old man, in his halting Spanish Broussard asked him how he felt. In a voice that was barely a whisper Fonseca told him that he must go on without him, that his time to die was very near and that he'd seen *Santa*

Muerte, the Angel of Death, and she had beckoned to him.

Broussard said, *"Despues de descansar, pronto te sentiras mejor,"* hoping like hell it meant, "After some rest, you'll feel better."

But the old man shook his head and said no more. He died just before sundown.

Broussard and the Mexicana buried Fonseca as best they could under sand and loose rocks and then took to the dark trail south again. The gambler knew the odds and figured their chance of survival was slim to none and slim was already saddling up to leave town. The water would soon give out . . . and that would be the end.

Two hours later, they found Luna Talbot. Or the coyotes did.

The coyotes were yipping close to the walking men, skulking silver shapes in the moonlight, flickering in and out of the brush. Broussard thought it strange that the animals would come so near to them, men being the most dangerous of their traditional enemies. But he dismissed the coyotes from his mind and continued walking. But then the yips grew more frequent and excited and it was one of the young Mexicans who first heard the sound that did not come from an animal or an injured deer.

The man's face puzzled, he said to Broussard, "*Señor, es una mujer?*"

Is it a woman?

The only woman who could be alone in the wilderness and cry out like that was Luna Talbot. But Brossard had thought her dead, killed by the

Rathmores . . . or the desert. Could it really be her? The question struck him like a blow. Then he was running, charging into the murk, whooping like an Indian to scare away the coyotes.

In the gloom, he at first thought the dark shape on the ground was in fact a deer or some other animal, but as he ran closer he made out the unmistakable form of Luna Talbot. The woman sat upright, a small pistol in her hand.

She recognized him immediately. "What took you so long?"

Broussard kneeled beside her and said, "Are you all right?"

"Apart from being almost eaten by coyotes and stranded in the middle of a wasteland with a busted ankle, I'm just fine," Luna said.

Broussard shook his head. "I thought you were dead."

"Likewise. At least for a while there."

Luna's canteen was still over her shoulder and Broussard said, "Let me get you some water."

"No, leave it," she said. "Save the water for later when I really need it."

"Then let me take a look at the ankle," Broussard said. "I'll need to take off your boot."

"No, my ankle is too swollen." She looked up at the gawking Mexicans and then said, "Mr. Broussard, you have a story to tell."

"Yes, I do," the gambler said. After a while he added, "The ankle is moving freely, and I don't think it's broken. It seems like you've got a sprain. How did it happen?"

"I stepped into a hole in the dark."

Broussard smiled. "Careless of you."

"Yes, wasn't it?" Luna said. "I'm glad to see you, Mr. Broussard, but you look awful."

"A few days without much water can do that to a man."

"And to a woman. I look awful myself.'

"Mrs. Talbot, you could never look awful. Can you walk on the ankle?"

"If I could walk on it would I be sitting here getting attacked by a pack of man-eating coyotes?"

"Then I'll have to carry you," Broussard said.

"I could be very brave and tell you to leave me," Luna said. "But I'm not brave."

"You're brave enough," Broussard said. "Here, let me help you to your feet and we'll go from there."

He helped Luna stand and then said, "Now, can you put any weight on it?"

Luna tried and flinched in pain. "No, I can't. I'm so sorry."

"A turned ankle can happen to anybody," Broussard said. "I'll need to carry you."

"All the way to my ranch?"

The gambler smiled. "No, not all the way. Chances are we'll never make it that far."

She said, "Now I feel much better."

As Western men went, Arman Broussard was as strong as most, but he was grateful to share the carrying chores with several of the younger Mexicans. Despite years of poor food and backbreaking work, they managed Luna Talbot's weight with ease.

But water was a problem.

Luna's canteen was still half full but added to the

little Broussard had remaining, it was not enough to keep ten people alive for very long.

They trudged through the night and into the next morning, when they each took a sip of water and settled down to sweat out the long, burning day. Hunger had begun to gnaw at them, but the Mexicans gathered piñon nuts that were surprisingly tasty and helped with the pangs.

Exhausted as they were, sleep turned out to be almost impossible as a rising wind blew stinging dust that covered everyone and made breathing difficult. After a couple of hours, the breeze dropped, and the heat returned with full force, making the surrounding landscape ripple. Luna Talbot's sprained ankle was obviously punishing her, but she didn't utter a word of complaint. Using her fingers, she combed the sand out of her hair, brushed off her shirt and riding skirt, trying to make herself presentable. Arman Broussard thought she looked just fine.

It was about two in the afternoon, the day a furnace set ablaze by the burning sun, when a dozing Broussard was shaken awake by one of the Mexicans. The man said nothing but pointed south where a dust cloud smeared the horizon like a dirty thumbprint. The gambler got to his feet. What the hell? Was it a party of Rangers? No, there weren't enough Rangers in Texas to raise that much dust. A train of freight wagons maybe? That was possible.

"It's a cattle herd," Luna Talbot said, sitting up, shading her eyes with a hand. "Probably my cattle."

"Why drive cows up here?" Broussard said.

"I don't know," Luna said. "But I reckon we'll find out soon enough. Help me to my feet, Mr. Broussard."

The gambler did as Luna asked and said, "Call me Arman, for God's sake."

"Hell of a name," Luna said. "You must be the only man alive with a ten-dollar name like that. But I'll call you Arman if you wish, and you may call me Luna."

"I was once introduced to a dog named Luna," Broussard said. "She was female, a real bitch."

A half-smile played on the woman's lips. "She was a fine dog then."

Broussard shook his head, grinning. "Here we are bandying words with each other and, depending on who's driving those cattle, we could be dead in a few minutes."

"You mean rustlers?"

"Or worse."

"I reckon we'll soon—"

"Find out. I know."

A moment later they heard the distant *Pop! Pop! Pop!* of guns, and the gambler said, "Sounds like somebody chasing rustlers all right."

"That will be my segundo Leah Leighton and the Talbot hands," Luna said. Worried, she bit her lip. "I never taught them how to handle a running gunfight."

"I'm sure they know," Broussard said. "Luna, if they're anything like you, they know."

The dust cloud came closer and riders and cattle were visible in the haze. The shooting became ragged and then died away into silence.

"I see her!" Luna said.

"See who?" Broussard said.

"Leah Leighton. That's her paint mare with the white blanket. I'd recognize her anywhere."

"Is she winning or losing?" Broussard said.

"She's won, Arman. She's carrying her rifle, and so are the others."

"Can they see us?"

"I don't know. We're covered in sand," Luna said. "Fire a couple of shots in the air."

Broussard thumbed off two rounds and waited. The Mexicans were excited, waving their arms and letting out with dry, croaky yells.

Finally, Broussard saw clearly. The woman on the paint rode forward fifty yards and then drew rein. She put field glasses to her eyes and studied the terrain ahead. Four more rifle-toting riders emerged from the dust and joined her. The woman lowered the glasses, turned her head, and said something to the hands. Then they shook out into a skirmish line and come on at a walk, rifles at the ready.

"Careful gals, those," Broussard said.

Luna nodded. "I taught them, and they learned." She leaned on Broussard and waved. "Leah!"

The woman riding the paint stopped, took off her hat, and held it over her head, shading her eyes from the glaring sun.

"Leah!" Luna called out again, waving.

Leah Leighton recognized her boss and kicked her horse into a canter. The other woman followed. A few yards away, she reined the paint to a skidding halt and leaped from the saddle. She ran to Luna, and the two women embraced. Luna winced a little as her weight shifted to her injured ankle.

Horrified, Leah said, "Boss, you're hurt."

"Only a sprained ankle," Luna said.

"But . . . but what happened?" Leah said, her pretty, sunburned face concerned. "What about the mine? Why are you here? Where are—"

"I'll tell you later," Luna said. "First, you tell me what happened? Those are my Herefords, aren't they?"

"Rustlers," Leah said. "They rounded up about fifty cows and drove them north. Eliza Holt was out checking the range and they shot her."

Luna felt a jolt of alarm. "Is she . . ."

"She's fine, boss. A bullet burned across the side of her head and knocked her out cold for a spell, but she got back on her horse and raised the alarm. She's a flighty gal, is Eliza, but she's got sand."

"And then you went after the rustlers," Luna prompted.

"Yes, five of them. We caught up with them, and there was a fight. We killed three and captured two others. I guess we'll hang those two when we find a suitable tree." Leah looked over Luna's shoulder. "Where did you find all the Mexicans?"

"This gentleman here is Arman Broussard," Luna said. "They belong to him."

The gambler gave a little bow. "It's a pleasure to meet you, Miss Leighton."

"Likewise I'm sure." Leah's eyes moved from the handsome Broussard to Luna and then back again, obviously trying to make a connection.

Luna recognized the look and said, "Arman saved my life last night. But that's for later. I'd like to talk to the two rustlers you caught . . . after we share your canteens, that is. We're dying of thirst and pretty much used up."

The Talbot hands shared their water and the beef jerky they'd packed in the event that the chase took them all the way to the New Mexico Territory and after Luna and the others were refreshed, she sat on a limestone rock shelf and ordered that the prisoners be brought forward.

They were an oddly matched pair, and Luna was surprised. The older of the two was a graybeard with tired, washed-out blue eyes, his companion a boy of about fourteen, tall and gangly and frightened. He kept his eyes on the Colt in Broussard's waistband.

"You rustled my cattle," Luna said. "What do you have to say for yourself?"

"I have nothing to say, lady. I saddle my own broncs and fight my own battles and I know what I done was wrong. But I needed money, and Billy Head showed me a way to get some."

"Who is he?" Luna said.

"He's one of the dead rustlers, boss," Leah Leighton said. "Before he died, he gave me his name and asked if I'd tell his sister what had happened to him. He said she lives on the Pecos, down Cowbell Creek way."

"We all lived on the Cowbell," the old man said. "Me, Billy Head, Tom Battles, and John Hawke—all of them three are dead now. This boy's name is Tim Meadows. He's an orphan boy and he ain't quite right. I've been taking care of him since he was six years old and I brought him with me. I reckon you'll hang me as a cow thief, lady, but spare the boy. He didn't know what he was doing, on account of the way he is, being slow an' all."

"Where were you taking my cattle?" Luna said.

"We figured to sell them in El Paso, lady."

"Cattle prices are low this year," Luna said. "Fifty head would bring you two thousand dollars. That means that four grown men risked their lives for five hundred dollars each. Mister, five hundred dollars isn't worth dying for.'

"We were all poor folks down on the Cowbell, lady. Five hundred dollars is a fortune for the likes of us. You should know that Billy Head and them were never outlaws. Oh, when the young'uns were hungry they wasn't above stealing a chicken or two, but they were not bandits."

"And then they heard about my ranch," Luna said. Her face was hard and the breeze tossed strands of hair across her face.

"Yes, a passing feller told Billy Head there was fat cattle for the taking," the old man said. "Billy said we'd keep to lifting just fifty head because they wouldn't be missed. Well, that's what we done and then we were caught." He shook his head in wonderment. "By some mighty sharpshooting ladies with Winchesters."

The boy spoke for the first time. "Don't hang us, ma'am. We didn't mean no harm."

"There's an old cottonwood that stands alongside a dry creek bed near my ranch house," Luna said. "Crows go there sometimes, especially when the tree grows dead men. A few weeks ago, if I'd caught you rustling my cattle I'd have hanged you both from the same branch and put I AM A RUSTLER placards around your necks. Do you understand?"

"I understand," the old man said, his head drooping. He looked up, "But please, lady, I beg you, spare the boy."

"However," Luna said as though she hadn't been listening, "the strange thing is that you and your fellow rustlers saved my life. I and all the men who you see standing here would have died of thirst long before we reached the Talbot. I'm sure of that."

"That's a natural fact," Broussard said, nodding.

"Yes, thank you, Arman." Luna looked at the old man. "I will not hang you or the boy. You are free to go. Leah, bring them their horses."

Tears sprang into the old timer's eyes. "Thank you, lady. And God bless you." Then, his words tentative, "Can we have a spare horse? I'd like to take our dead back to the Cowbell for Christian burial."

Luna smiled slightly. "Pushing it, aren't you? What's your name?"

"Owen Mollohan, lady. Man and boy, it's been Owen Mollohan."

"Leah, bring all five of the rustler horses," Luna said. "They're the only spare mounts we have."

Broussard looked at her in surprise. "Spare mounts?"

"I need a horse and a gun," Luna said. "The hands need to take the herd back, and I don't want them riding double."

"You're not thinking about . . ."

"About heading back to the Cornudas? Yes, I am. No man abuses me and puts a slave rope around my neck and lives to boast of it. I have a score to settle with the fat man."

"And I promised Buttons Muldoon and Red Ryan that I'd return," Broussard said. "So make that two horses. What about your ankle?"

"It's fine."

"It hurts, I'm sure."

"I can bear it. Anger helps numb the pain."

The running gun battle had scattered the herd and the rustlers' horses, and it took a good thirty minutes before a couple of punchers led the mounts to where Luna sat. She was less than impressed by the five hammer-headed mustangs with worn-out

McClennan saddles on their backs and bridles held together with string. Poor men's horses.

"Take your pick, Arman," Luna said, smiling.

"Ladies first," Broussard said, also smiling.

"The sorrel," Luna said.

"Good choice." Broussard stepped to a mouse-colored mare that must have weighed no more than eight hundred pounds and patted her neck. "I'll take this one." He turned to the old man. "The rest are yours."

He and the Mexicans helped load the dead men onto the remaining horses and with Luna's approval gave Mollohan a rifle. "Old-timer, don't even think about taking up the rustling profession again," Broussard said, "That cartridge sure don't fit your pistol."

"Mister, I'm done," Mollohan said. "And so is the boy."

He kneed his horse forward, him and the youngster, leading dead men east toward the Cowbell under a clear blue sky.

After Mollohan left, Luna Talbot said to Leah Leighton, "Who started the shooting?"

The woman seemed surprised, but said, "They did when they saw us coming after them." Then after a pause for thought, "They weren't very good."

"They were rubes," Luna said.

"Yes, boss, they were. Rubes with Winchesters, one with a Sharps fifty."

Luna nodded and smiled slightly, "Yes, there is always that to consider."

Guessing that Mrs. Talbot was suffering a pang of

conscience, Leah said, "I would've preferred to have taken them alive, but they gave me no choice."

"Of course, they didn't," Luna said. "You did the right thing."

"Yes, boss," Leah said. "I did."

Luna accepted that last and ordered her segundo to send the hands back to the ranch with the herd. "But I want you with me, Leah. Where I'm headed I may need your fast gun."

The woman didn't even blink. "Tell me about it, boss."

"We're headed back to the Cornudas."

"To the mine?" Leah said.

"Yes, to the mine." Luna hesitated and then said, "It could be dangerous. If you want to leave with the herd, I'll understand."

"I ride for the brand," Leah said. "I'll stick."

CHAPTER THIRTY-ONE

Dave Sloan was Ben Kane's gunman, and he was mighty close . . . close to putting a bullet in his own head. He'd coughed up blood that morning, a bucket-load lot of bloody phlegm, and his breathing had been agonizing. It was no way for a man to live . . . but sure as hell a good reason for him to die.

Sloan sat on a wooden bench outside the barn, his face turned to the sun, basking in its healing warmth. Inside, the shadows were fading and the big draft horses shifted their feet in their stalls, rattled their halters, and snorted, impatient for hay and oats. Birds fluttered in the piñon trees near the corral and the cook's cur dog barked at the two tomcats he hated with a passion. He'd chased those cats a hundred times and caught up with them once. After that, he'd never chased a cat again.

Sloan never got far from his gun, and the holstered Colt lay on the bench beside him. A young hand nodded to him, gave his bloodstained lips a second glance, and hurriedly looked away. The cowboy pitched hay and then scooped oats into feed buckets. As he worked he sang, "The Old Gray Mule," and the horses seemed to like it.

When the puncher left, Sloan was breathing easier and the pain in his chest had eased.

Milt Barnett walked purposely toward him.

Barnett had been with Jake Wise when the Rathmores killed him, so Sloan doubted his spunk. Since the puncher wore a gun he was handy with and Sloan was not a trusting man, he moved his hand an inch or two nearer to his Colt.

If Barnett noticed the play, he didn't let it show.

"Boss wants to see you, Dave." Barnett stood with his right arm away from his body, putting a discreet distance between his hand and his gun. "It's about that Rathmore trash."

Sloan got to his feet and buckled on his gun belt and holster.

The man was wasting away, Barnett thought. Soon the only thing left of him would be his shadow.

"Bad morning, Dave?" Ben Kane said, looking the man over.

"You could say that," Sloan said.

"Sorry to hear it. Too early for whiskey?"

"It's never too early for whiskey."

Anse Dryden, Kane's foreman, was already there. He nodded to Sloan but didn't speak.

It was about eight o'clock in the morning and the sun angled through the windows of the ranch house parlor and made the dust motes dance. Kane poured amber bourbon into crystal glasses and handed one to Sloan, the other to Dryden.

Sloan raised his glass. "Barnett said you wanted to talk about the Rathmores."

"Yes, I do. I want to talk about the Rathmores." But Kane seemed in no hurry. Finally he said, "Dave, before we go blowing up them mountains, what have you heard about a gold mine?"

"What everybody else has heard," Sloan said. "That there's a lost gold mine in the Cornudas."

"And maybe the Rathmores found it," Kane said. "That's a real possibility."

"You've seen those people, boss," Sloan said. "They ain't exactly living high on the hog."

"Could Mace Rathmore be keeping all the gold for himself?" Dryden said.

"It's possible, I suppose." Kane shook his head. "Nah, he'd share it among all those sons of his. If there was a gold mine they'd all be prospering instead of living among the rocks like wild animals."

Dryden said, "Maybe there is a gold mine, maybe there's not, but we shouldn't use dynamite to blow the Rathmores out of their holes. I never liked the idea anyhow."

"You mean we might cave in the mine?" Kane said.

"Yeah, if it's there."

Kane turned to Sloan. "Dave, what do you think?"

"Dynamite and gunpowder are messy and hard to use," Sloan said. "I say we just ride in there in force and kill 'em all."

"How many of our own will we lose?" Dryden said.

"If we hit them hard and sudden, not many," Sloan said. "The Rathmores won't stand and fight. I reckon we'll have to hunt them down like jackrabbits."

"You sure about that?" Kane said.

"If Mace Rathmore had any sand he'd have attacked this ranch before," Sloan said.

"We killed some of the hired hands he had working for him, but as far as I know, none of his kin," Dryden said. "Maybe Mace wasn't mad at us enough to tackle the Rafter-K."

"I didn't know the Rathmores had hired hands," Sloan said.

"They started out with some," Kane said. "Hardrock miners mostly and some toughs. But after we killed a few the rest lost heart and lit a shuck out of there. Now he has Mexicans working for him, still trying to find the lost mine, I reckon."

"So Mace Rathmore believes there's a gold mine in Cornudas?" Sloan said.

"That would seem to be his way of thinking," Kane said.

Anse Dryden drained his glass and then stood. "So, what about the explosives, boss? Do we use them or not?"

Kane thought about that before he spoke, then said, "Just suppose there is a mine, I don't want to blow it up. So we go in there with guns blazing and kill all them Rathmores once and for all and get rid of their taint forever."

"When, boss?" Sloan was a man for whom time mattered.

"Soon, Dave, mighty soon." Then, pinning it down, Kane said, "Within the next few days. I'll let you know. In the meantime, take care of yourself."

Sloan gave one of his rare smiles. "Too late for that."

Watching him, Anse Dryden thought the man

looked terrible, and his galloping consumption made him all the more dangerous. Sloan wouldn't allow himself to pass away in bed . . . he'd go out in a moment of hell-firing glory and spit in the eye of death.

CHAPTER THIRTY-TWO

Red Ryan and Buttons Muldoon were bound hand and foot and left alone in the mine shaft. The heat of the day had turned the place into a furnace. The dry air was thick as molasses and smelled of dust and rotting wood.

"Well, it's about time," Buttons said. "You plan to sleep your whole life away?"

Red stirred, and his eyes fluttered open. "Where am I?"

"In the mine shaft, all tied up."

Red said, "I thought I was dead."

"So did I, at least for a spell, but you sure as hell fooled me, huh?" Buttons said.

"I can't move," Red said, struggling a little.

"That's because you're trussed up like a turkey ready for the oven," Buttons said.

Red lay quiet for a few moments then said, "The Rathmores gave me a beating, didn't they? I feel like I was whipped with a bois d'arc fence post."

"They damned near killed you, Red," Buttons said. "Fact is, I'm surprised you're still kicking."

"How long have I been out?"

"A couple of days."

"I can't move to test for broken bones."

"Well, don't be too surprised if you got some."

"What's been happening?" Red asked.

"I'll tell you later. Right now rest up some. You're as weak as a two-day-old kitten."

"I'm thirsty, Buttons." Red said. "Wait, a minute. Hell, you're all tied up, too."

"Damn right I am. I bit Papa Mace's leg and took a beating, kinda like you did."

Red managed a ghost of a smile. "You bit him?"

"Sure did. Hung onto his leg like a Louisiana alligator."

"I would have loved to have seen that," Red said.

"The fat man squealed and squealed, and they beat the hell out of me, but I still chomped down on him," Buttons said.

Red managed a laugh. "Damn, that must've been a sight to see." He tried to stretch, but his bonds hampered him. "Buttons, I'm thirsty. Do we have any water?"

"No, I don't see any." Buttons maneuvered his body until he lay on his back, then took a deep breath and shouted, "Hey, you damned heathens. A man in here needs water!"

There was no answer.

Buttons tried again with the same result.

Red said, "Maybe they've forgotten about us."

"I doubt it," Buttons said. "I'm sure they'll bring us food and water presently. Can you hold out that long?"

"Food, I don't need. I can wait for water, even though I'm thirsty enough to spit cotton. Buttons, what the hell have they got planned for us?"

"Pardner, you don't want to know," Buttons said. "It ain't good."

"Then don't tell me."

"I won't."

"Where is the gambler feller?"

"Broussard? He escaped."

"Maybe he'll come back and rescue us."

"That's a good notion, Red. Keep thinking that way." Buttons yelled again. "We need water in here, you damned savages!"

"I wonder if Luna Talbot made it back to her ranch."

"I'm sure she did," Buttons said, though he was sure she had not.

"Right pretty lady, with plenty of sand." Red's voice was weak and the shadows under his eyes were as black as soot. "Damn, Buttons, these ropes hurt."

"You take it easy, pardner," Buttons said. "Just try to relax."

Red's fevered mind wandered, and he said, "Buttons, you recollect that time in Dallas when I climbed out of that lady's bedroom window . . . what was her name?"

"If it's the one I'm thinking about, her name was Lizzie. *Mrs.* Lizzie Schumacher. Her husband was a sea captain as I recall."

"Remember, I climbed onto the roof with my boots and clothes under my arm and it was winter. All those chimney pots were red-hot, every one of them smoking like a saloon stove with the flue closed?"

"Burned your bare butt, I recall," Buttons said. "Both cheeks, if memory serves me right."

"Yeah, I did, and for a week it hurt like hell to sit."

"You got a bad burn," Buttons said. "As I recollect,

I had to slow down the stage over the rough patches, no bouncing with you up on the seat with a cushion under your ass."

Red smiled and said, "Do you remember her husband stood in the front yard and took pots at me with a brace of Remingtons and cussed enough that he singed all the grass within ten yards from where he stood?"

"I remember. You were lucky that day," Buttons said. "If the captain's old lady hadn't stood naked in the window, singing 'Come All Ye Fair and Tender Ladies,' and beckoned for him to join her, he would've plugged you fer sure."

"She was a pretty lady," Red whispered. "What was her name again?"

"Lizzie . . . Lizzie Schumacher."

"Yes, I remember . . . Lizzie . . . Lizzie . . ." Red lapsed once again into unconsciousness.

Buttons said, "Best you sleep, Red." Then fully aware of what was ahead for both of them, "Best you sleep and never wake."

"Water!" A male voice bellowed from the mine entrance. "Does somebody want water?"

"Yes, in here, you damned brigand," Buttons yelled.

A few moments passed, and Mace Rathmore limped inside, a fat bandage on his bitten leg. He held an earthen crock, condensation beading on its sides. "Who's thirsty? I got cool water here." His smile was unpleasant, sadistic, bordering on the deranged grimace of the criminally insane.

"Over here," Buttons said. "Damn your eyes."

"Certainly." Papa Mace took a waddling step forward, pretended to trip, and upended the pot, spilling its contents onto the ground. Looking down at the puddle at his feet, he said, "Oh, dear. I tipped out all that nice, cool water, fresh from the spring."

"You damned animal," Buttons said between gritted teeth. "One day, I'll kill you."

"You've said that before. I'm still here and you're the one that's all tied up . . . and I must say, dying very slowly." Rathmore smiled again. "Ah well, never mind. I'll bring you more water, but not today. Maybe tomorrow or the next day. We'll see." He fixed his eyes on Red. "My, my, is he dead already?"

"Not yet, you sorry piece of trash," Buttons said.

"Looks like he will be soon." Rathmore grinned. "Until tomorrow, then. Or the next day."

Buttons watched the fat man go . . . and all of a sudden, he became aware of his raging thirst.

Maybe she'd been expecting too much too soon. Clementine Rathmore was sure the gambler had escaped, but when would he come back and rescue her from this place? Next week, next month . . . never?

She'd no answer to that question, but she still had an iron in the fire, the Patterson stagecoach driver and his shotgun guard. As far as she knew the guard was dying, if he wasn't dead already, but the driver was still alive. Could he be the one to bring her the freedom she craved? The word around camp was that because of the wood shortage Papa Mace wanted the prisoners to die of thirst. That was a lingering death, but with her help the strong, stocky driver could yet be healthy enough to make his break. It was a long shot, she knew, but it was worth trying.

Using a sponge she'd bought in Forlorn Hope years before, she stripped naked and began to wash herself all over, getting rid of the sweat stink her husband had left on her. At sundown, Asher was due to go on guard duty at the mouth of the arroyo and would be there until midnight. As soon as darkness came, she'd make her move.

The newspaperman A. B. Boyd always claimed that, on what would be the last day of her life, Clementine Rathmore was certifiably insane. He based his opinion on interviews he conducted in 1935 with two of the surviving Rathmore women who both stated that Clementine was "tetched in the head" and that they both feared for the safety of her children. Admittedly, the women still believed that Papa Mace was some kind of demigod and their evidence may have been biased, but the fact remains that Clementine's plan had no hope of succeeding. It could well have been the demented act of a crazy woman.

CHAPTER THIRTY-THREE

The day wore on, and Clementine Rathmore thought the darkness would never come. In the late afternoon several women talked to her about getting Asher to kill and butcher another of the stage horses for meat, but later they decided to wait for a couple of days until he was no longer on guard duty. Then more gossip—Esther Rathmore was sick with female hysteria and a wandering womb, but she hoped to feel better soon. And one of the men had seen a pack of gray wolves near the arroyo and had scared them off with a rifle shot and . . .

Clementine didn't listen but nodded in all the right places and waited impatiently for darkness, when she'd wear the gloom like a cloak.

With agonizing slowness, the sun dropped lower in the sky, shadows lengthened in the arroyo, and the light shaded into an ashen gray. She slipped a knife into her pocket and prepared to do what she must, make another bid for freedom.

Full dark. The stars were out, and the moon had started its climb into the night sky. Out in the wilderness where scuttling and squeaking things lived, the hunting coyotes were already yipping their hunger. A silence fell over the arroyo and only the fluttering flames under the perpetual cooking pot moved.

Four words, casually spoken, sealed Clementine's fate that night . . .

"She's up to something." Reta Rathmore, one of the women who'd talked to Clementine about killing a horse, said those words to her husband.

"Up to what?"

"I don't know. But it's something."

Women are sometimes more sensitive than men to the emotional state of other women. But Reta had thrown the observation out there as a passing comment at a time when topics of conversation in the claustrophobic atmosphere of the arroyo were few.

Since Papa Mace had a paranoid fear of any of his followers "getting up to something" and challenging his authority, Reta's husband thought the comment important enough to pass it on to his father.

And so it was that Clementine thought she'd made it to the mine shaft unseen . . . unaware that the night had eyes.

It was dark in the mine shaft, and Clementine felt her way to the recumbent forms of Red Ryan and Buttons Muldoon. She made out Buttons's stocky bulk and shook him awake.

"You have to leave," she said, the knife in her hand. "You must bring help."

Buttons struggled to regain consciousness. The woman stood over him in the murk, her long hair wild, her face a pale oval, the eyes sunken in shadow.

"Did you bring water?" Buttons's voice sounded raspy to his ears.

"No water. I'll cut you free and then bring some. A canteen. I'll bring a canteen."

"And a gun," Buttons said. "Can you find a gun?"

"I don't know," Clementine said. "Maybe I can."

The knife blade glinted in the gloom . . . and then turned the color of bronze as a pair of lanterns splashed the shaft with light. Buttons heard the woman's sharp intake of breath as she turned and then her body stiffened, frozen in place.

"What the hell are you doing here, woman?" Papa Mace said. He held a Winchester. Asher and another son held lanterns.

Asher spoke. "You were going to free them, wife, weren't you?"

Her throat paralyzed with fright, Clementine did not respond. After a moment she found her courage, or plumbed her madness, and said, "Yes, I was going to cut them free. I planned to make them say a solemn vow that they'd come back for me and free me from this terrible place and rid me of you, Asher. Yes, above all, rid me of you."

Asher Rathmore roared his rage and tried to grab the rifle from his father's hands, but Papa Mace pushed him away. The fat man's voice was a serrated knife blade. "Woman, out of your own mouth you are condemned, and you must surely die."

"Let me shoot her, Pa," Asher said. "She's my wife and I got the right."

"I'm the only one with rights here," Mace said. "If there's shooting to be done, I'll do it."

"Then kill me and get it over," Clementine said. "I'd rather be dead than suffer this living death any longer."

Asher's hate-filled eyes were fixed on the woman. "Pa, it was me jumped the broom with her. I got the right."

"No," Papa Mace said. "The women have the right. They are the ones that have been betrayed. Bring them in."

"Pa . . ."

"Bring them in, Asher, or by God you'll feel the butt end of this rifle."

The Rathmores had a firewood shortage, but there seemed to be no lack of wood for clubs. When the six women stepped inside, their eyes immediately went to Clementine, read what had happened, and slowly advanced on her. The eyes of Ella, the youngest and prettiest, were malevolent, her smile wicked.

Buttons Muldoon watched in horror as Clementine was beaten to death. More dreadful still was the sight of Asher Rathmore's sadistic, grinning face as he savored every blow, took pleasure in every shriek that came from his wife's mouth.

When it was all over, and the woman's broken body had been dragged away, Buttons Muldoon, for the first time in years, whispered a prayer . . . for Clementine, for himself, for Red Ryan . . . and for a blessing on the terrible vengeance he intended to bring down on Papa Mace Rathmore.

CHAPTER THIRTY-FOUR

"Dust cloud to the west of us, Johnny," Dave Quarrels said.

"I see it," Johnny Teague said. "Looks like a herd on the move."

"Ain't the Talbot ranch over that way?" Quarrels said.

Crystal Casey drew rein beside the two men. "Yes, that's the Talbot range. Why would they move cattle at this time of the year?"

Teague said, "Well it ain't Apaches lifting a few head, so it's probably rustlers."

"Any profit in it for us, Johnny?" Slim Porter said.

Teague shook his head. "Nah, I was never much interested in rustling cows. I don't like them that much. We'll show some professional courtesy and leave them rustlers to their work."

"Listen," Crystal said. "I hear shooting."

"Yeah, so do I," Teague said. "Seems like the Talbot hands have caught up with their stolen herd. I wonder if Luna Talbot is there?"

"I reckon she's still searching for her mine in the Cornudas or digging out gold already," Crystal said.

Teague said, "I hope she's found it before we get there. Save us some time and work."

"The shooting has stopped," said Daphne Loveshade, now Dumont.

"Time we were on our way," Teague said. "We're wasting daylight."

The two women fell in behind Teague and then Slim Porter, leading the mustang packhorse, fell back to join them.

"What do you think, Slim," Crystal said. "Will Johnny share the gold we find?"

"If we find it," Porter said. "But if there's gold to be found, I'm sure Johnny will split it up in equal shares, and that includes you . . . ah . . . Miss Dumont."

The girl smiled. "I could be a rich whore."

Porter laughed. "Lady, if you're rich you won't need to be a whore."

"I know, but even if I'm rich I'd like to keep busy," Daphne said.

Crystal and Porter laughed at that.

The girl was genuinely perplexed. "What did I say that's so funny?"

"Nothing, nothing at all," Porter said. "I'm sure you're going to make a mighty interesting whore, rich or not."

Crystal looked at Teague, Dave Quarrels, and Townes Pierce who were riding twenty yards ahead of her. As he always did, Juan Sanchez was out front on point. "Slim, I don't want Johnny to hear this, but if Mrs. Talbot has found the mine, will there be a gun battle?"

"You mean when Johnny takes it? Yeah, I think that's possible. But maybe he and Mrs. Talbot can reach some kind of agreement."

"To share the gold, you mean?" Crystal said.

"Yeah, they may work something out, so it might not come to shooting." Slim's smile was grim. "Right now, after what happened with Arch Storm and them, I think Johnny has had a bellyful of gunfighting. At least for a spell."

"I certainly hope so," Crystal said. "I wouldn't like it if something bad happened to Mrs. Talbot."

"I'm sure Johnny wouldn't like it either," Porter said. "We'll wait until the cards are dealt and play our hand from there."

The day was moving toward dusk when Johnny Teague and the others rode up on the Cornudas Mountains. The evening promised to be dreary. Gray clouds dominated the sky and there had been a steady drizzle for the past hour.

"Smoke rising," Teague said, drawing rein.

"The Talbot woman's campfire, you think, Johnny?" Dave Quarrels said.

"Seems like," Teague said.

"How do we play it?" Quarrels said.

Teague considered that for a few moments, then said, "We ride in grinning, like we're visiting kinfolk. Let Luna Talbot make the next move."

"Johnny, she ain't gonna welcome us with open arms like we was kissin' kin," Quarrels said. "She'll know we're there because of the mine."

"Which maybe she ain't found yet," Teague said. "Maybe she'll welcome the help." He turned in the saddle. "Hey, Crystal, how will Mrs. Talbot react when she sees us?"

"She'll either offer us coffee or shoot us. Take your pick."

"My money is on the coffee," Teague said.

"Not mine," Crystal said. "Mrs. Talbot can be a hardcase when she feels like it."

"So can I." He kneed his horse forward. "Let's go find out which way the wind blows."

Teague found out in a hurry when a volley of rifle fire kicked up dirt around him and filled the air with angry hornets. "What the hell!" he yelled, fighting his restive horse. "They're shooting at us."

"Just found that out, huh, Johnny?" Crystal said.

Teague studied the drifts of gun smoke along the rocky slope of the nearest mountain. "Five shooting. Back up everybody, I ain't riding across two hundred yards of open ground into rifle fire."

After retreating out of range, he said, "Crystal, go talk to Luna Talbot. She won't shoot at a woman, and she knows you. Tell her we're friendly. Tell her anything you like that gets her to stop shooting."

"I quit her, remember," Crystal said. "She might plug me out of spite. Besides, there are four other people shooting."

"And I bet it's them damned Patterson stage men," Quarrels said. "Shotgun guards are always handy with a gun."

"They won't shoot at a woman," Teague said. "Now give it a try, Crystal."

"Johnny, if they put a bullet in me, I swear to God I'll come back and haunt you." She took off her hat, shook out her long hair, and finger-combed it over her shoulders. "Now I look like a woman. I hope."

"Crystal, you could show your tits," Daphne said,

her face serious. "Then they'll know you're a woman for sure."

"The hair is enough," Crystal said, grimacing. "Thanks for the suggestion, though."

That pleased Daphne and it showed in her smile. "I always have good ideas."

Crystal glanced at the gloomy sky. "It's getting dark, and this damned rain doesn't help. I hope they can see me well enough to recognize me as a female."

"They'll see you all right," Slim Porter said. "A pretty girl like you."

"Well, here goes." Looking closely at the mountain, Crystal urged her horse forward. "I sure hope you aren't nursing any hard feelings, Mrs. Talbot."

She rode out waving, smiling, a sweet, attractive girl coming for a friendly visit. At least Crystal hoped that's how she looked. But her hopes were shattered when gunfire again erupted from the mountain's slope. She turned and galloped back in a hail of bullets.

"She tried to kill me!" Crystal said after she'd reined her horse to a skidding stop. "She tried to shoot me right out of the saddle. For a minute there, I thought I was a goner. Mrs. Talbot can sure hold a grudge."

Teague shook his head in disappointment. "It didn't work, did it?"

"No, it didn't work," Crystal said, her eyes blazing. "Johnny, don't ever ask me to do something like that again."

Townes Pierce and Slim Porter looked glum, and then Dave Quarrels asked the question that was on their minds. "Where do we go from here, Johnny?"

"It seems that Luna Talbot is mighty anxious to keep folks away from the Cornudas. That tells me she's found the mine and discovered gold in it. Now all we have to do is take it away from her, or at least make her give us our fair share."

"And how do we do that?" Quarrels said.

"I'll study on it," Teague said. "I've never been one for nighttime gunfighting, but that doesn't mean we can't do some walking in the dark. Let me think it through. In the meantime we'll camp here. Rustle up anything that will burn and put on the coffee and bacon. I'm mighty hungry." He looked up at the dark sky. "At least the rain's stopped."

CHAPTER THIRTY-FIVE

Arman Broussard raised his nose and sniffed. "Yes, it's coffee. And bacon frying."

"I smell it too," Leah Leighton said. "And there's a fire right ahead of us. Do you see it?"

"I see it," Luna Talbot said. "It could be the Rathmores."

"I don't think so," Broussard said. "I never smelled bacon in the arroyo. If they ever had any, it ran out a long time ago. And why would they camp so far off their home range?"

"Well, I'm worn out and hungry enough that I'm willing to take a chance that it's not the Rathmores," Luna said.

"Could be Rangers," Leah said.

"Could be anybody," Luna said. "Let's go find out."

Broussard felt reassured by the weight of the Colt in his waistband and that Luna and Leah were armed. But it was late to be calling on strangers in this wild country that seemed to nurture even wilder men.

Luna must have read his thoughts. "Ride in easy,

but be on your guard. We don't know if we're about to meet up with friend or foe."

"Or a little of both," Broussard said.

With the dark of night tight around them and under a sky without a moon, Luna held up a halting hand and drew rein when they were as yet a good distance from the fire. "Hello, the camp!" she called out.

Silence.

Luna saw shadow figures move in the fire glow and then the distinct *click-clack* of a Winchester lever.

A moment . . . and then a man's voice called out, "What do you want? State your intentions."

"We smelled your coffee and would admire to share your fire," Luna said.

"How many of you?"

"Three. Two women and a man."

Another pause, then, "Who's the man?"

"My name is Broussard. It's well-known in some quarters."

The silence dragged on longer before a man said, "Arman Broussard, out of New Orleans?"

"The very same."

"I heard you'd been hung."

"You heard wrong."

"Then come on in real slow. And Broussard, keep your hand well away from your gun. There's some mighty excitable gents around here, and they ain't trusting men."

"We're coming in," Broussard said. "Grinning like visiting kinfolk."

The three riders approached the campfire at a walk, and then as frontier etiquette demanded, sat their saddles until they were asked to step down.

"Light and set," Johnny Teague said. "There's coffee in the pot and bacon and cornbread in the pan."

Broussard didn't dismount with the women. His eyes hard on Teague he said, "It's been a while, Johnny."

"Four years. That time in Galveston," Teague said. His hand hung close to his gun. "You were dealing faro in the First Chance saloon when I shot Charlie Banks."

"I recollect, Johnny," Broussard said. "Banks was no good. Neither was his brother."

"You joined the posse that went after me though, Arman. Ran me for three days before y'all gave up."

"Johnny, I was a pillar of the community, a new experience for me. I was expected to do my duty. The others took pots at you, but I didn't. I always figured that Banks only got what was coming to him."

"Well, let bygones be bygones, I say. Water under the bridge, huh? Now light and set."

"We still got a problem, Johnny. I have to say it straight out, no holding back."

"Tell it. I'm listening."

"I killed a man in New Orleans, a rich man's son, and his pa put a price on my head," Broussard said. "I've been dogged by bounty hunters ever since."

"I figured that's why I thought you'd been hung already," Teague said. "I got my information wrong."

"Seems like. The thing is, I'd take it real hard if you try to collect that bounty. I mean, given our past history and all."

"Men in my profession don't cotton to bounty hunters. Too close to the law for our liking," Teague said. "If there's a bounty on you, I won't be the one cutting off your head and taking it to New Orleans. You savvy? You have my word on it."

Broussard nodded. "Your word is good enough for me." He swung out of the saddle. "Now where's the coffee?"

"Aren't you going to introduce the ladies first?" Teague said.

"Of course. That was remiss of me. Johnny Teague, this is Mrs. Luna Talbot and Miss Leah Leighton, her ranch segundo." Broussard might have said more, but the stunned expression on Teague's face stopped him in his tracks.

"But . . . Mrs. Talbot . . . but you shot at us," the outlaw said.

"When, Mr. Teague? Recently or at some time in the past?"

"Just before sundown when we rode up on the mountains," Teague said. "And then you shot at Crystal Casey, who used to work for you."

Luna smiled. "I see you, Crystal. You look well."

The woman smiled. "No hard feelings, Mrs. Talbot."

"Not hard enough to shoot you, my dear." Luna looked back at Teague and said, "I assure you, I didn't shoot at you, either, nor did Miss Leighton or Mr. Broussard."

Teague looked doubtful, as though he was unconvinced. "Arman, give me the right of it."

"Mrs. Talbot didn't shoot at you, Johnny. But I can tell you who did."

"Who?" Teague was angry. "Give me names."

Broussard shook his head. "All in due time. Johnny, as a host you leave much to be desired. Do I ever get the coffee you promised?"

"Mrs. Talbot, I'll get your coffee, and yours too, Leah," Crystal said, anxious to make amends for her betrayal.

"Arman, help yourself and then tell me who I can add to my list of enemies," Teague said. "It seems to grows longer by the day."

"And of course you'll want to know all about the Lucky Cuss gold mine, won't you, Mr. Teague?" Luna said.

That caught the outlaw flat-footed, but he managed to say, "It had crossed my mind."

Luna smiled. "I'm sure it had. And I'm afraid you're in for a huge disappointment."

CHAPTER THIRTY-SIX

"Well, I got no reason to doubt what you and Broussard told us about them Rathmores, Mrs. Talbot," Dave Quarrels said. "So my question is for you, Johnny . . . what the hell do we do now?"

"Do?" Teague said. "We pickax our way into the rock and see if the gold vein is really disappearing. That's one thing we can do. Only I'm not about to fight a war with them Rathmores to do it."

"So what the hell do we do *now,* Johnny?" Quarrels repeated.

"Head back to east Texas and take up our profession again," Teague said. "We cut our teeth in the bank- and train-robbing business. That's where we belong."

"We'll need to hire more men," Quarrels said.

"I know Brad Ward and Mitch Mills are still around," Teague said. "Those fellers are train specialists, especially Mills, but he's a cantankerous cuss when he's in drink."

"And he can be quick to go to the trigger," Slim Porter said. "Remember he shot Danny Elliot that time for laughing at his new top hat."

"Good man, though, Mitch," Townes Pierce said. "Dependable, and he never demands more than his fair share. Got a widowed sister in Fort Worth that he supports. Her name's Mildred, I think."

"Gentlemen, the Lucky Cuss wasn't much to begin with, and now it's played out," Luna Talbot said. "We three are here for two reasons. One is that I want to even the score with the animal who calls himself Papa Mace—"

"And the other is that we want to rescue two men from his clutches before he kills them," Broussard said.

"And that would that be the stage driver and the shotgun guard," Quarrels said.

"It would," Broussard said. "I set store by them."

"With all that in mind, I have a proposition for you and your men, Mr. Teague," Luna said.

"I'm listening," Teague said.

"Help us, and I'll give each of you a hundred dollars," Luna said.

"What kind of help?"

"It won't be easy," Luna said. "I've told you how savage the Rathmores are."

"What kind of help?" Teague repeated.

"Mrs. Talbot means gun help, Johnny," Broussard said. "There's no way around the matter. It will all come down to a shooting scrape."

Suddenly Teague looked serious. "I got burned, Arman, burned bad. Now I'm wary. I've turned cautious and kinda lost my taste for gunfighting."

"How burned?" Broussard said.

"Had it out with four wolfers. I didn't think it would come to a gunfight, but they fooled me. I lost five good men that day. I got burned bad." Teague shook his head. "And it was a yellow butterfly lost me those men. Don't that beat all?"

"With or without the butterfly, the fight would've happened anyway, Johnny," Quarrels said. "Arch Storm wanted the women. Simple as that."

Juan Sanchez listened and then said, "The Sioux and the Blackfoot say the butterfly brings luck and will not allow it to be killed. Maybe some good will come of this, I think."

"Of course it will. Mr. Teague, a man in your line of work can expect to get burned now and then," Luna said. "Jesse James got burned at Northfield, but he hired more men and kept on going. Sure, the new men he hired were trash, but you can do better."

"Ward and Mills are good men, Johnny," Quarrels said. "They're mighty rough in speech and deed, but they ain't trash like Bob Ford and Charlie Pitts and them."

"Mrs. Talbot, do you have a plan in mind for them Rathmores?" Teague said.

Before she answered, Luna took a sip of coffee and then carefully laid the cup on the ground beside her. "I have no clever plan. We just hit them hard, go in with guns blazing, and kill them all. But leave Papa Mace to me."

"After what you told us about him, I've a mind to gun him myself," Porter said.

"Well, Mr. Teague, do we have a deal?" Luna said.

"We can't do anything until sunup," Teague said. "Until then I'll study on it for a spell. I got burned. I have scars, Mrs. Talbot, deep scars."

"Yes, I know you have burn scars," Luna said. "One way or another we've all been burned, Mr. Teague."

The drizzle had long stopped, and the clouds melted into starlight.

"Someday you'll have to tell me about the butterfly, Johnny," Broussard said.

"But not tonight. I've got some thinking to do."

On the eastern side of the Cornudas Mountains another man was deep in thought.

Sleepless, Ben Kane lay in his bed and stared at the ceiling. The rain had stopped, and the moon was high in the sky, adding points of crystal light to the water drops that dripped from the roof of the ranch house.

He had no illusions about what the dawn would bring. He would conduct a massacre, a mass slaughter that would remove the loathsome Rathmores from the face of the earth and end the pestilence that had for too long threatened to destroy his ranch

In the pearly gloom his eyes were drawn to the portrait of his wife, dead these two years. Martha had been a gentle soul and she'd abhorred violence of any kind. Even when he and the hands had fought Apaches, she'd cried over the Indian dead. Martha would not approve of what was to happen come morning.

"Ben," she'd say, "you must find common ground with the Rathmores. Let us have peace, not war."

Kane asked himself why, at this late stage, was his conscience troubling him?

Of course he knew the answer.

In his time he'd killed many men. He'd shot them, hanged them, dragged them behind horses until their flesh ripped from their bones . . . but women and children . . . he'd never in his life killed a woman or harmed a child.

Kane got out of bed, took his Colt from the holster on the table beside him, and stepped to the window. The wheels were already in motion and there was no stopping them. The hands would assemble at dawn, heavily armed, and Dave Sloan and a few others would push it, wanting it done. Anse Dryden, a decent man with quiet eyes, would go along with the rest.

The old man gazed out at the still, moonlit night and the deep, almost mystical shadows by the corrals, the bunkhouse, the outbuilding. They were made dark by darker memories.

Dead men. Skinned cowboys. The bloody bodies of hard-rock miners pretending to be gunmen. Hanged rustlers, piss running down their kicking legs, tongues sticking out of mouths with ashen lips . . . all the black memories of the passing years from which shadows were made.

Ben Kane turned his head and looked at the portrait on the wall. "I don't want to do this any longer, Martha. I've lived too long at war. I want peace. I need to close my eyes and sleep."

And Martha said, "Then sleep, Ben. Good night, my old friend."

Kane smiled. "Good night, Martha."

He clicked back the hammer, shoved the muzzle of the Colt into his mouth, and pulled the trigger.

CHAPTER THIRTY-SEVEN

The gunshot woke Dave Sloan. His room was at the back of the ranch house, far enough away that his nighttime coughing didn't keep others awake. Ben Kane was slightly deaf and didn't seem to mind.

But the gunshot had seemed to come from Ben's room.

Sloan jumped out of bed, put on his hat—a habit of his long-gone cowboying days—and pulled on his pants. Gun in hand, he made his way through the dark house toward Kane's room. From outside, he heard the hands yelling to one another and the sound of pounding feet. The bedroom door was ajar, and its hinges creaked when Sloan opened it.

Helped by the moonlight that streamed through the windows, he took in the scene at a glance, a stark image that burned itself on his consciousness . . . the disheveled bed, the Navajo rug on the floor, the polished furniture and trimmed oil lamps, the painting of Robert E. Lee on the wall and the picture of Kane's dead wife Martha. Ben had once told him he wanted to remove her portrait because it broke his heart to look at her as she was in life, but he never did.

The focus of Sloan's attention was the body on the floor. Ben Kane, never a big man, looked even smaller in death. He lay on his back, the Colt still clutched in his right hand. Blood spread from under his head like a pool of spilled ink. Sloan took a knee and placed his hand flat on Kane's chest. The old man's breathing had stopped, his heart had stopped . . . and the stillness of death was on him. His face showed no pain. His features were serene, as though he was sound asleep.

Sloan heard footsteps behind him, looked up, and saw Ansley Dryden looming over him, a revolver in his hand.

"Ben killed himself." Sloan rose to his feet and started to cough, his frail body racked by hacking, choking barks that doubled him over, sent him staggering across the room, and stained scarlet the handkerchief he'd hurriedly pulled from his pocket.

The other hands drifted into the room and gathered around their boss's body. No one said a word or looked at Sloan until his coughing attack ended and he straightened up, his face a white, bleached skull.

"You are wrong, Dave," Dryden said. "Ben Kane didn't kill himself. The Rathmores killed him."

No one questioned that statement.

One young puncher said, "Mr. Kane was getting old and couldn't take it any longer." Then slightly embarrassed for speaking up, "It seems to me."

Dryden nodded. "I saw it on him. He was getting worn out. The Rathmores were wearing him out."

Breathing hard, Sloan said, "For a spell there, we were the same, Ben and me, but at different levels. He was ahead of me in the race, dealing with the same hell but different demons."

"Well, he's at peace now," Dryden said. "If a man who blows his brains out can find peace."

"Ben served his time in hell. The Rathmores saw to that," Sloan said. "He's at peace."

"I say we bury the boss with a Rathmore at his feet," the young cowboy said.

"Anse, did Ben have an heir?" Sloan said.

The foreman shook his head. "Not that I'm aware of. He told me once he hadn't written a will because too many hopeful people would want him dead." Dryden smiled slightly. "He was making a funny joke."

"This is no funny joke," Sloan said. "Anse, as far as I'm concerned, you're the new boss of the Rafter-K." He gave a series of short, dense coughs and then said to the hands, "How do you boys see it?"

The young puncher, a tough kid named Pete Harker, said, "I can only speak for myself, but I say Mr. Dryden is the new boss of this ranch. He served his time."

That brought a murmur of agreement from the rest of the hands.

Sloan said, "You heard them, Anse. Now you call the shots around here."

Suddenly Dryden seemed angry. "Look at us. The boss isn't even cold yet and you want me to take his place. It ain't right." He kneeled and put his hand on Kane's bloody forehead. "Hell, Ben, you were the one always gave the orders. Give me one now. What do I do?"

"He can't talk to you," Sloan said. "He can't say anything to you. Ben Kane's time for giving orders is over."

"Dave, I've worked for wages all my life," Dryden said. "I don't know how to be a ranch owner."

"You make one decision at a time," Sloan said. "That's how it's done. Ben's dead, but the Rathmores are still aboveground, and that ain't right. Come dawn, we were to attack their nest and wipe them off the face of the earth. Do we still do it? Or do we sit back and do nothing? That's your first decision, Anse."

Dryden ignored that and said, "You men get shovels. We'll bury Ben beside Martha and we'll do it now. I don't want to see him laid out in his parlor like a side of beef. Does anybody know the words?"

An older hand with a canvas patch over his left eye, partly covering a deep knife scar, said, "I am the resurrection and the life. He who believes in me, though he may die, he shall live. And whoever lives and believes in me shall never die."

"How do you know that, Cogan?" Dryden said.

"I heard it said often enough. Ben Kane must've said it a score of times. A stickler for the proprieties, was Ben."

Dryden nodded. "Then you'll say that at his grave." He turned to Sloan. "Give me until an hour before sunup to study on things, Dave."

"A man's got that right," Sloan said. "Now we got a burying to do."

When the others filed out, the puncher with the eyepatch said to Dryden, "Anse, is this the end of the Rafter-K? I fit Comanches with Ben and I fit Apaches and I fit rustlers and I fit the Rathmores. Do all that go for nothing, like a hill of beans?"

"I don't know," Dryden said. "I haven't even seen the books yet. Hell, maybe Ben was broke. Maybe he wasn't. We'll know soon enough."

"Tell me when you got it figured all out," Cogan said. "Man gets to my age and all he's ever known is cowboying, he has to make plans. The boss dying like this, well, it brung all that to mind."

"We all got to make plans, Cogan," Dryden said. "After today, we'll talk on it."

CHAPTER THIRTY-EIGHT

"Do we have a plan yet?" Arman Brossard said.

Luna Talbot smiled. "You can't sleep either, huh?"

"Worrying about Ryan and Muldoon. I told them I'd come back for them. I plan to keep my word."

"And so you will," Luna said.

"But are they still alive? Will they know I kept my word?" Broussard said. "Those are questions that vex me considerably."

"As I said before, there is no clever plan. Johnny Teague knows that."

"Johnny doesn't want to get burned again. Losing those men . . . their ghosts are in his head."

"If he'll ride with us, we can overwhelm the Rathmores real quick. Take the fight out of them so there's less killing to be done."

"Well, that's a plan. Of a sort," Broussard said.

Luna looked at the sky. "I don't think I've ever seen so many stars."

"They're always that way before a fight," Broussard said. "Real bright. Brighter than you ever seen them before."

Luna looked at him. "Really? Why is that, I wonder?"

"I don't know why. Maybe the possibility of dying sharpens a man's senses." Broussard smiled. "Or a woman's."

"You know that from experience?" Luna said.

"Yes, I do."

"Tell me about it."

"I'll bore you. I think sometimes I bore people with my talk."

Luna smiled. "Maybe it'll help me sleep."

"All right, here goes . . . I first realized how a man sees, hears, and tastes things with a heightened sense of appreciation years ago when I first became a professional gambler," Broussard said. "I was . . . what? . . . twenty-two years old at the time."

"Young," Luna said. "Young to be a gambling man."

"Yes, very young. I was playing poker in the Number Seven saloon in Abilene when a lumberman by the name of Archie Kirk called me out. He'd been losing big all night and claimed I was cheating."

"And were you?" Luna said.

"No. I don't cheat. I'm a good poker player."

"I'm sure you are. So what happened?"

"Well, the bartender and a couple of bouncers knew Kirk's reputation as a troublemaker and took his gun away from him. It seems that he'd killed a man a few months before over the affections of a fallen woman and was a bad hombre to cross.

"About an hour later a man came in with a message for me. It was from Kirk, telling me to leave Abilene because he intended to shoot me on sight." Broussard was silent, remembering. "I wasn't about to let Kirk, a bully and a blowhard, put the crawl on me and knew I was facing a gunfight come morning. That night the stars were brighter than I'd ever seen them before and the whiskey in my glass was like . . . I don't know, nectar, I guess."

"Because you thought you were about to die," Luna said.

"I figured there was a good chance that I might. Kirk had a reputation as a shootist and boasted that he'd killed five men. Looking back, I really didn't believe his claim, but I didn't disbelieve it either."

"Had you killed a man before?" Luna said.

"No, I had not. I never even had to draw my gun before. After I got the message from Kirk, the bartender offered to saddle my horse and bring it out front, so I could make a clean getaway."

"Where was the city marshal?" Luna said.

"Hickok was out of town serving a warrant, and his deputy was nowhere to be found."

A mesquite limb dropped in the fire and sent up a shower of sparks. A man mumbled in his sleep, rolled over and was silent.

"To make a long story short, Archie Kirk saw me again next morning outside Murphy's Grain and Feed Store on Walnut Street. He said something like, 'Now I've got ye,' and he went for his gun." Broussard shook his head. "The gun had been returned to him that morning by Hickok's deputy, for God's sake."

"You're still here, so obviously he didn't kill you," Luna said.

"An astute observation, Mrs. Talbot. No, he didn't kill me, and for the first time in my life, I was aware that I was fast on the draw and shoot."

"You killed him?"

"I dropped Kirk with my second shot. He joined his shadow in the dirt and didn't shoot back. I heard later that my bullet had severed his spine and he died six months later. It was self-defense, but I knew Wild Bill Hickok might not see it that way, so I got out of town in a hurry. In those days Bill's method of keeping the peace was *Bang! Bang! Bang!* 'Now what seems to be the problem here?'"

Luna smiled. "So I've heard." She stretched her arms and said, "There's still a few hours until sunup. I think I'll try for some sleep."

"Me too," Brossard said. "All this storytelling has worn me out."

Arman Broussard managed to drop off but dreamed of a pair of dancing skeletons in a cobwebbed mine shaft. He woke with a start, his heart thumping and his eyes wild.

Ben Kane was laid to rest by lantern light, and Len Cogan said the words.

"He and Martha are together now," Anse Dryden said. "I think that's what he always wanted."

His eyes glittering, Dave Sloan looked across the grave at the foreman. "That, and an end to the Rathmores."

"I hear you, Dave," Dryden said. "That was an obsession. In the end, I think it killed him. Made him not right in the head."

Milt Barnett said, "Jake Wise always said that afore the Rathmores killed and skun him."

"Jake said what?" Dryden said.

"That Mr. Kane wasn't right in the head about the Rathmores."

"How would he know?" Cogan said. "Jake wasn't right in the head either."

"How come you never told Jake that to his face, Len?" Barnett said.

"Quit that, both of you," Dryden said. "I won't have squabbling over Ben's grave. All of you, go see to your guns and saddle up. We ride out at dawn."

"Made up your mind, Anse, huh?" Sloan studied the big foreman for a few moments and then said, "You're doing the right thing."

"I want it done," Dryden said. "I want the damned thing over with. It's gone on too long."

The punchers walked away from the grave, and only Sloan and Dryden remained. The two men stood in the gloom, measuring each other. Sloan was dying. He was dying fast.

Dryden considered what Sloan had said—"You're doing the right thing." Didn't dying men always tell the truth? In Sloan's mind at least, making war on the Rathmores was the right thing to do. Dying men don't lie.

As though he'd read Dryden's mind, Sloan said, "Anse, Ben is dead and now you got it to do. You wouldn't tolerate sheep on your range, and the Rathmores are worse than any sheep. By their very presence, they'll eventually destroy the Rafter-K. They have to be stopped before it's too late."

"You don't need to lecture me, Dave. I know what's at stake here. The boys are saddling up and the die is cast," Dryden said. "By suppertime tonight, there won't be a single Rathmore left alive in Texas."

"And Rafter-K cows will graze in the Cornudas," Sloan said. "That's how God intended it to be."

CHAPTER THIRTY-NINE

Papa Mace rolled off Ella Rathmore, sated. Free of the pressure of his great bulk, the girl managed to breathe again, taking in great gulps of air that Mace mistook for passion.

He smiled. "Don't worry, my dear. Soon you'll have me all to yourself."

"I . . . so . . . look . . . forward . . . to . . . that." Fighting for each breath, she spoke with little conviction.

But Papa Mace didn't notice, wrapped up as he was in his future plans. "I think my speech tonight was received very well."

"Yes . . . everyone believed that you've had another great vision about the promised land," Ella said, breathing easier. A swig from Mace's whiskey bottle helped.

"Did Malachi?"

"Yes. My husband most of all. He even believed the part about you breeding with a younger woman to produce another leader when you retire." She smiled. "He's very excited about it, and that's why I'm here."

Papa Mace grinned. "And the bit about us riding

into the wasteland to have the second part of the vision, the location of a new gold mine?"

"Hook, line, and sinker," Ella said, her face hard-planed in the firelight. "Malachi don't know his butt from a watering hole."

"He's a whore's spawn. What do you expect?"

"How did you get in tow with all them whores, Papa?" Ella said.

"It took a few years," Mace said. "I've always been partial to whores. Then I decided to keep the sons and get rid of the rest. I had a vision of my future. Instead of a small-time conman, I saw myself as the leader of a clan, my own blood, with me as master."

"But, Papa, you got that right here," Ella said.

"No, I don't," Mace said. "At first I had enough gold from the mine to pay for the hired hands who did the digging, but Ben Kane hung some of them and the rest were ready to quit."

"Malachi told me the miners were hung for rustling," Ella said.

"Yeah, it was my intention to take Kane's cattle and then his ranch, but he was too tough for me," Mace said. "I skun a couple of his cowboys, figuring to scare him off, but all I did was start a feud. I lost all my remaining hands and then there was a standoff. Kane wasn't strong enough to attack me, and I wasn't strong enough to attack his ranch, so we've been sniping at each other ever since." Mace grimaced. "And now the gold seam has run dry and so have all my hopes for this place."

Ella snuggled against Mace's naked, sweating body. "Well, now you got me, Papa. Tell how it's gonna be, Papa."

"I already told you all about it."

"Tell me again."

"Well, I've hoarded enough gold to last me and you quite a few years," Mace said. "So we'll head for Fort Smith and stay in the best hotels, eat in the best restaurants, and live pretty damned high. You'll have new clothes—"

"And a pink parasol."

"And a pink parasol, and we'll never walk anywhere. We'll ride in a carriage that will take us wherever we want to go. For a while at least, we'll be gentry, you and me."

"And what happens when the money runs out?" Ella said, frowning.

"It won't run out, Ella. You can do some whoring on the side, and I'll be working a con or two. Before I ended up here, I was one of the best bunco artists around."

Ella smiled and snuggled closer. "Papa, I'll be so glad to get away from this dump."

"Yeah, it's a dump, all right." Mace sat up, lit a cigar with a brand from the fire, and then lay on his back again, exhaling blue smoke. "Like I said, things didn't work out the way I planned. The mine playing out and the trouble we've had with Ben Kane and his ruffians spoiled everything. The best of my sons are dead, and them that are left don't amount to much, so I won't regret running out on them."

"And their ugly women and kids."

"Yeah, them too," Mace said.

Ella's frown deepened. "Papa, I don't want to be a two-dollar whore again. I've had enough of that. It's no kind of life for me."

Mace shook his head. "You won't be. Ella. You've got class. Your clientele will be fine gentlemen with deep pockets and dutiful little wives waiting for them at home. I mean, clean gentlemen, nothing but the best. I'll see to that."

"You'll be so good to me, won't you, Papa?"

"You'll want for nothing. Fine clothes, jewelry, it will all be yours." Mace said. "Pass the bottle, will ya? We're going on a visit."

"Visit who?" Ella said.

"Them two in the mine shaft. Time to tease them again."

Ella smiled. "I thought they'd be dead by this time."

"Probably close, one of them at least. The shotgun guard with the red hair is on his last legs, damn him," Mace said. "They call the other feller Muldoon. He bit my leg, the dirty rat, and he's paying for it now." He tied on his loincloth and donned his sandals as Ella hurried into her clothes.

"Now let's go have some fun," Mace said.

"Buttons, I'm thirsty," Red Ryan said, his voice a husky whisper. "So thirsty. Where's the water?"

"We'll have some soon, Red," Buttons Muldoon said. "It's on the way. Just you rest for a while."

Red was quiet for a few moments and then he said, "Buttons, give it to me straight." His words were weak.

Buttons strained to hear him. "Give you what straight?"

"Am I dying? It feels like I'm dying. I'm kinda numb all over."

"No, you're not dying," Buttons said. "I won't let you die. You're the best shotgun guard I ever had. And as for feeling numb all over, why, that's because you're all trussed up. By and by, once the ropes are loosened you'll be as fine as dollar cotton."

"They hurt me bad, didn't they? Then Rathmores."

"No, not too bad," Buttons said. "You're tough, Red, mighty tough."

"Bad enough though, huh?" Red said.

"Yeah, maybe that," Buttons said. "They hurt you bad enough."

Red whispered, "God, I'm thirsty."

"Soon," Buttons said. "We'll have water soon." He saw that Red's lips were white and cracked, his green eyes feverish. "You rest now."

But there was to be no rest for Red Ryan that night.

Papa Mace and Ella Rathmore, half-drunk, mean, and grinning, burst into the mine shaft arm in arm, the whiskey bottle in the man's hand. Ella carried a lantern that spread a fitful light.

"Is he still alive?" Mace said, eyeing Red.

"He's alive, and he'll stay alive long enough to see me kill you," Buttons said, scowling.

"And that ain't never gonna happen," Mace said. "You've lost, driving man. You tried to take what was mine and you couldn't do it. You lost . . . lost. Let it sink in . . . you lost."

"Trash, I haven't lost yet. I said I'll kill you, and I will," Buttons said.

"Papa, why don't you just shoot him?" Ella said. "You shouldn't let him talk to you like that."

"Too quick, my dear. He's got a lot of suffering still to do." Mace stepped to Red, took in the cracked lips and ashen face, and grinned, "Look, Ella, the red-head needs a drink. I'll give him one." Mace tipped the bottle and splashed whiskey into Red's face. He was delighted when Red desperately attempted to lick the bourbon as it trickled down his cheeks and over his mouth. "There," Mace said, smiling like a devil. "I reckon that will make him even thirstier."

Buttons's killing rage exploded. He snarled like a trapped animal as he tried to get to his feet, a movement that earned him a kick from Mace that knocked him flat on his back again.

Papa Mace grinned. "You want a drink too, big man? Here, have a swig." He threw the remaining bourbon into Buttons's face and then tossed the empty bottle at his head. The bottle hit Buttons on the forehead and cut him above his left eye, drawing blood.

The sight of the scarlet rush of blood that ran down Buttons's face sobered Ella and she said, "Papa, I want to leave here. These two are no fun."

Mace nodded, "As you wish, my dear." He picked up the lantern where Ella had left it and stepped toward the mine entrance. "You lost, both of you!" he yelled through a laugh. The tunnel of rock made his voice boom and sound hollow, like the voice of a fiend.

CHAPTER FORTY

It was two hours before sunup.

Papa Mace and Ella Rathmore returned to the fat man's lair, the private niche in the arroyo hidden from prying eyes. Mace opened a trunk and said to her, "No more dressing like a poverty-stricken Indian for me. That didn't work a damn. My sons didn't turn out to be noble savages."

"Malachi is a savage," Ella said.

"Maybe so, but he ain't noble." Mace dressed, taking his time, into the clothes he'd worn when he and his criminal clan were run out of east Texas and like a seedy Moses, he'd led them to the Cornudas Mountains. He'd promised his family a wonderful new life but had brought them nothing but starvation, disease, and death. He was abandoning them and dressing for the occasion.

"Very smart, Papa," Ella said. "You look like a banker or maybe a lawyer."

And indeed, in his black frock coat, striped pants, white, frilled shirt, and elastic-sided boots, he did have the look of a businessman of some kind.

"And soon you will look like a Denver hostess, my

dear," he said as he buckled on a fancy tooled gun belt, an ivory-handled Colt in the holster. "That is once you shed those rags and get into a pretty dress."

"It can't come soon enough for me," Ella said. "I've worn these duds for way too long."

"Patience, my dear, patience," Mace said. "You told Malachi to bring the horses?"

"Yes, I did. And a Winchester like you said. The fool thinks we'll return once you have your vision in the desert."

"We're not coming back here, ever," Mace said. "I never again wish to be a king without a kingdom. Damn Ben Kane for keeping us poor."

"You should have taken over his ranch, Papa," Ella said.

"Yes, I could, but my worthless sons didn't have the belly for it, made the hired help do the fighting." He shrugged. "The hell with the ranch. Who wants to be a cow nurse anyway?"

"Not us," Ella said. "We're . . . what did you say we were?"

"Gentry," Mace said, smiling. "And come dawn we'll leave the poverty stink of this place behind us."

"It will take me a dozen baths before I feel clean again," Ella said.

An hour before sunup.

Malachi Rathmore, a thin, slack-jawed young man with vague, unintelligent eyes, brought the horses, slat-sided animals that had been feeding on grass and not much of that. Both were saddled, and Papa Mace's Winchester was shoved into the rifle scabbard. "Pa,

I'll take care of things here while you're gone," he said. "I'll be in charge."

Mace nodded. "Yes, you will be, Malachi. You'll take my place as head of the family until your wife and I return."

"Pa, why are you wearing them fancy clothes?"

"It was made known to me by the prophet Habakkuk that I must wear them for my great vision," Mace said. "These clothes are a sign of respect."

"Where will you lead us, Pa?"

"That will be made known to me in the desert. When I return, I'll reveal our destination to all my people."

"California, maybe?" Malachi said. "They say it's a great place to live off the fat of the land."

Mace said, "Who says?"

"Folks."

"Well, them folks told you right. There's gold in California. So much gold that you can pick it up off the streets. And the trees . . . well, there are trees everywhere . . . and you can eat the fruit right off the branches anytime you want, and nobody around to say, 'No, you filthy Rathmores, leave them peaches alone.'"

Malachi was excited. "Is that where we'll go, Pa, California?"

"Could be," Mace said. "Of course, it all depends what I see in my vision. Maybe there's an even better place that nobody knows about."

"Me an' Ella could be happy in California, Pa," Malachi said. "Couldn't we, Ella? Me an' you?"

"Sure, Malachi, sure," the woman said. "We'd pick up gold from the street and eat peaches all day."

"You got that right, Ella," Malachi said. "Now, you

take good care of Pa out there in the desert and help him with his vision."

"Oh, I will, Malachi, I will." She wanted badly to giggle.

"Oh, and Pa, what about them two in the mine?" Malachi said. "You need me to kill them while you're gone?"

"No, let them die by themselves," Mace said. "I want it to be slow. Understand? No food and no water."

"Sure thing, Pa. No food and no water. I understand."

Papa Mace and Ella Rathmore rode out of the arroyo just before sunup and headed east. Unbeknownst to them, lost in darkness, they passed within a mile of ten men from the Rafter-K riding in the opposite direction toward the Cornudas Mountains.

As the curtain of the night lifted, the stage was set for what one later historian would call the Cornudas Massacre . . . and with it would come the violent death of Papa Mace Rathmore, one of the vilest creatures to ever walk the face of the earth, destroyed by a much better man.

CHAPTER FORTY-ONE

Johnny Teague had thought things through and had reluctantly decided to join Luna Talbot and the others for their attack on the Rathmores. But as he stood in the gray predawn light drinking coffee, he was already second-guessing his decision.

"I got burned, you see," he said to Luna Talbot. "Puts a sight of caution in a man."

"I know it does." She smiled as she took a cup of coffee from Arman Broussard. "Mr. Teague, if it doesn't set right with you, I won't hold it against you if you cut a trail away from this."

Teague shook his head. "I can't do that. I'd show yellow, a bad thing in my profession."

"You're not yellow, Johnny," Juan Sanchez said. "If I thought you were, I'd have killed you by now."

Teague stared at the breed, surprised. "I never expected to hear that from you."

"Well, now you heard it," Sanchez said.

"You think I'm yellow?" Teague said.

"I just told you that you are not."

"I wanted you to hear you say it again," Teague

said. "I got burned, Sanchez. Arch Storm and them burned me. That's all I'm saying."

"Mr. Teague, I'm sure we all know you won't be stampeded by anyone," Luna said. "I'm glad you've decided to join us."

"I'll stick." Teague angled a look at Sanchez. "I figured to stick all along."

"We knew you would," Townes Pierce said. "Slim, Dave, didn't we know Johnny would stick?"

"Damn right," Dave Quarrels said. "You got burned, Johnny, but there's no backup in you, and that's a natural fact."

Teague glanced at the dawn lightening the sky to the east. He threw away the dregs of his coffee and said, "Enough of this damned talk. Let's saddle up and get it done."

Luna rose to her feet and said to Crystal Casey and Daphne Loveshade, now Dumont, "You ladies stay right here until the shooting is over. If you see anybody but us come out of the arroyo, light a shuck, and I mean, get away from here fast."

"Good luck, Mrs. Talbot," Crystal said.

"Thank you," Luna said.

"Yes, good luck," Daphne said. "I wish I could come with you."

"Maybe another time," Luna said.

Broussard brought her saddled horse. "Are we ready? Then let's—"

Gunfire erupted in the arroyo and shattered the quiet morning into a million shards of sound.

Dave Sloan led the charge into the arroyo and shot one of the drowsy guards and then he was past and galloping deeper into the arroyo. The second guard was shot by Anse Dryden and several others. Rafter-K bullets pounded the man against a wall, his body jerking in a mad jig as he was hit a dozen times.

Malachi Rathmore was busy exploring Papa Mace's throne room when he heard the gunfire. He grabbed his Winchester and ran outside into the clearing and into path of a charging horseman. Malachi instinctively raised the rifle and snapped off a fast shot. The mounted man was hit and reeled in the saddle, but his lips peeled back in a wild grin and the Colt in his fist roared. Malachi took the bullet in his left shoulder just under the clavicle and it exited horribly an inch above the top of his shoulder blade. It was a devastating wound, sustained by a half-starved body unfit to endure it, and Malachi screamed and fell on his back. Dave Sloan pumped two more bullets into the shrieking man, silencing him, and then, hit hard himself, slumped over in the saddle.

Dryden and the rest of the Rafter-K riders rode into the clearing, the big foreman's eyes going to the slumped Sloan. The gunman held a hand to his chest that was covered in blood.

"Don't shoot! Don't shoot!" A man dressed only in a loincloth and crude leather sandals ran toward the riders, his hands waving in the air. Ten men shot at Zacharias Rathmore, the youngest of Papa Mace's sons, and all of them scored hits. The man went down under a hail of lead and would never rise again.

Moments later, five women and a dozen children, all of them underfed, dirty, and ragged, emerged from hiding places among the rocks and stood silently watching the riders, the children's eyes as big and round as dollar coins.

Dryden ignored them and rode beside Sloan. "Dave, you're shot through and through."

"I'm killed," Sloan said. "I wish . . ." The gunman went silent, fighting the approaching darkness.

"What do you wish, Dave?" asked Dryden, a man much inclined to kindness.

"I wish it could've been somebody else that killed me, somebody the history books will remember." He turned his ashen face to Dryden and smiled. "Wes Hardin, maybe. Or Bill Longley . . ." He shook his head. "Dave Sloan had his suspenders cut by a white savage in a breechclout . . . well, don't that beat all . . ."

Blood welled into Sloan's mouth and then slowly . . . with agonizing slowness . . . he fell from the saddle. Dryden tried to stop his fall but could not.

One of the most feared gunmen in the West died with his beard in the dirt and an expression of wonder on his face.

"Boss, what do we do with the women and their brats?" a puncher said.

"Line them up over yonder with their backs to the rock," Dryden said. "Then you boys line up facing them and shuck your rifles."

"The kids as well?" the puncher said.

"All of them," Dryden said, his face gray, devoid of expression.

CHAPTER FORTY-TWO

The shooting had stopped when Luna Talbot and the others arrived at the mouth of the arroyo. They drew rein to look to the two dead men.

Johnny Teague said, "There's enough lead in those boys to use them as sinkers."

"Mr. Teague, is it Texas Rangers?" Luna said.

"I don't know, but let's go find out," the outlaw said.

"Riding in uninvited on a bunch of Rangers with their blood up and guns in their hands isn't a good idea," Juan Sanchez said. "Better tell them we're coming."

"I'll do it." Luna stood in the stirrups and called out, "You in there! This is Mrs. Luna Talbot of the Talbot ranch."

There was a silence and then a man yelled, "What do you want? State your intentions."

"Justice," Luna said. "I have a score to settle with the Rathmores, and that is my intention."

"That's already settled, or most of it," the man yelled. "Who do you have with you?"

"A party of armed and determined men," Luna said.

A longer silence, as though the men in the arroyo

were having a parley, and then, "Ride in slow, keep your guns holstered, and don't let us see any fancy moves. We're mighty salty men here and we mean business."

"And so do I mean business," Luna said. In a lower tone of voice she said to Teague and the others, "Case the rifles and holster the six-guns."

"Damn, they sure sound like Rangers," Dave Quarrels said to no one in particular. "Makes a man uneasy."

"Makes a man think of a hanging posse and a hemp noose, you mean," Teague said. "All right, boys, put away the hardware. Rangers don't like guns unless they're holding 'em."

Luna led the others into the arroyo at a walk and they were met with a single rider.

"Name's Ansley Dryden. I'm the foreman of the Rafter-K Ranch, and we've been at war with the Rathmores for years. The war ended today. All the rustlers are dead." He shifted in the saddle and then said, "Heard there was a ranch to the south owned by a pretty lady, and you're a pretty lady."

The compliment was casually given with no other implications beyond the words, and Luna Talbot accepted it as such. "You're very gracious, Mr. Dryden. We thought you were Texas Rangers."

"No, ma'am, we're just punchers," Dryden said. His measuring eyes flicked to Broussard and then to Teague, and one by one the men with him. "You keep rough company, Mrs. Talbot"—he nodded in the direction of Leah Leighton—"with one lovely exception."

"Thank you," Leah said. "But I can be rough myself when the occasion calls for it."

Dryden smiled, but it slipped some when Broussard

said, "Mister, this rough character has two friends in the mine shaft. They may be dead by now, but I have to find out."

"Mine shaft? I didn't know there was a mine here. What kind of mine?" Dryden said, pretending ignorance.

"A gold mine, and it belongs to me, but it may be played out," Luna said. "Now, please allow Mr. Broussard to see to his friends,"

"Go right ahead, gambling man." Dryden took a canteen from his saddle horn and tossed it to Broussard. "Take this. They might need it."

Broussard nodded his thanks and swung out of the saddle.

"Hold on," Dryden said. He turned his head and called out over his shoulder, "You boys back there. Man coming in. Let him pass." Then to Broussard, "Go right ahead. See to your friends."

"Obliged," Broussard said, not liking the man because of his rough company comment.

After Broussard walked hurriedly away, Luna said, "Where is Papa Mace?"

"He was the headman around here, wasn't he?" Dryden said.

"Yes, he was the big auger," Luna said.

"So far, we've killed four Rathmores, well, three dead and when I last saw him, the fourth was breathing his last," Dryden said. "Could be he's Papa Mace."

"Mace is a fat man," Luna said.

Dryden shook his head. "None of those boys was fat. They were all as skinny as slats."

"Then Papa Mace escaped," Luna said.

"You holding a grudge against him?" Dryden said.

She nodded. "Yes, I plan to find him and kill him."

"That's holding a grudge, all right," Dryden said. He looked at Teague. "You got a stake in this as well?"

The outlaw shook his head. "I'm just along for the ride.'

"Or maybe for the gold mine, huh?" Dryden said.

Luna said, "Mr. Teague offered his protection, and I accepted."

The big foreman had no problem with that. "Mrs. Talbot, the final act is about to start, but maybe you should give it a miss. It could be hard to watch."

Suddenly Luna felt a pang of alarm. "What are you going to do?"

"I'm going to get rid of the last of the Rathmores," Dryden said.

Arman Broussard stepped into the mine shaft, going from morning sun into gloom, the strange, eerie half-light that is seen only underground. Triangles of tangled gray cobwebs hung between the beams holding up the roof and then along the angle between the floor and the walls rats as big as tomcats scuttled. The place smelled musty, like old parchment manuscripts, and was as silent as a shadow.

As his eyes adjusted to the change of light, Broussard made out the recumbent shapes of two men. They were still and made no sound. He kneeled beside Buttons Muldoon and stared into his face. The man's eyes were shut, and at first Broussard didn't know if he was alive or dead. Gently, he shook Buttons's shoulder, and the driver's eyelids fluttered.

"Buttons, it's me," Broussard said. "I came back for you."

Without opening his eyes, Buttons croaked. "It's about time. Where the hell have you been?"

"Are you hurt?" Broussard said, his gaze taking in the ropes that cruelly bound both men.

"Damn it, man, I'm dying here and you're asking me questions," Buttons said, his voice as dry as the rustle of straw. "Have you any water?"

"Right here." Broussard uncorked the canteen and held it to Buttons's lips.

But the driver shook his head and then nodded in Red's direction. "Him first."

"Buttons, I think Red Ryan's dead," Broussard said. "I'm sorry, real sorry."

"He ain't dead. He's shamming."

Broussard tilted the canteen to Red's mouth. To his joy, Red stirred, his eyes flew open, and he drank greedily.

"Easy, shotgun man," the gambler said. "Not too much at first."

"Told you he was shamming," Buttons said.

After Red drank his fill and Buttons had done the same, Broussard said, "You're hog-tied, and I have to get you out of those ropes." But the knots were tight, and the gambler's slender fingers were no match for them. "I'll get a knife." He smiled. "Don't go anywhere."

"I'm dying, and the gambler is making funny jokes," Buttons said to the barely conscious Red. "Remind me to shoot him first chance I get."

Something stirred in Red's addled brain and he said, his voice weak, "As a representative of the Abe

Patterson and Son Stage and Express Company, I forbid you to do that. He's a passenger and under our protection."

"Red, he ain't a passenger," Buttons said. "Your mind's in a fog."

Broussard smiled at this exchange and stepped out of the mine entrance. To his left a line of mounted cowboys, rifles in hand, faced a group of women and children who had their backs to the wall of the arroyo. The woman seemed frightened, clutching children to their skirts, and the tension in the breathless air was as taut as a fiddle string. Broussard, a rational man, could not think the unthinkable. As far as he was concerned the women and children were temporary prisoners, nothing more.

When heads turned to look at him, he said, "I need to borrow a knife. Got some ropes to cut." When none of the punchers acknowledged him, he said, "Any kind of knife will do."

Finally a man tossed him a Barlow and said, "Bring it back, you he'ah?"

Brossard nodded. "I will. And thank you kindly."

The puncher waved a dismissive hand and turned to renew his watch on the women and children.

It was the work of a moment to cut Buttons and Red free of their bonds, but it took several minutes of trying before Buttons could stand again. Stiff and sore from rope burns, he watched Broussard gently stretch Red's arms and legs, working to get circulation back, and he was impressed that the gambler cared.

"I heard the shooting," Buttons said in a friendlier tone than he'd used before. "Did they get Papa Mace?"

Without looking up from his task, Broussard said, "I don't know. I saw dead men, but I don't know if he was one of them."

"If he ain't dead, I want him," Buttons said.

Broussard smiled. "Get in line, stage driver."

CHAPTER FORTY-THREE

Luna Talbot was horrified. She stared at Anse Dryden in disbelief. "No!" She kicked her horse into a startled run and behind her Dryden yelled, "Wait! Don't go back there!"

But the woman ignored him.

She galloped past the entrance to the mine shaft, swung her mount between the Rafter-K hands and the Rathmore women and children and violently drew rein, forcing her horse to its haunches. Dryden was right behind her, cursing up a storm.

"What are you men doing?" Luna said as she rode up and down the line of tight-faced horsemen. "Have you all gone stark, raving mad?" She waved a hand. "These are women and children. Are you going to shoot down women and children?" She picked out a young puncher and stared into his startled blue eyes. "Which of the children are you planning to kill? The littlest one over there holding the ragdoll?"

The cowboy looked flustered and turned his head away, saying nothing, but Dryden yelled, "They're Rathmores, damn it! Scum. Trash. They ain't fit to live."

"Everybody is fit to live," Luna said. "Their husbands

were your enemy, not the wives and certainly not the children."

"Mrs. Talbot, stand aside," Dryden said. "Let justice take its course. Are you men ready?"

A few of the punchers looked uneasily at Dryden and then gaped in surprise as Luna leaped from the saddle, ran to the women, and took a place among them.

"If you kill these people, you'll have to kill me too," Luna said, her angry eyes defiant.

"If that's what it takes," Dryden said.

"It's gonna take a sight more than you got, mister." A woman's voice.

Dryden swung his head around and saw Leah Leighton and Johnny Teague and his four gunmen, all with guns drawn.

"This is none of your concern," Dryden said. "And it's none of Mrs. Talbot's concern."

"You threatened to kill my boss, so I'm making it my concern," Leah said.

"Seems like you got a decision to make, Dryden," Teague said. "I don't want to influence your thinking, but you were right about us. We're mighty rough men."

Juan Sanchez eyed Dryden and smiled like an alligator. "I'll kill you first, señor, I think."

A silence fell on the compound, and tension tied the air in knots as fighting men became fingers looking for triggers. All that was needed to set off an explosion of hell-firing fury was a few spoken words from Dryden or Johnny Teague.

And everybody knew it . . . men, women, and children.

Long seconds ticked past. A horse tossed its head and jangled its bit, and a child cried from fear. Her mother tried to calm her in hushed, soothing tones. The cooking pot bubbled over and water hissed over the coals, raising steam. Above the arroyo, the cloudless sky was as blue as a sapphire.

Buttons Muldoon broke the tension.

Moving stiffly, he stepped out of the mine with Red Ryan in his arms. He read the signs and recognized a Mexican standoff when he saw one. But his only concern was the man he carried. "I've got a feller here needs help. Somebody help him."

All eyes turned to Buttons and the tension leaked out of the atmosphere, pent-up breaths hissing from tight mouths like steam escaping from a boiler.

"Mr. Dryden, stand your men down," Luna Talbot said. "There will be no massacre of the innocents here today."

Buttons reinforced that statement by pushing through the horsemen who pulled aside to let him pass. He walked to a grassy area close to the wall and gently laid Red on his back. "Mrs. Talbot, take a look at him. I think he's real bad and he ain't thinking straight."

As Luna kneeled beside Red, Johnny Teague kneed his horse forward and Juan Sanchez, with his significant guns, went with him. He followed Teague's lead when the outlaw drew rein a couple of feet from Dryden.

"Looks like you're done here, cowboy," Teague said.

Dryden's anger flared. "Who the hell are you, mister?"

"Name's Johnny Teague, originally out of the Harris County country, but I've traveled around a fair piece."

"I've heard of you," Dryden said. "You're an outlaw."

Teague nodded. "And like you said, mighty rough and so wild I can buck in eight directions at the same time."

Dryden had his back to the wall. He doubted that his men would obey an order to kill the woman and children in cold blood, and he no longer wished to put it to the test. To save face, he retreated into bluster. "Mrs. Talbot, the Cornudas Mountains are now part of the Rafter-K range and those Rathmore women are trespassing. What do you intend to do about it?"

"They can come with me and live on my ranch until they get settled elsewhere," Luna said. "In the meantime they are grieving for dead husbands, so I suggest you let them be."

"You've got a week, seven days, to get them out of here," Dryden said.

"I know how many days there are in a week," Luna said. "I'm attending to a sick man here, Mr. Dryden, so call off your dogs and go. You're wearing out your welcome."

Dryden salvaged his dignity. "A week, Mrs. Talbot. Come on, boys. Back to the ranch."

In later years, Dave Quarrels insisted that if it was not for the presence of Luna Talbot and Johnny Teague, the massacre of the Rathmore women and children could easily have become a grim reality.

"It would've taken only one shot from one puncher to commence everybody to shooting," he told A. B. Boyd. "Nowadays all the talk is about the O.K. Corral street fight in Tombstone back in 1881 and that began with one shot."

Luna Talbot never talked about the incident nor did Johnny Teague, and Anse Dryden took his silence with him to the grave. The consensus of opinion among historians is that the Rafter-K hands would not have shot the women and children . . . but unless a letter or a diary written by one of the participants turns up, no one will ever know.

"How is he?" Buttons Muldoon said. He'd just watched Dryden and his hands leave, one of them dead and hanging over his saddle.

"Red is very weak, but with proper medical care he'll live," Luna said. "I advise you to take him to El Paso, where there are doctors." She looked up at Buttons. "He was given a dreadful beating."

"And that's why I aim to kill Papa Mace," Buttons said. "He was the instigator."

"I plan to go after him myself," Luna said. "He aimed to use me as his slave and do whatever he wanted to me."

"No, I'll kill him," Buttons said. "If it takes me the rest of my life, I'll rid the ground of his shadow."

"Mr. Muldoon, right now you're in no shape to go anywhere, except to a doctor's surgery with Red," Luna said. "You were badly beaten and starved into the bargain. Don't look into a mirror. You won't like what you see. You've been through it and it shows."

The woman was right. Buttons's usually ruddy face was ashen and the ordeal he'd experienced showed in his sunken cheeks and hollow eyes. He looked like an exhausted man teetering on the edge of collapse.

"Mrs. Talbot is right, old fellow," Arman Broussard said. "You need food and rest. Above all, rest."

Then, a small weak voice said, "Lady . . ."

The women were gathered around Malachi Rathmore, who lay on the ground, leaning on one elbow and staring at Luna. His chest was covered in blood that was already clotting over at least two bullet wounds. "He took all the gold . . ."

Buttons stepped toward him. "Who did? Was it Mace?"

"All the gold . . ."

"Was it Mace?" Buttons said again.

Luna left Red who was unconscious and took a knee beside the dying man. "Did Mace take all the gold?"

Malachi nodded. "Yes, he took it all . . . with my . . . wife."

"Where did he go?" Buttons said. "Answer me or I'll put another bullet in you."

"Please, Mr. Muldoon, let me talk to him," Luna said. Then, "Do you know where Mace is headed?"

"East," Malachi said. "He took the gold . . . betrayed us . . ." Those were the last words he'd ever speak. He made a sound in his throat and then fell dead on his back.

"East," Buttons said. "That's all I need. No, I need a horse."

"And a gun," Johnny Teague said. He carried a couple of gun belts and holstered Colts. Behind him Dave Quarrels held a scattergun. "I found these back there. I guess one of these is yours, huh?"

Buttons nodded and took a gun rig. "Yeah, this is mine. The other belongs to Red. And that's his Greener. I'll take it."

As Buttons checked the loads in the Colt and

shotgun, Luna said, "Mr. Muldoon, you're not in a fit state to go after Mace Rathmore. Look at you. You're so weak you can barely walk.'

"A horse will do the walking for me," Buttons said.

"Mr. Broussard, talk some sense into him," Luna said.

"I'll go with you, Buttons," Broussard said.

"That's not talking sense," Luna said. "We'll all go with him."

The driver shook his head. "No, not today. There has to be a reckoning, and it's a thing I must do by myself."

"A man knows his own mind," Broussard said. "I won't stand in your way."

Luna said, "Your mind is made up, Mr. Muldoon. I can see that. Then at least ride a decent horse. Leah, let this stubborn man borrow your paint."

Leah Leighton smiled. "It's all yours, driving man. I'll see that your friend is well taken care of."

"Thank you, thank you kindly," Buttons said. Stiffly, he got down on a knee beside Red. "Can you hear me?"

Red's eyes fluttered open. "I heard you on the brag as usual."

"I'll bring you back Mace's head on a stick," Buttons said. "And that's not a brag."

Red reached out and he clutched Buttons's thick bicep. "Bring yourself back. You hear?"

"Depend on it," Buttons said.

A few minutes later, he rode out of the arroyo and turned east at a canter. The sun was warm on his bruised face.

CHAPTER FORTY-FOUR

Papa Mace Rathmore was aware of the limitations of the horses and didn't push them hard. They'd fed on grass and not much of that and were not in good shape. He didn't expect a pursuit and was content to hold them to a walk.

Ella turned her pretty but hard-bitten face to Mace and said, "What do you think happened back there, Papa? That sure as hell was gunfire we heard."

"I don't know, and I don't care," Mace said. "Maybe Malachi shot the prisoners."

"He used a lot of cartridges to kill two men," Ella said. Mace had given her Red's plug hat and she wore it tilted back on her head, her dirty blond hair falling over the shoulders of her dress.

"Malachi ain't much of a shot." Mace took a cigar from a silver case with the initials *TL* engraved on it, lit the smoke, and passed it to the woman. He lit another for himself and said, "When we reach Fort Worth, we'll turn this gold into cash and then set up in business. I got it all planned."

"Is whoring still part of it?" Ella said, frowning. "I figured I was all through with that."

"Yeah, but only for a while, until we're well set up, and then you can quit." He gave her a sidelong look. "We all got to make sacrifices, Ella. You sell your body, and when I'm working a con, I sell my words. In the end it's all the same."

"Maybe, but you'll get out and meet hifalutin folks," Ella said. "All I'll do is lie on my back and count the cracks in a boardinghouse ceiling. That ain't the same."

"You'll meet folks," Mace said. His great belly juddered with every step of the horse. "I already promised you, no two-dollar tricks. You'll be a lady whore, the kind that makes the big money."

"I wish I was in Fort Worth already, away from this damned desert, making big money and wearing all them nice clothes like they do," Ella said from behind a blue curtain of cigar smoke.

"Soon, my love, soon," Mace said. "There's a long, dusty trail ahead of us and not much grub, but when we arrive in Fort Worth, we'll look back and say, 'Well, there was value in every miserable mile we rode to get here.'" Mace smiled, "Yup, value all right. Fort Worth is a burg with snap, and it's crying out for sporting folks like you and me, Ella."

By noon the sun was a fireball in the sky that scorched the wasteland and all who were foolish enough to move across it. Papa Mace removed his frock coat and tied a rust-colored bandana around his bald head before replacing his hat. He sweated like a pig, and his thick-lipped mouth was open, gasping for air. And he smelled rank.

Not for the first time, Ella thought him a repulsive creature, and the thought of his dank hands exploring her again made her skin crawl. But, at least for the time being, he was a necessary evil. She made up her mind to dump him at the first opportunity . . . after he'd cashed in the gold. She clenched her cigar between her teeth and smiled inwardly at the thought she'd just had . . . *Killing him is not out of the question.*

The afternoon wore on, and Ella Rathmore and Papa Mace drowsed in the saddle, the only sound the creak of saddle leather and the soft fall of the horses' hooves.

Something made Ella jerk wide awake. A woman's intuition perhaps.

She looked uneasily at Mace, but his head nodded in sleep, his many chins rolled around his throat like a string of sausages. Ella turned and studied their back trail . . . and spotted a thin column of dust behind them.

She shook Mace awake and said, "Dust behind us." She looked again. "And it's coming on fast."

Mace drew rein, swung his horse around and stared.

"Do you see it?" Ella said.

"Hell, yeah, I see it," Mace said, irritated. "I'm not blind."

"Who could it be?"

"How the hell should I know?" Mace said.

"Malachi. It could be Malachi."

"Whoever it is, he's seen us," Mace said. "We can't outrun him on these horses. They're about done for the day as it is."

"Can you kill him?"

"Yeah, I can kill him." Mace slid the Winchester from the boot under his knee. "I can kill him easy . . .

and I plan to do just that." He held his rifle at the ready and watched the rider come on at a run. What he needed was the patience to make sure of his shot. Around him the silence was so profound he heard the short, nervous gasps of Ella's breathing.

The rider closed the distance. He carried some kind of long gun, held straight out at his side, and a ribbon of dust trailed behind him.

Soon . . .

Papa Mace threw the scarred stock of the Winchester to his shoulder . . .

And it was then he made the biggest mistake of his life.

Mace recognized the blue coat with the silver buttons and the stocky shape of the rider. It was Muldoon, the man he'd left to die of thirst in the mine shaft. The feller was still alive and bearing down on him. What had happened back there?

Papa Mace was a man filled with hatreds, and he directed all of that hate at the stage driver. In that moment, Mace's loathing for the man possessed him like a form of insanity. Muldoon had to die . . . and Mace had to watch him die . . . and gloat . . . and torment him as he drew his last breath.

Mace screamed in demented fury and fired. A miss. The rider galloped closer.

Shrieking curses, Mace raked his big-roweled spurs across his mount's flanks and the abused horse lurched into a run. As he rode, the fat man levered shot after shot at Buttons but scored no hits. Buttons held his fire, closing the distance.

A hit!

A bullet burned across Buttons's left shoulder, gouging deep, drawing blood. It would have made a careful man wary, but Buttons threw caution to the wind and relentlessly advanced on Mace.

The two riders were madmen, each bent on destroying the other, roaring curses, eyes blazing with crazed anger. Then a disaster struck Mace that he'd not anticipated.

The hammer of his rifle snapped on an empty chamber. He levered again and again . . . Snap! Snap! But there could be no retreat. He was too close to the hated Muldoon.

The two men closed, cursing their loathing for one another.

Mace reined in his horse and grabbed his rifle by the barrel. He raised it above his head, planning to bring down a crunching blow on Muldoon's skull. But Buttons ducked the blow, and for an instant Mace's motion exposed the left side of his belly and chest. As the riders passed, Buttons triggered the scattergun. Two barrels of buckshot ripped into Mace and almost turned him inside out. Blood exploded everywhere. The fat man screeched in pain and terror, the Winchester cartwheeling away from him. Mace rode on for a few yards and then toppled out of the saddle, dead when he hit the ground.

Buttons drew rein and walked his paint to the sprawled body, a great mound of bloody flesh slowly turning the desert sand red.

"Dead, ain't he?" Ella Rathmore said. She'd dismounted and led her horse to the obscene corpse, staring down at it.

"As he's ever gonna be," Buttons said, a dreadful weariness on him, sapping what remained of his strength. He looked at Ella with dull eyes. "He wasn't much, but he was a man who needed killing."

A silence grew between them until Ella said, "No, he wasn't much. But he was my only hope."

"Hope for what?" Buttons said, short and tight, not liking the woman.

"Hope for a new life in Fort Worth. Mace told me I'd wear all the nice clothes and eat nice food and live off the fat of the land."

"He promised you that?"

"Yes, he did. And more."

"And you believed him?"

"No, I didn't believe him, but I *wanted to* believe him. I needed hope. A woman like me, a two-dollar whore and common as dirt, needs hope."

Buttons warmed to the woman, but only slightly. Above them, a hawk suddenly dived into the brush and something small died in the waning afternoon.

"Well, everything happens for a reason." Buttons said. "I heard that once."

Ella's smile was slight. "Hell, mister, I wish I knew what the hell that reason was." Then, "Are you planning to shoot me?"

Buttons shook his head. "As a general principle, I don't shoot women. I bet the Abe Patterson and Son Stage and Express Company has a rule about shooting women, and it's wrote down somewhere, I'm sure."

"You look all used up," Ella said. Then after a while, "I wanted Mace to kill you, blow you away."

Buttons nodded. "You didn't want to lose all hope, such as that was, huh?"

"Yeah, something like that. You've spoiled everything."

"Go bring in his horse."

"Mace's gold is on the horse, if you want to take it," Ella said. "He left me to carry the grub."

"Bring it in." Buttons waited until the woman led the horse back to where he stood, and he found the gold in the saddlebags, divided between two burlap sacks. Buttons opened one of the bags and let a handful of small nuggets and flakes, mixed with some quartz, trickle through his fingers. "Gold. That's the color of hope, ain't it?"

"It's what hope is made of," Ella said. "But now that hope is gone, it might as well be ashes."

"Take it," Buttons said. "Take the gold."

She was shocked. "What did you say?"

"I said for you to take the gold," Buttons said. "It's yours." Then, after some thought, "Lady, it's a long way to Fort Worth, and you'll cross some mighty rough and hostile country, to say nothing of outlaws or bronco Apaches or wolf packs. This gold brought nothing but death and misery to the Rathmores, and do you know why? I'll tell you why . . . because it's cursed. Now, after all that, are you sure you want it?"

"I'll take my chances," Ella said. "What have I got to lose? My life? Without the gold I don't have a life."

"Then all I can say is good luck, and God help you." Buttons pointed east. "That's the way to Fort Worth. Now give me the hat you're wearing. It belongs to a friend of mine."

The woman handed over Red's plug hat and then said, "What about him?"

"What about who?"

"Papa Mace. You just gonna leave him there?"

"The coyotes will take care of him," Buttons said.

"No they won't. They'll gag on him," Ella said. "He'll still be lying there ten years from now."

Buttons Muldoon watched the woman ride into the gathering dusk. He then mounted and pointed his horse back toward the Cornudas Mountains . . . and reckoned that you couldn't put a silver dollar on any part of him that didn't hurt.

CHAPTER FORTY-FIVE

"You couldn't put a silver dollar on any part of me that doesn't hurt," Buttons Muldoon said to Luna Talbot.

"You need to rest up, driving man." She handed him a cup of coffee and smiled. "You're not as young as you were when you first rode onto my ranch with a coffin on the roof of your stage."

"When was that? A hundred years ago?" Buttons said.

Luna nodded. "About that long."

"I can't rest up," Buttons said. "I got to take Red to El Paso. Anybody checked on my team?"

"I did," Arman Broussard said. "You've got four left. The Rathmores ate the other two."

"Damn, I hope it wasn't the leaders," Buttons said. "I need that pair."

Broussard shrugged. "I don't know which pair they ate."

"Damn them Rathmores," Buttons said.

Red Ryan was covered with a blanket up to his

chin. Buttons sat down beside him, groaning from the effort. "How are you feeling, old-timer?"

Red groaned. "I reckon I'd have to be dead three days before I felt better, and that's a natural fact."

"I'll get you to a doctor," Buttons said. "He'll fix you right up."

"I can ride shotgun to El Paso," Red said.

"No you can't. You're as weak as a two-day-old kitten," Buttons said. "You'll set inside with the rich folks."

"What rich folks?" Red said.

"I don't know. But maybe we'll pick up a few," Buttons said. "You heard me tell what happened to Mace, huh?"

"I heard. My Greener came in handy." Red said.

"Both barrels of it did," Buttons said. "Shot a sight of daylight into him."

"What about the woman he took with him?"

"She's headed for Fort Worth." Buttons didn't think it would be a good idea to mention the gold.

"Hey, you!" Leah Leighton stomped toward Buttons leading her horse, her expression furious. "What happened to my Daisy?"

"Who's Daisy?" Buttons said.

"My mare, that's who. This mare. She's been shot."

"Shot? Where?" Buttons said.

Hands on her hips, Leah said, "You mean, you didn't notice?"

Buttons sighed and rose to his feet. "I was kinda busy, lady. Let me see this wound."

Leah turned the horse and pointed. "Look, right there on the flank. She's scarred for life."

"It's dark. I can't see anything," Buttons said.

"Here, use this." Luna held a lantern high. "Yes, I see it."

"Where?" Buttons said. Then, "Hell, it's only a scratch."

"Only a scratch!" Leah said. "Look how upset she is. Daisy will never be the same again."

"Leah, she'll be fine," Luna said. "When we get back to the ranch, a little iodine will heal her just fine."

"And sting like crazy." Leah glared at Buttons. "Mr. Muldoon, you may mistreat your own horses, but you'll never mistreat Daisy again . . . because you'll never ride her again. So there!"

"After this, I don't reckon I want to ride her again," Buttons said.

Red Ryan giggled, and Crystal Casey and Daphne Loveshade, now Dumont, his self-appointed nurses, scolded Buttons for getting his guard overexcited.

"Now we'll never get him to sleep," Crystal said, frowning.

Not a word of criticism was directed at Leah Leighton, who'd begun the fracas, and Buttons decided enough was enough. He fled into the darkness, found a place where the rock was softer, and lay down and went to sleep.

The womenfolk, with the exception of Leah Leighton, who was still annoyed about her wounded horse, insisted that Buttons Muldoon remain for a few days to regain his strength.

"And Red isn't yet fit to travel," Luna Talbot said. "He may have injuries that we can't see."

"You mean to his insides?" Buttons said.

"Yes. He took some powerful kicks to his body."

Buttons reluctantly agreed and spent his time with his team, now reduced to four horses. Townes Pierce shot a deer, and that and what was left of the bacon and flour helped feed everyone reasonably well. Johnny Teague and his boys worked in the mine shaft, an increasingly dangerous undertaking since the roof was collapsing one beam at a time.

On the third day he had some bad news for Luna Talbot. "We cleared away the rock ahead of the gold vein."

"And?" Luna said.

"It just plays out . . . and then nothing."

"Does that mean there's no more gold?"

"Seems like," Teague said. "Unless there's another vein somewhere that we don't know about."

"Any chance of that?" Luna said.

"I don't know. But you could search these mountains for the rest of your life and never find one. Most prospectors never hit pay dirt."

Luna sighed. "Well, I guess it was worth the effort."

"Was it?" Teague said, one eyebrow lifting. "Was it worth the effort?"

After a moment's hesitation, Luna said, "No, it wasn't. That was silly of me. I only need to look at Red Ryan and know it wasn't worth it." She smiled. "There's no gold, Mr. Teague, so what will you do now?"

"Me and the boys are heading up to El Paso," Teague said.

"Will you go straight now? Stay on the side of the law?"

"No," he said. "That just ain't in our nature."

Luna said, "If you ever need a place to hide out . . ."

Teague smiled. "I'll keep that in mind."

"Then good luck . . . Johnny."

"You too, rancher lady. Good luck."

CHAPTER FORTY-SIX

The day after Johnny Teague and his men left, the roof of the mine shaft collapsed, bringing down an avalanche of rubble. When the dust cleared, it looked as though the Lucky Cuss had never existed.

That same day, Luna Talbot told Buttons Muldoon and Red Ryan that she was leaving and taking the Rathmore women and children with her. "They're all in pretty bad health, but I've sent Leah Leighton ahead to meet us with wagons and food. It will be a long trek across the desert, but I think the Rathmores will make it all right."

"What are you going to do with them?" Buttons said.

Luna smiled. "Find homes for them, I guess. When they get stronger, some of them will just leave."

"Well, good luck with that," Buttons said.

Luna nodded. "Thank you. I think I'll need it. I hear Daphne wants to go with you and Red to El Paso."

"Yeah, she does," Buttons said. "It's the policy of the Abe Patterson and Son Stage and Express Company not to accept nonpaying passengers. That's a rule, and it's wrote down somewhere. But in the girl's case, I guess we can make the exception."

"She still intends to be a whore," Luna said. "Nothing I can say will change her mind."

"Well, if that's her chosen profession, El Paso is the place to hang out her shingle," Buttons said. "Plenty of business to be had there with the railroads an' all."

"Mr. Muldoon, I hesitate to ask you this, but could you take care of her for a while till she's settled?" Luna said. "I've grown quite fond of her."

"Me and Red will see that she's settled," Buttons said. "Red is one for the ladies, so I'll tell him to give her some teaching on the whoring profession. He can be a regular schoolmarm when it comes to lecturing folks." Buttons dropped his voice to a whisper, fearing Daphne was within earshot. "Trouble is, that little gal ain't real pretty. In fact, she ain't pretty at all."

Luna shrugged. "We all have our crosses to bear."

"Ain't that a natural fact," Buttons said.

"Mr. Muldoon, I wish to thank you and Red for all you did for me," Luna said. "Day and night, any time of the year, my door will always be open to both of you. I want you to know that."

Buttons said, "Well, thank you kindly, Mrs. Talbot, and let me say just one thing. If'n you ever want a stiff delivered again . . . use a different stage line."

Arman Broussard had decided to return to the Talbot ranch with Luna. Used to the ways of humanity, Buttons guessed at a budding romance, a notion that Broussard reinforced.

He said, "I'm giving up my wandering ways and have decided to settle down."

Buttons grinned. "Gonna do some cowboying, huh, gambling man?"

Broussard winced, and Luna said hurriedly, "Arman will do my bookkeeping. He's very good with figures."

Farewells were made. Crystal Casey, who'd also decided to return to the ranch in the face of Johnny Teague's indifference, kissed Red good-bye and wet his gaunt cheeks with her tears. In spite of the Rathmore women insisting on taking their cooking pots and their few belongings, Luna Talbot fussed over them and their children like a mother hen as she herded them south.

Buttons and Red, who was finally standing on his feet, his plug hat on his head where it belonged, watched them leave until their dust cloud settled and they were gone from sight. The arroyo was deserted

After a few years, it would look like no one had ever lived . . . or died . . . there.

CHAPTER FORTY-SEVEN

Red Ryan felt better . . . if aching all over and hurting to breathe could be defined as such.

Buttons Muldoon was concerned. "Red, if you're up to it, we'll detour to Bill Stanton's station and change the team."

"I can stand it. Have you any money? The Rathmores took every cent I had."

"Took mine as well. All the dinero Luna Talbot gave us for bringing in the stiff is gone," Buttons said. "And Bill Stanton charges for everything. He's a tight-fisted man."

"Think he'll give us credit?" Red said.

"Stanton ain't a big believer in tick. And since the Leah Leighton gal killed Charlie Brownlow in Stanton's place, he might hold it against us."

"Hell, we didn't kill him."

Buttons said, "I know, but stage station men have a heap of time on their hands and they start into thinking. Maybe Stanton is thinking what we're thinking . . . and that is that we started the Brownlow fight. Maybe that's what he's thinking."

Red groaned, both from pain and his driver's tangled logic. He shook his head. "That didn't make a lick of sense."

"That's what you think," Buttons said.

"Wait . . . I have money." Daphne Dumont stood watching the two men, a small, forlorn figure in a shabby dress holding a tattered yellow parasol above her head, her carpetbag at her feet. She saw the expressions on the faces of Buttons and Red close down in disbelief.

"I do too," Daphne said. "I took it from Mr. Loveshade."

"How much money?" Buttons smiled. "A whole dollar?"

"Twenty dollars," the girl said. "I can loan it to you, and if you want, you can pay me back when we reach El Paso."

"Show us," Buttons said.

Daphne reached into her bag and came up with a gold double eagle. She held out the coin. "Do you want it?"

Red smiled. "Best you keep—"

"Yeah we want it." Buttons grabbed the money and said, "We'll pay you back in El Paso."

Buttons Muldoon held the stage door open. "Inside with you, Miss Daphne," he said, refusing to tackle the girl's name change. "And you too, Red."

Red Ryan held his shotgun and wore his Colt. "I'm the guard. I'll ride up on the box."

"Red, you ain't fit—"

"I'm fit enough." Red closed the door on Daphne and said, "I hope you'll be comfortable."

"I've never been in a stagecoach before," Daphne said. "This is exciting."

Red grinned. "A trip with Mr. Buttons Muldoon is always exciting."

"Buttons, what the hell happened to your team?" Bill Stanton said, his hound dog eyes puzzled.

"Hungry folks ate two of them," Buttons Muldoon said from his perch in the driver's seat.

"Not you and Red?"

"No, other hungry folks."

"You got a tale to tell," Stanton said.

"Later," Buttons said.

Stanton looked in the stage window and saw Daphne. He was alarmed. "Here, Buttons, I don't want no trouble."

"What trouble?" Buttons said.

"Your female passengers keep shooting my best customers. I can't have that. It's bad for business."

"She ain't a shootist like the last one," Buttons said. "Her name is Daphne, and she's a learner whore. Who you got inside? No kin of the late Charlie Brownlow, I hope."

"I got a Texas Ranger by the name of Sam Flowers," Stanton said. "Seems like a nice enough feller, but he'll pay me in Ranger scrip that I can never collect on."

Red Ryan said, "It's worth it for the goodwill. Rangers are fine men to have on your side."

"I suppose you're right," Stanton said, "but it depends how much he eats, don't it?"

"Talk about eating, what's for supper, Bill?" Buttons said. "I'm feeling gant."

"Got a nice pork stew," Stanton said.

"From the same hog we had the last time we was here?" Red said.

"I salted down the meat. It's right tasty." Stanton looked up at him. "You look like hell. You been through it, Red?"

"You could say that, Bill."

"Seems like you and Buttons both have a story to tell."

"Same story. Long in the telling."

"All I got in this place is time," Stanton said. "Buttons, I'll help you put up your horses. I have oats, and they need 'em. Red, you come inside and set. You look like you got an axle dragging." He smiled at Daphne. "And you, too, young lady. Just don't shoot anybody."

Red stepped into the cabin and sat at the table. Daphne set her parasol and bag on the floor at her feet and then settled beside him.

The Ranger sat opposite, a bowl of stew in front of him, a spoon in his right hand, a chunk of fry bread in his left. "Howdy." He laid down his spoon and touched his hat to Daphne. "Ma'am."

Back to eating, he finished quickly, pushed the bowl away, and took the makings from his shirt pocket. As he rolled a cigarette, he saw the tobacco hunger in Red. He tossed the papers and a full sack of Bull Durham across the table. "Help yourself, shotgun guard."

"Obliged." Red's eager fingers built a smoke, and the Ranger thumbed a match into flame and lit it for him.

"Keep the makings," Sam Flowers said. "I got more."

Red was happy to accept the man's offer.

"Saw you come in on the stage," the Ranger said. He was a tall young man with frank, hazel eyes, and he sported the huge dragoon mustache that was a Texas Ranger rite of passage. "Where are you headed?"

"El Paso." Guessing that some sort of clarification was needed, Red said. "Came up from the Rio Bravo way."

Flowers nodded, accepting that without comment, and then said, "See any riders on your travels?"

"A few. You looking for anybody in particular?"

"Yeah, a feller by the name of Johnny Teague," the Ranger said. "Him and his boys have been playing hob, robbing and killing. They're the worst of the worst."

Suddenly a man thrust into conflicting loyalties, Red stalled. "Worse than the James boys?"

"As bad, I'd say." Flowers thought for a moment, drumming on the table with his fingers, and then added, "Yeah, I'd say just as bad."

"I'll keep a lookout for him." Red figured it was a statement of fact, or could be, not an outright lie.

"Yeah, you do that and if you come across him, tell the local law enforcement. His name is Teague . . . *T-e-a-g-u-e* . . . Johnny Teague. Only don't try to tackle him yourself. Leave it to the law."

"I won't. He sounds like a desperate character."

"Oh, he is," Flowers said. "That's a guaranteed natural fact."

"Quick on the draw, huh?" Red said.

"I don't know about that, but I'd guess he is," the Ranger said. "Outlaws who are slow shucking the Colt's gun don't live real long." He looked at Daphne.

"You got a situation waiting for you in El Paso, young lady? A teacher's post, maybe?"

The girl smiled. "No, sir, I want to be a whore."

It took a lot to surprise a Ranger, but Flowers was surprised. "Say again?"

"I want to be a whore," Daphne said. "It is the oldest profession, you know."

"After undertaker, maybe." Flowers shrugged. "Well, good luck in your chosen calling." He stared at the girl, obviously unimpressed by what he saw. "Well, if that don't beat all." Rising to his feet, he stretched. "Time for some shut-eye. The most comfortable place in this station is the hayloft, if you don't mind the rats who share the same opinion."

Buttons passed the Ranger in the doorway. They exchanged greetings, and Buttons took the man's vacated chair at the table.

"The Ranger asked me if I'd seen Johnny Teague," Red said after the driver sat.

"What did you tell him?"

"That I hadn't."

Buttons considered that and said, "We rode with him, Red, ate his grub. Seems hardly right to sell him down the river."

"That was my thinking."

"Say no more about it to anybody," Buttons said. "So long as he ain't holding up the Patterson stage, it ain't really any of our business." His gaze took in Red, assessing him, the hollow eyes and gray pallor under the tan, the sag of his shoulders and the weakness in his voice. "I'll get you a cup of coffee, then lie down and rest."

Red nodded. "I reckon I will. My tail is dragging."

Buttons poured coffee from the pot simmering on

the fire and placed it in front of Red. "I told you to ride inside the stage."

"And I told you, I'm the shotgun guard. I take my place in the box."

Buttons shook his head and then said, "Where did you get the makings?"

"Ranger gave them to me."

"He's a smart man, that Ranger, knows you're ill. He was being considerate."

"Maybe so. Anyway, I sure appreciated the gesture."

"Yes, he's a nice man," Daphne said. "I hope I meet him again in El Paso."

CHAPTER FORTY-EIGHT

When Buttons Muldoon drove the Patterson stage into El Paso, the city was booming thanks to the arrival of the railroads—the Southern Pacific, Texas and Pacific, and the Atchison, Topeka and Santa Fe. Ten thousand people—merchants, entrepreneurs, ranchers, and young men on the make—rubbed shoulders in the crowded, roaring streets. Undesirables also sought to make their fortunes. Flashy gamblers, careful-eyed gunmen, wild young cowboys, thieves, murderers, and prostitutes crammed into the scores of jangling saloons, dance halls, gambling dens, and brothels that lined the streets. The proud boast of the lawless was that El Paso was the "Six-Shooter Capital of the World."

Amid this cacophony of sin, violence, and debauchery was the modest, two-story depot of the Abe Patterson and Son Stage and Express Company, managed by seventy-five-year-old Ira Cole, one of the saltiest stage drivers to ever crack a whip. A wreck up Lincoln County way in the New Mexico Territory had broken both his legs, and a road agent's bullet still lodged somewhere in his vitals had slowed him some, but the greeting Cole gave Buttons and Red was exuberant and energetic enough to refute his age.

After the whiskey was poured, drunk, and the glasses refilled, Cole said, "Well, Buttons, and be damned to ye fer a lost soul, you were supposed to be here in El Paso weeks ago. We thought for sure you were a goner."

"It's a long story, Ira," Buttons said. "I'll write up a full report for Abe Patterson and explain the loss of two horses."

"No need to write it up. Abe is here in El Paso," Cole said.

"Here? Because of me?" Buttons said.

"Partly. But mostly it's to close a deal with the Texas and Pacific," Cole said. "Abe says railroads are the future and he wants to get in on the business afore it's too late." The old man smiled. "Of course, he ain't exactly as happy as a pig in a peach orchard with you two. He's got his son with him, and that high-yeller gal of his, and they're writing down new rules for stage drivers every day."

"Then he'll have to wait," Buttons said. "I need to get Red to a doctor."

Cole looked at Red. "Figured you'd took poorly with some misery or another, sonny. You look a mite green around the gills."

"I'm fine. I don't need to see a doctor," Red said. Doctors will kill you quicker 'n scat. Everybody knows that."

Daphne spoke or the first time. She laid down her whiskey and said, "Mr. Muldoon is right, Mr. Ryan. You must get checked out and get a clean bill of health before you ride shotgun again."

"Wisely spoke," Cole said. "And who are you, young lady? A passenger?"

"Yes, I was a passenger," Daphne said. "I'm here in El Paso to practice the whore's profession."

With the truthfulness of the old, Ira Cole shook his head. "No offense, young lady, but it seems to me that you don't have the trappings for that line of work."

"But I do have the equipment, Mr. Cole," Daphne said. "That should see me through."

"Well, I hope that's the case, young lady, and good luck to ye," Cole said. "Some ladies get rich from lying on their backs, but it ain't real usual." He directed his attention back to Red. "There's a doctor just down the street, a man named McKenna. He learned his trade during the War Between the States, and he'll fix you right up. They say he can saw off a rotten leg in less than two minutes."

"Damn it, I don't have a rotten leg."

"I know," Cole said. "But he'll fix you up just the same."

"You're a strong man, Mr. Ryan," gray-haired Dr. John McKenna said. "I can't find anything wrong with you that can't be fixed by a week of bed rest. You can put your shirt on now."

Red pulled his buckskin shirt over his head and then glanced at the disapproving portrait of a bearded Confederate colonel on the wall. "Is he kin of yours, Doc? He's been staring daggers at me since I came in here."

"No, not kin," McKenna said. "That's Lieutenant Colonel Booker C. Hadden. I amputated his left arm after the Battle of Gaines's Mill. He was very grateful and later sent me his picture."

The doctor took a small brown bottle with a tan-colored label from a glass-fronted cupboard and passed it to Red. "This is a tonic. Take a spoonful twice a day and it will help build your strength. Meantime, don't work too hard and try not to get overexcited."

Neither the doctor nor Red knew it then, but soon his strength would be put to the test . . . and he'd get very overexcited.

"Well?" Buttons Muldoon said, an eyebrow lifting.

"Well, what?" Red Ryan said.

"What did the doctor say?"

"He gave me a tonic." Red held up the bottle. "Told me to take a spoonful twice a day."

"And have you taken it yet?"

"No."

"Then take a swig now." Buttons made a face. "What does it taste like?"

Red tilted the bottle to his mouth, swallowed, and then put the cork back in place.

"Well?" Buttons said.

"It tastes mostly like gin."

"Gin?" Buttons said, looking doubtful.

"You asked me, and I told you. It tastes like gin."

"Let me try that." Buttons took a swig and then said, "You're right. It does taste like gin and maybe lemon juice." He handed the bottle back. "It's good."

"And don't you be getting any ideas. This stuff is a tonic to build up my strength. It ain't for the likes of you."

He and Buttons were in the depot's back room, where there were cots and shelves above them for the drivers and shotgun guards to rest and put their belongings. Oil lamps were lit against the growing darkness and a small, four-paned window gave a view of the corral and barn outside. A potbellied stove stood in one corner with its always simmering coffeepot, the Arbuckle strong enough to float a Colt revolver. The room smelled of coffee, man sweat, tobacco, wood smoke, and gun oil. A print of Indians attacking a wagon train hung askew on one wall.

Red sat on the creaking corner of his cot and said, "Where's the girl?"

"Daphne? As far as I know she's gone whoring."

"We have to pay back her twenty dollars."

Buttons said, "Right as soon as we get paid."

"We ain't gonna get paid. Abe is likely to dock us pay for losing the stiff's fare and the two horses."

"If he don't give us the boot," Buttons said.

"We'll find the twenty somewhere. I have a feeling that little gal is sure gonna need the money."

CHAPTER FORTY-NINE

The One Note Saloon where Daphne Dumont chose to start her chosen career was probably the worst dive in El Paso. Patronized mainly by cowboys, railroad workers, and a seasoning of gamblers, con artists, and sporting gents, more dead men had been carried through its batwing doors than any other drinking establishment in town.

When the place burned down in 1889, the citizens of El Paso breathed a collective sigh of relief, but that was still a few years in the future.

When Daphne stepped into the One Note for the first and last time, it was a Friday night. Everybody had folding money, and the guy at the piano was playing a rousing rendition of "I'm a Good Old Rebel" that drowned out the ten chimes of the railroad clock above the bar.

The saloon was a dangerous, violent cesspit, the kind of place where the first thing a new bartender learned was when to duck and the whores wore bulletproof corsets. The last preacher who tried to reform the drunks was hung in the belfry of his own church. It was said he kicked so hard and for so long the bell clanked for fifteen minutes.

Daphne, confused by the noise, peered shortsightedly through a haze of smoke that was so thick it seemed to have been knitted together by giant spiders. She stood at the edge of the dance floor, her folded parasol in her hands and an expression of dazed bewilderment on her face.

A tap on her shoulder from behind made Daphne turn to a woman in a yellow dress, a brassy blonde with heavily made-up eyes and a scarlet ruby of a mouth. Her voice rose above the din. "You lost, honey?"

"I want to be a whore," Daphne said. "Am I in the right place?"

The woman's smile was thin. "Oh, you're in the right place, no doubt about that." She looked Daphne up and down from her scuffed ankle boots to the top of her head and was obviously not impressed. "You sure you want to be a whore, honey? It's a demanding profession."

"Yes. I . . . I think so . . ." the girl said. Her chin took on a determined set. "Yes, I am sure."

"Then you'll need to talk with Pete Pace. He runs the place." She steered Daphne to an empty chair. "Sit there and I'll bring him over. Maybe you can work the cribs. My name's Pearl, by the way."

"Nice to meet you, Pearl. My name is Daphne."

"Oh my God," Pearl said before she swept away, her silk petticoats rustling under her dress.

Pete Pace was a splendid creature with slicked-down black hair parted in the middle and a pencil-thin mustache. He wore a brocade vest, boiled white shirt and string tie, and on his feet patent-leather shoes with pointed toes. He extended a beringed hand to Daphne and said, "Up. Let's take a look at you, little lady."

Like Pearl before him, he was less than impressed. "Daphne . . . that's your name?"

"Yes. Daphne Dumont."

"Well, Daphne Dumont, you ain't much to look at," Pace said. "And I mean no offense by that. It's just that what you have to sell, men may not be willing to buy."

Pearl untangled herself from a sporting gent and stepped to the table. "Pete, I figured she could work the cribs," she said, almost shouting above the bedlam of noise, the roars of men, and the high, false laughter of women.

"Maybe." He stared at Daphne. "Back there against the far wall are three small, curtained-off rooms. Nothing in them except a cot and a chamber pot. Those are cribs, understand?"

The girl nodded. Pace wasn't sure if she understood or not.

"The house takes forty percent of all you earn," he said. "Set your price at two dollars and on a good night you can still clear fifteen, sixteen dollars. Does that set all right with you?"

Again Daphne nodded. She seemed a little dazed by the commotion going on around her.

Pace sighed as though he'd made a decision that displeased him. "Pearl, can you fix her up with a dress and shoes? Maybe do something with her face and hair?"

"I'm sure I can find a dress and shoes to fit her," Pearl said. "The rest won't be easy."

"I know, but do what you can, huh?" He shook his

head and said to Daphne, "Girl, you know why I'm doing this? It's not on account of you being pretty, because you ain't. It's because I have a heart of solid gold."

An hour later Daphne Dupont was transformed from a plain Jane to a plain Jane trying to look like she wasn't. She wore a red dress two sizes too large for her that had once belonged to a well-endowed whore who'd quit the business, and red shoes adorned with a gold fleur-de-lis that were a size too small. Her hair was piled, more or less, on top of her head and held in place with pins. Her face was made up with cheek rouge and lipstick, hastily applied by Pearl since, for her, time was money. The end result was . . . disastrous.

But Daphne, embracing her new role, thought she looked beautiful.

His name was Barney Koerner, a tall, muscular man who'd been in several shooting scrapes and had a minor reputation in and around El Paso as a gunman. When the deadly shootist Dallas Stoudenmire was city marshal, Koerner had kept his head down and stepped softly, but now that Stoudenmire was dead, Koerner claimed he was "the cock o' the walk in El Paso." A bully and an abuser of women, he was drinking in the One Note the night Daphne made her dreadful debut . . . and the stage was set for a display of Koerner's latent sadism.

The girl's ordeal began innocently enough. She stood on the edge of the dance floor, knock-kneed in her short dress, her eyes wide as she beheld sights and sounds she'd never experienced before in her life. She smiled at the big, yellow-haired man who strode across the floor toward her, shoving aside dancers in his path.

"Well, well, what do we have here?" the man said.

"My name is Daphne Dumont," she said.

"I bet it is." Koerner grabbed Daphne by her thin arm. "Let's rub bellies, lil darlin'."

For a couple of minutes, to the tune of "Clementine," the big man cut a rug, displayed some fancy footwork and knocked around the other dancers on the crowded floor like a bowling ball striking pins. But then he steered Daphne toward the bar and yelled, "Hell, that's enough. Lady, you're just too damn ugly to be dancin' with!" He pushed her hard toward a man at the bar, a puncher with rodent eyes in a small, triangular face. "Here, Ellis, you take her."

The man ginned and said, "Hell, Barney, I don't want her." And he pushed her back.

"Over here, Barney!" another man yelled.

Koerner laughed and threw Daphne at him.

"Hell!" the man yelled. "I ain't dancin' with her. She's as homely as a mud fence. Here, take her back."

Soon a circle of men formed and to the cheers, clapping, and laughter of the crowd, Daphne was thrown from man to man like a ragdoll. At first she laughed, thinking it was all part of the fun, but then it began to hurt. The game got rougher, more violent and bruising. Strong fingers dug into Daphne's arms and shoulders, tugged at her breasts, and Koerner, his face a vicious mix of cruelty and amusement, slapped her around.

Suddenly for Daphne Dumont, the game wasn't fun any longer.

Ira Cole was playing poker with some other old-timers when the horseplay on the dance floor began. He watched for a while, but when he saw the girl who'd come in with Buttons Muldoon and Red Ryan being abused, he threw in his hand and quietly slipped out of the saloon door.

CHAPTER FIFTY

When Ira Cole stepped into the Patterson stage depot, Red Ryan lay on his back in his cot and Buttons Muldoon sat at the table playing solitaire, a glass of whiskey beside him.

"Sorry to intrude, gents," Cole said. "But that little gal you brought in with you—"

"What about her?" Buttons seemed absorbed and didn't look up from his cards.

"She's being slapped around in the One Note by Barney Koerner and them," Cole said.

"She's learning to be a whore," Buttons said. "What does she expect?"

"This ain't whoring. They're throwing her around and beating her up." He hesitated and then said, "Well, anyway, I thought you'd like to know."

"Ain't our concern." Buttons slapped down a card with the flat of his hand and made the table jump.

"The hell it ain't." Red rolled out of the cot and got to his feet. "She was a passenger of the Abe Patterson and Son Stage and Express Company and is still under our protection."

"Red, she wasn't a fare-paying passenger," Buttons said. "We owe her nothing."

"We still owe her twenty dollars, or did you forget about that?" Red buckled on his gun belt and holster and then put on his hat. "Buttons, you coming?"

"Maybe. When I finish this game. We'll pay her back the twenty, you know."

"If she lives that long," Cole said, "After Koerner gets through with her."

Red said, "Ira, take me there."

After Red and Ira Cole left, Buttons stared at his cards for a while and then shook his head. "Damn it all. We'll pay her the twenty dollars," he said to no one but himself. He sighed, used both hands to mess up his cards, and stood. Like Red before him, he put on his hat and gun belt and walked out the door.

When Red Ryan stepped into the One Note, he at first saw no sign of the incident Ira Cole had witnessed. The floor was crowded with slow dancers, every table in the place hosted cardplayers or dedicated drinkers, the bar was lined with noisy men, and the guy at the piano played, "Juanita." Red moved here and there through the smoke, his eyes searching, the smell of stale sweat, cheap perfume, and spilled beer so familiar to him.

Then he saw Daphne . . .

She sat at a table on the edge of the dance floor and a blonde woman sat next to her, holding a bloody rag to the girl's nose. When Daphne saw Red, her eyes lit up and she managed a weak smile. A man vacated a seat at the table and Red drew the chair over and sat. He saw bruises all over the girl's neck, shoulders, and upper arms. Someone had spilled beer over the front of her dress. Daphne's nose was bloody and swollen, and she had the suggestion of a black eye.

Red decided to confine himself to two questions. First he asked, "How do you feel?"

"Mr. Ryan, I don't want to be a whore anymore," Daphne said, her bottom lip trembling.

He pointed to her nose and asked the second. "Who did this to you?"

The blonde woman answered that question. "See the big, towheaded feller standing at the bar? His name is Barney Koerner and he did it . . . and a lot more."

Red nodded. "I'll talk to him. Daphne, stay here. I'll be right back."

Red Ryan crossed the dance floor and stepped behind Koerner. The big man's back was to him, so Red tapped him on the shoulder.

When Koerner turned, Red smiled and said, "Care to dance?"

The man was immediately belligerent. "What the hell?"

"Oh, you want to be a wallflower. Too bad." Red hit him smack on the chin with a straight right. Anyone who's been punched in the mug by a man trained as a prizefighter knows how Barney Koerner felt that night. Red had lost strength, but his wallop was still a force to be reckoned with.

Koerner took the punch flatfooted, and it staggered

him. On rubber legs he stumbled backward, his arms cartwheeling, and he crashed into the saloon wall, dislodging a sign that read, HAVE YOU WRITTEN TO MOTHER? that fell neatly across his chest.

Red, used to men with sand, expected Koerner to come up fighting, but the man stayed down. Then an attack came from his right. The man with the rodent eyes charged at him swinging, but Red blocked his clumsy right hook and countered with a left cross of his own that slammed the puncher against the bar and dropped him to the sawdust. Ellis's legs twitched, saliva leaked out of his bloody mouth, and then he took a nap.

Red turned and glared at Koerner. "On your feet. We got a Pecos promenade to finish, and I'm not a little girl you can slap around."

Koerner wiped blood from his nose, leaving a scarlet smear on his mustache, and held up a hand. "I'm done. I'm not fighting you."

A gawking crowd surrounded the two men, and everyone knew that Barney Koerner was finished in El Paso . . . and Koerner knew it, too.

Suddenly Red was angry. "You stinking piece of trash. I ever hear of you abusing a woman again, I'll pin your dirty hide to the outhouse door." He waited a moment. "Do you understand?"

Koerner made no answer.

"I said, do you understand?" Red bunched his fists.

"I understand," Koerner said, hatred burning in his black eyes.

Red gave the man a final, contemptuous look and turned away. At the same moment Koerner got to his feet and pulled a Webley Bull Dog revolver from his pocket. He went after Red and two things happened . . . a man in the crowd yelled, "Here, that won't do!" and a bullet kicked up splinters an inch in front of Koerner's right boot.

Buttons Muldoon's voice was loud in the ensuing silence. "You got a choice to make, mister. Drop the stinger, or I'll ventilate you." The stage driver stood with his legs apart, stern, stocky, and significant, his gun in his hand.

Koerner wanted no part of him. He dropped the revolver.

Buttons said, "Now git the hell out of here and don't come back."

His head hanging, Koerner left the saloon to a chorus of jeers and cheers from the sporting crowd. He fled the town of El Paso and was never heard of again, though it's believed he died of yellow fever in 1904 while working as a laborer during the construction of the Panama Canal.

Daphne Dumont quickly referred to herself as Daphne *Loveshade* and insisted on changing out of her saloon finery and into her own clothes. Buttons and Red took her to Dr. John McKenna. Irritated at being awakened after midnight, he nonetheless gently treated Daphne for a broken nose and cuts and abrasions.

"She can stay here tonight where I can keep an eye on her," the doctor said. "She's in considerable shock."

Red nodded. "We'll look in on her in the morning."

Dr. McKenna said that was just fine by him and pointed out that it already was morning.

But come the gray dawn, Red Ryan and Buttons Muldoon found themselves in the El Paso hoosegow after being arrested for disturbing the peace. Acting Marshal Thomas P. Moad indicated darkly that other charges of a more serious nature could be pending.

CHAPTER FIFTY-ONE

Buttons Muldoon planned to spend the morning yelling protestations of innocence through the bars of his cell, but he decided to eat first after breakfast turned out to be coffee, beef and beans, and a chunk of good rye bread. Chewing, he said, "Hell, Red, I just thought of something."

"What is it?"

"We can't pay a fine. What does that mean?"

Red looked grim. "It means we'll be writing our names on the walls of this cell for a long time."

Buttons poised a forkful of beans between his plate and mouth and said, "Well, you can always sell your belt gun. But not the Greener. We need that."

"If we both sold our belt guns, I reckon we still wouldn't have enough money to pay our fines."

Buttons chewed, thinking, and then said, "It would probably be enough for one fine."

"Which one?"

"Mine, of course. I have to take care of the team."

"Ira Cole is taking care of the team," Red said.

"I know he is. But I don't trust him with my horses."

Red shook his head and was silent, unable to find a way around Buttons's logic.

A loud voice from the office out front said. "This is an outrage! Bring those two scoundrels to me."

Then came Moad's soft drone that neither Red nor Buttons could hear, and then again, an angry bellow. "My dear sir, you are talking to Abe Patterson of the Abe Patterson and Son Stage and Express Company, and I have some mighty powerful friends in this town. Now release my driver and shotgun guard instanter!" A pause as Moad spoke, and then, "Yes, I'll pay the fine, although after I'm through with them, you might well find those miscreants back in your dungeon."

"I thought I recognized the voice," Buttons said. "That's ol' Abe."

"And he sounds like he'll be real happy to see us." Red said.

Buttons scraped his plate, scraped Red's, and then stood. "Make yourself look presentable," he said around a mouthful of beef and beans. "Comb your hair."

"I already look presentable. And I don't have a comb."

"Well, stand up straight," Buttons said.

"Two horses dead, all my money lost. I should have you two hung," Abe Patterson said.

Moad smiled. "That could be arranged."

"Mr. Patterson, I told you what happened." Then with a suitable note of pathos in his voice, Buttons added, "It wasn't our fault."

"It was all your fault. Every bit of it was your fault,"

Abe Patterson said. He was a short, wiry, feisty, banty rooster of a man in a black ditto suit, the bottom of the pants tucked into a pair of embroidered boots. He wore a revolver of the largest size on his hip and a wide-brimmed Stetson that made him look like a poisonous mushroom. "After you delivered Morgan Ford to the Talbot ranch, you should've immediately turned around and headed for El Paso."

"Mr. Patterson, Morgan Ford was a stiff," Red said.

"What difference does that make?" the little man said. "Dead or not, he was a fare-paying passenger of the Abe Patterson and Son Stage and Express Company."

Buttons said, "We were trying to make more money for the company by getting involved in Luna Talbot's troubles, but it didn't work out the way we planned."

"Like gallivanting around, searching for a gold mine." Patterson shook his head. "The height of folly that almost got Ryan killed. I've wrote down eight more rules to the book because of you two."

"Sorry, Mr. Patterson," Buttons said.

"*Sorry* doesn't even begin to describe how you should feel," Patterson said. "Cuthbert said, 'Pop, you should fire those two,' and I was inclined to agree with him. But seeing the pitiful state you're in, I reckon you've suffered enough. Besides, I have a job for you both."

Buttons smiled, thinking that he should shoot fat Cuthbert Patterson the first chance he got. "You can rely on us, boss."

"No, I can't, but you're the only men I have available for the task I have in mind." After a last, scathing, sidelong look at Buttons and Red, Patterson said,

"Come now Marshal Moad, how much to spring these wretches?"

"The bail for disturbing the peace is set by the city," Moad said. "At twenty dollars each, that will be—"

"I know how much it is," Patterson said. "Too much." He took a fat wallet from the inside of his coat and thumbed a pair of twenties onto the marshal's desk. Then to Buttons and Red, "You two retrieve your guns and come with me."

"You're getting off light," Moad said. "Grisome Bell, the owner of the One Note, wanted you hung for putting the crawl on Barney Koerner. Seems he was a big spender."

Buttons opened his mouth to speak but abruptly shut it again when the door opened, and Daphne Loveshade stepped inside. She quickly crossed the floor to the desk and put her arm around Buttons's shoulders. "I heard you'd been arrested. And I was so worried about you and Red."

Daphne had a plaster across her nose and both her eyes were swollen and bruised, making the homely girl homelier still.

"My God, what happened to you?" Moad said.

Red said to Moad, "Your big spender did that to her."

"I didn't know . . ."

"So now you do know, lawman. Give Mr. Patterson his forty dollars back."

Moad ignored that, and Abe Patterson said, "What's your name, girl?"

"Daphne Loveshade, sir."

"Good, good. A well-mannered girl. I like that," Patterson said. "Were you beaten?"

"Yes, sir, by Barney Koerner. I wanted to be a whore, but after last night I don't want to be a whore any longer."

"Good decision, my dear. The oldest profession offers steady employment, but it can be a hazardous occupation at times." Patterson studied the girl closely and then said. "Tell me, have you any desire to be a nun?"

Daphne shook her head. "No, sir. I've never thought about being a nun."

Patterson smiled. "Good, good. Have you had any thought about getting wed?"

"I am married, sir, but I'm separated from my husband, the Reverend Loveshade. I don't know where he is, and I don't much care, either."

"Splendid!" Patterson said. "The nunnery holds no attraction for you, and since you are already married, neither do the joys of matrimony."

"Why are you asking me all these things, sir?" Daphne said.

"Because I need a private secretary, now more than ever since I've recently entered the railroading business. I've had two already. One ran off to the nunnery and the other surrendered to the lure of wedded bliss."

"Mr. Patterson, are you offering Miss Loveshade a job?" Buttons said.

"I have been trending in that direction and being the soul of discretion at the same time. But, in short . . . yes, I am. Miss Loveshade, I'll be frank. I don't want a pretty private secretary who will attract scores of ardent young suitors and leave at the first sign of an offered wedding ring. Though, and

I must be careful what I say, with you I don't see that being much of a problem. Do you?"

"No, sir. I know I'm not pretty," Daphne said. "Gentlemen callers will not be a problem."

"Good! Then, we are in complete agreement," Patterson said. "I will pay you the handsome salary of twenty dollars a month and board, and an additional daily allotment of sugar, coffee or tea, and beer." The little man sat back in his chair as though he'd fairly stated his case. He then said, "Now, young lady, do those generous terms of employment please you?"

"Yes, sir," Daphne said. "And I am most happy to accept. Where will I be working?"

"Mostly at my home in San Angelo, but you can expect some train and stage travel." Patterson suddenly sat upright as though a dreadful thought had just dawned on him. "Here, you can read and write and do your ciphers?"

"Oh, yes, sir. I had a good teacher in my mother," Daphne said.

"And you read your Bible?" Patterson said.

"Yes, I do," Daphne said. "The Reverend Loveshade taught me much about the Good Book."

"Then we will be perfect friends," Patterson said. "I will introduce you to my son, Cuthbert."

"I look forward to meeting him, sir," Daphne said.

Abe Patterson smiled. "Apart from his sheer size, there's very little else to meet."

Buttons and Red's eyes met . . . each telling the other that Cuthbert was short in the brains department and a walking, talking tub of lard who never ate in a restaurant he didn't like.

"Now we'll find you some decent clothes, Mrs. Loveshade," Patterson said. "I'll deduct the cost from your wages." He clapped his hands. "Right, this was an excellent morning's work, apart from bailing out a couple of rapscallions who will also find the cost of lost fares and two dead horses deducted from their future wages."

Buttons opened his mouth to object, but Patterson held up a silencing hand. "Ah-ah, no more from you, Mr. Muldoon, or you either, Mr. Ryan. Let's hope in the course of future events you can redeem yourselves."

"What's the nature of those future events, Mr. Patterson?" Red was reluctant to put his entire trust in the little man.

"I cannot reveal them right now, but they will be perilous . . . oh, yes, mighty perilous." Patterson smiled with all the warmth of cobra rising from a snake charmer's basket. "There's a cannonball coming in from Kansas at four o'clock this afternoon. Meet me at the station at three-thirty and all will be revealed. And be armed." He softened his tone. "I know that deep down you boys are true blue and that you'll come through this with flying colors."

Buttons was suspicious. "Come through what, boss?"

"You'll find out," Patterson said.

CHAPTER FIFTY-TWO

Shortly after noon, another Patterson stage carrying two army officers en route for the Arizona Territory arrived at the El Paso depot to change horses. The driver was a talkative man named Hynick Pruitt who'd driven for Wells Fargo as a teenager. He and Buttons Muldoon went back a ways.

"Buttons, I seen not hide nor hair of anybody the whole trip from Fort Concho," Pruitt said, helping himself liberally from the company's whiskey jug. "Seen a buffalo, though, where once I seen thousands."

"Changed times," Buttons said.

"Sure enough." Pruitt pulled on his tobacco-stained beard, obviously thinking, and then he said finally, "Rumor going around, Buttons. And you too, Red. You might want to hear this."

Remembering Patterson's hints about the coming of perilous events, Buttons said warily, "What kind of rumor, Hynick?"

"Nothing I could write down and make sense of," the driver said. "Just whisperings, ye understand?"

"Let's hear them," Red said. "Whispered rumors are the worst kind."

Pruitt's shotgun guard, a surly man named Quinan, spoke for the first time. "I heard the army officers from Fort Concho talking and they say they heard it from Cuthbert Patterson. It seems there's an important person coming in on a train and the gov-ment is involved. It's being kept very secret. They's heading this way and on different trains that end up in El Paso."

"Do tell," Buttons said. "What the hell would an important government person want in El Paso?"

"The Patterson stage, if the rumor is right," Pruitt said.

"Taking him where?" Buttons said.

Pruitt said, "The government wants him hidden away in a godforsaken army post at the edge of nowhere and Fort Concho fits the bill." He stared at Buttons. "Maybe you'll take him there, Buttons, you and Red."

"What's so important about this government feller?" Buttons said. "Is he the president or something?"

"That's the strange thing of it, Buttons," Pruitt said. "Them two army officers we're taking to Arizony say that Cuthbert told them he's a whiskey drummer."

"Huh?" Buttons said.

"You heard it right," Pruitt said. "He's a whiskey drummer."

"The gubmint must be real worried about their whiskey supply, that's all I can say," Quinan said sourly.

Buttons shook his head. "It's a great mystery."

"Ain't it though?" Pruitt drained his glass. "I got to go see to my team. So long, Buttons, Red."

"Yeah, so long, Hynick" Buttons said. "And good luck."

Pruitt said, "You, too. Good luck."

It was the custom of a stage driver to showboat as he left town, standing in the box yelling and cracking the whip as the team leaned into the harnesses and broke into a thundering gallop. Buttons, a very critical judge, was impressed. Hynick Pruitt had it down to a fine art and passersby stopped in their tracks to cheer and applaud as the spinning yellow wheels of the Patterson stage kicked up clouds of dust on their way to places known and unknown.

Red Ryan and Buttons Muldoon were at the Texas and Pacific railroad station at three-thirty and Abe Patterson showed up five minutes later. He wore his Colt on his hip as did Buttons and Red, and he was not in a sociable turn of mind.

"I'm glad to see you boys can be on time," Patterson said. "More than your stage ever is."

Buttons let that slide and said, "Boss, we hear the passenger is some kind of a government man. Is that true?"

"Who told you that?" Patterson said.

"It was Hynick Pruitt," Red said.

"Pruitt never spoke an honest word in his life," Patterson said. "The passenger is a whiskey drummer, or he was. He got religion a time back and swore off peddling demon drink."

"All right then. How come a reformed whiskey drummer is getting so much attention from the government?" Buttons said.

"Because he is, that's how come," Patterson said, his banty rooster feathers ruffled. "That's all you need to know for now."

Buttons decided to avoid the whole subject, at least for a spell. But he did have one more question to ask. "What's the party's name, boss? We can hardly call him, 'Hey, you' all the way to Fort Concho."

Patterson though about that and said, "His name is Archibald Monday, but you can call him Mr. Monday."

"But only on a Sunday," Buttons said, grinning.

Patterson eyes became pieces of flint. "Is that your idea of a good joke, driver?"

Buttons shook his head. "No, boss. It was my idea of a bad joke."

Patterson said, "Ryan, if Muldoon comes up with another joke, good or bad, you have my permission to shoot him." Then, in his changeable way, he took out a silver case and proffered it to Buttons. "Here, have a cigar. Keep you occupied until the train gets here."

CHAPTER FIFTY-THREE

The train was only twenty minutes late and disgorged about thirty passengers who wasted no time clearing the station and heading for the city. The big locomotive belched clouds of steam across the deserted platform and then it cleared, revealing two men who stood side by side, both carrying small carpetbags. The larger of the two was a tall, wide-shouldered man who had a United States Marshal's star on the left lapel of his coat as regulations demanded. He wore a Colt with dull yellow celluloid grips in a cross-draw holster and carried a Winchester. Even from a distance, the marshal looked like a man to be reckoned with.

Red Ryan studied the lawman's companion who could only be Archibald Monday. In contrast to the marshal, he was a short, frail-looking man, dressed in a gray ditto suit and a bowler hat of the same color. The little man blinked like an owl behind his round spectacles and seemed nervous. Red mentally amended that observation . . . Archibald Monday seemed terrified.

For long moments five men stood on the platform

staring at each other until Abe Patterson broke the ice. "Mr. Monday, I am Abe Patterson of the Patterson stage line. A warm welcome to El Paso."

The big marshal whispered something in Monday's ear and the little man scampered like a scared rabbit to where Patterson stood.

Immediately, his face ashen, he said, "There's trouble brewing, Mr. Patterson. Big trouble."

He was right. It was trouble with a capital T, and it wasn't long in manifesting itself.

Three men stepped off the train, all of them big, all of them wearing shabby suits and bowler hats. They were a tough threesome, more gorilla than human, with fist-battered faces and huge hands that hung by their sides like anvils. Their deep-set eyes never left the trembling form of Archibald Monday, three predators studying their prey.

The marshal cleared his gun and turned to face them.

"Ryan, Muldoon, side him!" Patterson drew his gun, and then said to Monday, "You stay right here with me."

Today, there are those who question why Red Ryan and Buttons Muldoon would get involved in a scrap that really didn't concern them. They've forgotten, or didn't know, that the frontier era was a time of fierce loyalties and if you accepted wages from a man, you rode for his brand. That mind-set left no room for questioning. It was the keystone of the Code of the West, writ large in letters of fire. And Red and Buttons lived by it.

* * *

As Red Ryan and Buttons stood on either side of him, the marshal said in a strong Irish brogue, "Now what is it you gentlemen would be wanting?"

The three toughs didn't like this development. Instead of facing one man, they faced three, all of them armed. But they'd been paid to do a job, and confident of their fighting and killing ability, they'd see it through.

The biggest of the three thugs, a man with a broken nose and scar tissue above each eye, took a step forward and said, "We want no trouble here, copper. Give us Monday and we'll walk away."

"You want Monday, come and take him," the marshal said.

"Don't force us to do just that," the big man said.

"I'm forcing you. May I suggest that you lively lads go back to New York and to whatever slum spawned you."

"You force our hand, copper," the man said. "On your head be it."

The three hardcases were by instinct and practice, fist, skull, and boot fighters, also adept with the knife, billy club, and sap. During their various criminal activities, they used revolvers when the need arose, but in the street gang brawls and muggings that occupied most of their time, guns were not their weapon of choice. They were city boys who'd never before come up against a tough frontier marshal and a Texas draw fighter like Red Ryan . . . a fatal flaw in their education.

To his credit, the marshal didn't immediately try to shade them on the draw. He waited a split second, hoping for a change of heart on the part of the thugs, but in that he was disappointed. They unlimbered their revolvers, two from shoulder rigs, the other from his coat pocket. The three took up a duelist's shooting stance, using the sights as they'd been taught, right side to the opponent, arm extended, the left foot behind the heel of the right.

The marshal drew and fired and Red did the same. Two shots a fraction of a second apart. Two hits. Red fired at the big man who'd done the talking and his bullet slammed into the thug's chest, staggering him. The man to Red's left went down under the lawman's bullet, a killing wound that dropped him to the platform's timber floor. The third man, still unhurt, fired at the marshal, who took the bullet to his lower left side that rocked him and put him out of the fight. Red and Buttons shot at the same time and the thug screamed and went down, blood opening up like a scarlet rose between his collarbones. But when he struck the ground he lived long enough to fire, and Red heard Buttons gasp as he was hit. The big, talkative man wanted no more of Texas gunfighting. Mortally wounded, he threw down his revolver and yelled, "Quarter."

But Red, seeing the marshal down and blood seeping through Buttons's fingers as he clutched at a wound in his right shoulder, was not inclined to be merciful, at least not that day. He pumped two bullets into the big hoodlum, scored two hits, and when the man hit the ground he was already dead as a rotten stump.

Gun smoke drifted across the station platform as Archibald Monday stood behind Abe Patterson, held his hands to his ringing ears, and in a state of trembling anxiety said over and over again, "Oh, dear . . . oh, dearie me . . ."

Red stepped toward Buttons, and the driver said, "I'm all right, Red. See to the marshal." Then, for no apparent reason, "He's an Irishman."

The lawman sat on the platform, the left side of his shirt glistening with blood.

Red took a knee beside him and said, "You've been hit hard. We'll get you a doctor."

The lawman nodded and extended his hand. "Name's Sean Brannigan. Pleased to make your acquaintance."

"Red Ryan." He took the man's hand. "I'm a representative of the Abe Patterson and Son Stage and Express Company."

"And a credit to it, you are. How are the three boyos over there?" Brannigan said.

"All dead."

"Pity. They were likely lads but on the wrong side of the law. Was Monday hit?"

"No, he's fine. Mr. Patterson is taking care of him."

"He's an excitable little fella," the marshal said.

"Which one?"

Brannigan smiled. "Mr. Monday."

Red nodded. "Yes, he's all of that."

Acting city marshal Tom Moad arrived with gun drawn and doctor in tow. The lawman looked around at the carnage and fell into an agitated silence, obviously deciding who to charge with what. But a quiet word from United States Marshal Sean Brannigan calmed him down and convinced him he was dealing with circumstances beyond his control.

As Dr. McKenna worked on Brannigan, Moad said, "Marshal, I searched the bodies and found no identification. Between them, the deceased carried a sum of two hundred and five dollars and eighteen cents, three large knives, and three Smith and Wesson pistols, all of which I am confiscating."

"The spoils of war, Marshal," Brannigan said. "The three deceased, as you call them, were gang members from the Five Points neighborhood in New York City, a place where lives are short and violent and a place where infectious diseases ravage the mostly starving population. In short, it's a den of murderers, thieves, brothels, and terrible poverty—and it's ruled by the gangs."

"The bullet passed right through your side, Marshal Brannigan," Dr. McKenna said. "I don't think it struck anything vital, but it's done some damage and I will examine you further in my surgery."

"How is the other fella?" Brannigan said.

"Mr. Muldoon? It's a flesh wound," McKenna said. "Nothing too serious."

"Glad to hear it," Brannigan said. "The Muldoons hail from County Sligo in the old country. Fine people."

"I'm sure they are." McKenna hailed a couple of railroad workers. "Bring me a cart or something to transport this wounded man to my surgery."

One of the workers touched his cap and said, "Doc, there's a stretcher in the station storeroom."

"That will do nicely," the doctor said. "You gentlemen can carry him."

Irritated by the interruption, Moad said, "Marshal Brannigan, why are the Five Points gangs so interested in a whiskey drummer here in Texas?"

"Best you don't know, Marshal Moad," Brannigan said. "Jesus, Mary, and Joseph help me. I wish I didn't."

CHAPTER FIFTY-FOUR

Abe Patterson thought it better that Archibald Monday spend the night in the stage station, rather than a hotel. "Easier to keep an eye on him."

The little man was terrified, jumping at every noise in the street outside.

Finally Buttons Muldoon said, "What the hell is making you so nervous, Archibald?"

Monday hesitated, and then said, "Men are trying to kill me."

"Why would anyone want to kill a harmless little runt like you?" Buttons said.

"Not only me, but my lady wife," the little man said. "My dearest Prudence is a large lady and not easy to hide." He leaned forward in his seat, whispering, imparting a confidence. "She's at a Catholic convent."

"Huh?" Buttons said.

"The Sisters of Charity are keeping her safe in their convent in New York's Upper West Side. She's guarded night and day." shook his head. "My dear, dear Prudence, so large in size, yet so vulnerable."

"Why?" Buttons said.

"Because she eats a lot," Monday said.

"No, not that," Button said. He had a fat bandage under his shirt. "I meant, why is she guarded day and night?"

"Because she's my wife," Monday said.

"You're not catching my drift," Buttons said. "Let's try it from a different direction. Why are men trying to kill you?"

"I'm sworn to secrecy," the little man said. "You'll need to ask Marshal Brannigan."

As it happened, there was no need to ask Marshal Brannigan, because a boy came to the depot door with a message for Mr. Muldoon. He was to come to Dr. McKenna's surgery right away.

"You'll be all right by yourself, Red?" Buttons said. "You still ain't feeling frisky."

"Says a man with a shot-up shoulder." Red smiled. "Sure, I'll be fine. And Ira Cole hasn't let go of his scattergun since Monday got here. He claims it's become both wife and child to him."

Dr. McKenna met Buttons Muldoon at the door of his surgery and imparted some bad news. "I'm afraid Marshal Brannigan has a fever and he'll have to remain in bed for at least a few more days. His wound is more severe than I first thought."

McKenna saw that his tidings didn't have the effect he'd anticipated on the stage driver and added, "It means he will be unable to accompany Mr. Monday to Fort Concho."

Now Buttons understood the implication. He and Red could have used Brannigan's fast gun on the journey. It was an unwelcome loss.

"Sorry to hear that, Doc."

"And so was Marshal Brannigan," McKenna said. "He wants to talk with you. How does the shoulder feel?"

"Middlin'," Buttons said.

"I'll change the dressing before you leave for Fort Concho. Now go see the marshal."

The lawman was propped up on pillows and at first look seemed healthy. But then Buttons saw the blush of fever on his cheeks and the beaded sweat gathered on his forehead.

"How you feeling, Marshal?" Buttons said.

"The sawbones says I'm doing poorly, and judging by the way I feel, I guess he's right," Brannigan said. "I can't ride with you to Fort Concho."

"McKenna told me that," Buttons said. "I was some disappointed."

"Whatever you do, take care of Monday," Brannigan said. "Make sure he gets to the fort safely."

"Depend on it," Buttons said. "Red Ryan is the best shotgun guard in the business."

"I hope he's enough," the marshal said.

Buttons sat on the corner of the cot, making it creak. "All right, Marshal Brannigan. What's going on? I think I got a right to know."

"Yes, you do. And I'll tell you." The lawman took a drink from the glass of water on the table beside him and said, "The three men we killed today were from New York's Five Points neighborhood, a cesspool of crime and violence, an overcrowded, disease-ridden slum run by five or six major gangs. For years the gangs have waged war on one another, and hundreds have died."

"Sounds like a place to avoid," Buttons said.

"Indeed, it is," Brannigan said. "But recently a new leader, a man named Steven Wainwright, rose up and convinced the gang bosses that they should join together into one huge, crime syndicate, to rob, rape, and murder on an industrial scale and get rich in the process. He wants the Five Points to be wide open to opium trade controlled by the gangs, and he estimated they could create a thousand new addicts a day among the poorest and least fortunate, the immigrants and sweatshop workers—men, women, and children who live ten or twelve to a filthy, rat-infested room. What better way for people to dream away their dreadful existence than opium?"

"So where does Archibald Monday fit in all this?" Buttons said.

"I'm coming to that, Mr. Muldoon," Brannigan said. "A crusading Catholic priest got wind of Wainwright's plans and confronted him in the street, demanding that he disband the gangs and work to make Five Points a better place. Wainwright's answer was to draw his gun and shoot the priest down in the street. There were no witnesses, of course . . . except one."

"Archibald Monday," Buttons said.

Brannigan nodded. "The Five Points is a big whiskey market. Archibald Monday was standing in the doorway of a saloon talking with the owner when the priest was murdered. As you'd expect, the saloonkeeper saw nothing, but Monday, being a responsible citizen, went to the police and told them he could identify the killer. It was a bad mistake. Some crooked, high-ranking officer tipped off Wainwright that there was a witness willing to testify. He also told him that

Monday was being taken to Texas . . . and you know the result of that."

"Wainwright is still on the hunt for Monday," Buttons said.

Brannigan shook his head. "Wainwright is in jail, arrested by the Secret Service on a charge of vagrancy while they build a case against him. Archibald Monday will stay in hiding until the murdering thug goes to court."

"Wainwright can't do much harm behind bars," Buttons said.

"Oh, yes he can, because the drug trade is way bigger than him," the marshal said. "The criminal organizations plan to flood the Five Points with opium, morphine, and a new German drug made from opium that goes by the name of heroin. It's a test, and if it's successful, they'll move on to other American cities and towns and villages. They need Wainwright in the Five Points, and they'll do everything in their power to put him back there. That means Monday has to die, and the sooner the better."

Buttons shook his head. "Marshal, there ain't none of them big outlaw drug gangs in Texas."

"Mr. Muldoon, they're in every state of the union, including Texas," Brannigan said. "They can buy guns and the men to use them, and they're spreading like a cancer." He grasped Buttons by the arm. "There's talk of another Chiricahua Apache outbreak, so you can expect no help from the army until you reach Fort Concho. Until then, keep Monday safe. Do it for your country. Trust me. A lot is riding on you and Red Ryan. The Secret Service will send agents to Fort Concho, but until they arrive, Monday is your responsibility."

"When will them agents get there?" Buttons said.

Brannigan managed a wry smile. "We're talking about the government, so it will be whenever it gets around to it."

CHAPTER FIFTY-FIVE

"Brannigan has sand, and he's good with a gun," Red Ryan said. "We could've used him on this trip."

"Ain't that the truth." Buttons Muldoon looked toward the cot where Archibald Monday lay snoring, his head and the rest of him covered in a blanket. "How long has the little feller been like that?"

"For the past couple of hours," Red said. "Let him sleep. It keeps him quiet. He's got one of them Bulldog revolvers in there with him as a sneaky gun."

"Then how come he didn't draw it at the station when the shooting started?" Buttons said.

"Maybe Brannigan told him not to get involved in a gunfight, but it's more likely he was too scared to move. Hell, he stood so close to Abe Patterson, I thought he was trying to crawl inside his skin."

"And talking about Abe, he's coming in," Ira Cole said from his guard post at the window. "Got that Sophie gal and his son with him."

The depot clock chimed ten and the street outside was in darkness. A horse whinnied in the corral out back and knocked over a metal feed bucket.

Abe Patterson stepped inside, bringing with him the tinny gust of a saloon piano. Sophie, a brown-skinned, statuesque woman, hung on his arm and Cuthbert, as was his practice, walked a step behind.

"Good evening, fellers." Patterson motioned to his son, who laid a bottle of Old Crow and a handful of cigars on the table. "This is my way of thanking you for the fine work you put in this afternoon." He looked around. "Where is Monday?"

Red jerked a thumb over his shoulder. "Back there, asleep."

"Worn out from nerves, I'd say," Patterson said. "Poor little runt."

"Pa, I wish I'd been there today," Cuthbert said. "I'd have told the others to stand aside and let me get my work in. I'd have shown them city slickers a thing or two about gun handling."

"I'm sure you would have, Cuthbert," Abe said.

"Damn right," Cuthbert said.

Buttons, as mischievous as always, said, "You could ride with us to Fort Concho, Cuthbert. Maybe you'll get your chance to get into a shooting scrape."

The pudgy young man didn't miss a beat. "I'd admire to, Mr. Muldoon, but I've got a sore back and stagecoach travel is not for me."

Sophie looked at Buttons, smiled, and winked, surprising the hell out of him.

Abe didn't notice or pretended not to. "Cuthbert is plagued by sore backs." He clapped his hands together. "Now, let us make a trial of the whiskey and cigars."

"Where is Daphne Loveshade?" Red asked.

"Back at the hotel getting ready for her first train ride," Abe said. "She's very excited."

After some drinking and smoking, Abe Patterson said, "I have a fine team for you, Buttons . . . and Red . . . and a couple of boxes of shells made by the U.S. Cartridge Company. Crackerjack shells, Red. Top notch."

"I'm obliged, Mr. Patterson. Let's hope I don't have to use them."

"Indeed. That's what we all want," Patterson said.

"I'll say a prayer to Saint Peter Claver for you, Red," Sophie said. "And you too, Buttons."

Buttons said from behind a cloud of exhaled smoke, "Who is he?"

"Peter Claver is the patron saint of slaves," Sophie said. "My parents were slaves, and St. Peter answered many of their prayers."

Buttons nodded. "Well, it sure can't hurt, so pray away, Miss Sophie. In the meantime, we'll put our trust in the U.S. Cartridge Company."

"Sophie is always praying to somebody," Abe Patterson said. He smiled benignly at his mistress. "Saint Peter Claver keeps me on the straight and narrow.' He turned his attention to Buttons again. "You and Red will leave with Mr. Monday tomorrow morning before sunup. Keep it quiet, Buttons. No showboating. The least number of people who see or hear your departure, the better."

"They won't even know we're gone." Buttons said.

"Excellent. The good name of the Patterson stage company depends on you, Buttons," Patterson said. "And it's a heavy responsibility . . . a burdensome responsibility."

Buttons smiled. "Marshal Brannigan says the whole damn country is depending on me and Red to get Monday to Fort Concho."

"Ah, yes, that is true," Abe said. "But the needs of the Patterson Stage and Express Company must always come first. Please remember that."

The Patterson stage was alone on a sea of grass under a blue sky dominated by the burning sun.

Apart from the big, strong wheelers, the team that Buttons Muldoon had in hand was young and inexperienced, and he sweated heavily as he managed the reins. "Answer me a question, Red."

"Fire away," Red Ryan said.

"What are our chances of reaching Fort Concho alive?"

"Pretty good." Red was silent for a while and then added, "That is, if we don't run afoul of Apaches, big-city gunmen, and plain old Texas road agents."

"Damn it all, Red, couldn't you have said 'Pretty good' and let it go at that?"

Red grinned. "All right, then. Pretty good. There, I've said it."

"Yeah. But you don't mean it," Buttons said.

"Sure, I mean it. I wouldn't say 'pretty good' if I didn't mean it."

At that moment Archibald Monday stuck his head out the window and yelled up at the box, "What are our chances, Mr. Muldoon? I didn't hear Mr. Ryan's answer."

"Pretty good," Buttons and Red yelled back in unison.

AFTERWORD

It is pleasant to report that, thanks to the bravery, loyalty, and patriotism of Red Ryan and Buttons Muldoon, Archibald Monday lived to testify in court against Steven Wainwright, and the gang leader was later executed. His death spelled the end of the Five Points. The gangs were crushed, its slums were torn down brick by brick, and by 1910 little of the place remained. It is of interest to note that the Secret Service took all the credit for safeguarding Monday. Buttons and Red were not mentioned in official reports, and neither was the Abe Patterson and Son Stage and Express Company.

Turn the page for a special early preview of the new Western epic
from William W. and J. A. Johnstone . . .

THE SCAVENGERS
A DEATH & TEXAS WESTERN

EVERYTHING IS BIGGER IN TEXAS.
EVEN DEATH.

Cullen McCabe has always been a risk-taker.
But sometimes, taking a risk means
taking a bullet—unless you kill first . . .

Cullen McCabe knew he'd make a lot of enemies when he agreed to be a special agent for the Texas governor. But now that he's managed to keep the peace in the hopeless town of New Hope, he's hoping he can go home and get back to business as usual.

No such luck.

There's a trio of troubles waiting for him there—three gun-toting avengers by the name of Tice. This hardcase family of bullies and prairie rats blame McCabe for taking down one of their kin and stealing their horses. They want revenge, and they want it quick . . .

McCabe wants something, too. He wants to finish the job he started—and pick off the rest of these scavengers. . . .

Look for THE SCAVENGERS *on sale in April 2020,*
from Pinnacle books.

CHAPTER ONE

"Look who's comin' in again," Alma Brown whispered softly to Gracie Wright when the cook walked past her on her way back to the kitchen. Gracie paused and looked toward the front door. It was the second time this week that Jesse Tice had come in the dining room next to the hotel, appropriately named The Two Forks Kitchen. He had become a regular visitor to the dining room ever since his youngest son was killed there some weeks before. Usually, he came in only once a week. "Wonder what's so special about this week?" Alma whispered. They were never happy to see the old man, because he made their other customers uncomfortable as he hovered over his coffee, a constant scowl on his unshaven face, while he watched the front door and each customer who walked in. Coffee was the only thing he ever bought. Everyone in town knew his real purpose in haunting the dining room was the chance to see the man who had killed his son. Cullen McCabe was the man he sought. But McCabe was a bigger mystery than Jesse Tice to the people of Two Forks. Everyone knew Jesse as a cattle rustler and horse thief whose three sons were hell-raisers and troublemakers. Cullen McCabe, on the other hand, was a quiet man, seen only occasionally in town, and seeming to have no family or friends.

Alma's boss, Porter Johnson, owner of Two Forks Kitchen, had talked to Sheriff Woods about Tice's search for vengeance against McCabe. Johnson was not concerned about the fate of either Tice or McCabe. His complaint was the fact that Jesse used his dining room as his base for surveillance, hoping McCabe would return. "Doggone it, Calvin," he had complained to the sheriff. "I'm runnin' a dinin' room, not a damn saloon. Folks come in here to eat, not to see some dirty-lookin' old man waitin' to shoot somebody."

Sheriff Woods had been unable to give Johnson much satisfaction when he responded to his complaint. "I hear what you're sayin', Porter," he had replied. "I reckon you just have to tell Tice you don't wanna serve him. That's up to you to serve who you want to and who you don't. I can't tell folks where they can go and where they can't. As far as that shootin' in here, I told him right from the start that that fellow, McCabe didn't have no choice. Sonny started the fight and tried to shoot McCabe in the back, but he just wasn't quick enough. I told Jesse I didn't want any more killin' in this town, so I'd have to arrest him if he shot McCabe."

Looking at the old man now as he paused to scan the dining room before taking a seat near the door, Alma commented. "One of us might have to tell the ol' buzzard we don't want him in here. I don't think Porter wants to get started with him. He's probably afraid he'd start shootin' the place up."

"Maybe we oughta hope McCabe comes back to see us," Gracie said. "Let him take care of Jesse Tice. He took care of Sonny proper enough."

"Meanwhile, I'll go wait on him and take his order for one nickel cup of coffee," Alma said. She walked over to the small table close to the front door. "Are you wantin' breakfast?" She asked, knowing he didn't.

"No, I don't want no breakfast," he snarled. "I done et breakfast. Bring me a cup of coffee." She turned and went to get it. He watched her for a few moments before bringing his attention back to the room now only half-filled with diners. He didn't see anyone who might be the man who killed his son. The major problem Tice had was the fact that he had never actually seen Cullen McCabe up close. When he and his two sons had gone after McCabe, he had circled around them, stolen their horses, and left them on foot. Still, he felt that if he did see him, he would somehow know it was him. When the sheriff tried to talk him out of seeking vengeance for the death of his son, Jesse was tempted to tell him that McCabe was a horse thief. He thought that would justify his reason for wanting to shoot him, but he was too proud to admit how his horses happened to get stolen. Every time he thought about the night he and his two sons had to walk twenty-five miles back home, it made him bite his lower lip in angry frustration. When Alma returned with his coffee, he gulped it down, having decided there was no use to linger there. It was already getting late for breakfast, so he thought he might as well go back to join Samson and Joe, who were keeping a watch for McCabe in the River House Saloon.

* * *

It had been several days since he had returned to his cabin on the Brazos River after completing his last assignment from the governor's office. The long hard job in the little town of New Hope had turned out to the governor's satisfaction, and Cullen figured it would be a while before he was summoned for the next job. For that reason, he hadn't bothered to check in with the telegraph office at Two Forks to see if he had a wire from Austin. He needed to do a little work on his cabin, so he had waited before checking with Leon Armstrong at the telegraph office. When he was not on assignment for the governor, he usually checked by the telegraph office at least once a week for any messages, and it had not been quite a week since he got back. Halfway hoping there might be a message, he pulled up before the telegraph office and stepped down from the big bay gelding. He casually tossed the reins across the hitching rail, knowing Jake wouldn't wander, anyway.

Leon Armstrong looked up when Cullen walked in and gave him a cheerful greeting. "How ya doin', Mr. McCabe? I got a telegram here for you. Figured you'd be showin' up pretty soon."

"Howdy, Mr. Armstrong," Cullen returned. "Has it been here long?"

"Came in two days ago," Armstrong said as he retrieved the telegram from a drawer under the counter. "Looks like you're fixin' to travel again."

Cullen took only a moment to read the short message from Austin. "Looks that way," he said to Armstrong and folded the message before putting it in his pocket. "Much obliged," he said and turned to leave. It seemed kind of awkward that Armstrong always knew Cullen's plans before he did, but since he was the telegraph operator, there wasn't any way to avoid it.

"See you next time," Armstrong said as Cullen went out the door. As curious as he was about the mysterious telegrams the big quiet man received from the governor's office in Austin, he was reluctant to ask him what manner of business he was engaged in. And after the altercation between McCabe and Sonny Tice, he was even more timid about asking. For the most part, McCabe had very little contact with anyone in Two Forks except for him and Ronald Thornton at the general store. He had an occasional meal at Two Forks Kitchen and made a call on the blacksmith on rare occasions perhaps, but that was about all.

Cullen responded to Leon's farewell with a flip of his hand as he went out the door. All the wire said was that he should come into the capital. That's all they ever said, but it always meant he was about to be sent out on another assignment. So, his next stop would be Thornton's General Merchandise to add to his supplies. As was his usual practice, he had brought his packhorse with him when he rode into town, in the event there was a telegram waiting. Austin was north of Two Forks, while his cabin was south of the town. So, by bringing the packhorse with him, there was no need to return to his cabin. Taking Jake's reins, he led the big bay and the sorrel packhorse up the street to Thornton's.

Jesse Tice and his two sons came out of the saloon and stood for a while on the short length of boardwalk in front. Looking up and down the street, hoping to catch sight of the man who shot his youngest, Jesse figured it another wasted day. Both Samson and Joe were content to participate in the search for the man called Cullen McCabe as long as their watching post was always the saloon. There was not a great deal of gray matter between the ears of either Joe or Samson and what there was seemed easily diluted by alcohol. Neither son carried the same driven desire their father had to avenge their brother. They generally figured that Sonny was bound to run into somebody he couldn't outdraw in a gunfight and the results would be the same. "How 'bout it, Pa?" Samson asked. "We 'bout ready to go on back to the house?"

"Hold on," Jesse said, something having caught his attention at the far end of the street. At that moment, Graham Price, the blacksmith, walked out of the saloon, heading back to his forge. Jesse stepped in front of Price. "Say," he asked, "who's the big feller leadin' them horses to the general store?" He pointed to Thornton's.

Price paused only long enough to say, "His name's Cullen McCabe." Having no more use for Jesse and his sons than most of the other citizens of Two Forks, he continued on toward his shop. Had he taken the time to look at the wide-eyed look of discovery on Jesse Tice's face, he would have regretted identifying McCabe. As luck would have it, Jesse had asked one of the handful of people in Two Forks who knew McCabe's name. As Price crossed to the other side of the street, he could hear the excited exchange of conversation behind him as the three Tice men realized their search had paid off.

Joe, Jesse's youngest, now that Sonny was dead, ran to his horse to get his rifle, but Jesse stopped him.

"Put it away, you damn fool! You're too late, anyway, he's done gone inside the store."

"He'll be comin' back out," Samson insisted, thinking the same as Joe. "And when he does, we can cut him down."

"Ain't I ever learnt you boys anythin'?" Jesse scolded. "And then what, after ever'body in the whole town seen you do it? Take to the hills with a sheriff's posse after us?"

"Yeah, but he shot Sonny right there in the dinin' room, and ever'body seen him do it," Joe declared. "Sheriff didn't arrest him for that."

"Sonny called him out," Jesse said. "There's a difference. You pick him off when he don't know you're waitin' for him—that's murder, and they'd most likely hang you for it."

Confused now, Samson asked, "Well, ain't we gonna shoot him? Why we been hangin' around here waitin' for him to show up, if we ain't gonna shoot him?"

"We're gonna shoot him," his father explained, impatiently. "But we're gonna wait and follow him outta town where there ain't no witnesses."

"What if he ain't plannin' to leave anytime soon?" Joe complained. "I'd just as soon step up in front of him and tell him to go for his gun—see how fast he is when he don't know it's comin'. Then it would be a face-to-face shoot-out, and like you said, that ain't murder. Hell, I'm as fast as Sonny ever was," he claimed, his boast in part inspired by the whiskey he had just imbibed. He didn't express it, but he was also thinking about gaining a reputation by gunning down the man who killed Sonny.

Jesse smirked in response to his son's boastful claim. "You don't know how fast McCabe is. You ain't never seen him draw." He had to admit that it would give him great pleasure to have the people of Two Forks see McCabe shot down by one of his boys.

"You ain't seen me draw lately, neither," Joe replied. "I know how fast Sonny was, and I know how fast I am. I'm ready to shoot this son of a bitch right now."

"He is fast, Pa," Samson said, curious to see if Joe could do it. "He ain't lyin'."

The prospect of seeing McCabe cut down before an audience of witnesses was too much for Jesse to pass up. Joe was right, he hadn't seen how fast he was lately, and he knew both his boys practiced their fast draw on a daily basis. There had always been a competition between all three of his sons, ever since they were big enough to wear a gun. Sonny had been the first one to actually call a man out, though, and that hadn't turned out very well. But the fact that Sonny's death didn't discourage Joe was enough to cause Jesse to wonder. "All right," he finally conceded. "We'll go talk to Mr. McCabe. He owes me for three horses he stole. We'll see what he has to say for hisself about that. Then, if you think you can take him, that'll be up to you. If you don't, we'll follow him out of town and shoot him down where nobody can see us do it." They hurried toward Thornton's store, concerned now that he might finish up his business and leave before they got there.

Inside the store, Cullen was in the process of paying Ronald Thornton for the supplies gathered on the counter when Jesse and his two sons walked in. He had never had a close look at the old man or his two boys, but he knew instinctively who they were, and he had a feeling this was not a chance encounter. He decided to treat it as such until he saw evidence backing up that feeling. He purposefully turned one side toward them while he gathered his purchases up close on the counter, so he could keep an eye on all three. Jesse took only a few steps inside before stopping to stand squarely in front of the door. His sons took a stance, one on each side of him. Thinking the entrance rather odd, Thornton said, "I'll be with you in a minute, soon as I finish up here."

"Ain't no hurry," Jesse said. "Our business is with Mr. McCabe there."

Thornton was suddenly struck by the realization that something bad was about to happen. "Clara," he said to his wife, "you'd best go on back in the storeroom and put that new material away." When she reacted with an expression of confusion, he said, "Just go on back there." Seeing he meant it, she quickly left the room.

Up to that point, McCabe had not reacted beyond pulling a twenty-pound sack of flour and a large slab of bacon over to the edge of the counter, preparing to carry them out to his packhorse. "What is your business with me?"

"Maybe it's about them three horses of mine you stole without payin' me for 'em," Jesse snarled.

"I figured we were square on that count. I paid you the same price you paid for them," Cullen said, guessing Jessie and his boys had most likely stolen them.

"I'm callin' you out, McCabe," Joe blurted, unable to contain himself any longer.

"That right?" McCabe asked calmly. "What for?"

"For killin' my brother," Joe said. "That's what for."

"Who's your brother?" Cullen asked, purposefully trying to keep the young man's mind occupied with something other than the actual act of pulling his weapon. He had faced his share of gunfighters in his time and it was fairly easy to read the wide-eyed nervousness in young Joe Tice's face. The fact that his speech was slurred slightly also suggested that alcohol might be doing most of the talking. He understood the obligation the two brothers felt to avenge Sonny's death, no matter the circumstances that caused him to be shot. There was a chance, however, that he could talk the boy out of a gunfight, so he decided to give it a try.

"You know who he was," Joe responded to Cullen's question. "Sonny Tice, you shot him down in the Two Forks Kitchen."

"So, you're Sonny's brother, huh?" Cullen continued calmly. "Yeah, that was too bad about Sonny. I could see that he wasn't very fast with a handgun. I think he knew it, too, 'cause he waited till I turned around and then he tried to shoot me in the back. He mighta got me, too, but somebody yelled to warn me, so I didn't have any choice. I had to shoot him." He could see that his calm rambling was confusing the young man. He had plainly expected to see a completely different response to his challenge to a face-off. "Yeah, I felt kinda bad about havin' to shoot poor Sonny," Cullen went on. "I've seen it before; young fellow thinks he's fast with a gun and ain't ever seen a man who's a real gunslinger. You must figure you're faster than Sonny was, but I don't know about that. Judgin' by the way you wear that .44 down so low on your leg, I don't see how you could be. How many men have you ever pulled iron on?"

"That don't make no difference," Joe protested.

"That's my business." He was plainly flustered by the big man's casual attitude.

"That's what I thought," Cullen said. "This is the first time you've ever called anybody out. Well, we'll try to make it as quick and painless as we can. Let's take it outside this man's store, though." He pulled the sack of flour and the slab of bacon off the counter. "Here," he said, "you can gimme a hand with these supplies. Grab that coffee and that twist of jerky—save me a trip back in here."

Clearly confused by this time, Joe wasn't sure what to do. Accustomed to being ordered around all his young life, he did as McCabe instructed, and picked up the sack of coffee and the beef jerky, then started to follow Cullen out the door. Caught in a state of confusion as well, Jesse finally realized that McCabe was talking Joe out of a face-off. "Hold on there! Put them damn sacks down," he blurted and pulled his six-shooter when Cullen started to walk past him. It was not quick enough to avoid the heavy sack of flour that smacked against the side of his head, creating a great white cloud that covered him from head to toe when the sack burst open. With his other hand, Cullen slammed his ten-pound slab of bacon across Jesse's gun hand, causing him to pull the trigger, putting a bullet hole in the slab of side meat. The hand that had held the flour sack now held a Colt .44, and Cullen rapped one swift time across the bridge of Jesse's nose with it. Stunned, Jesse dropped like a rock.

His two sons stood paralyzed with the shock of seeing their father collapse and Cullen was quick to take advantage of it. "Unbuckle those gun belts, both of you." With his .44 trained on them, they offered no resistance. After laying his slab of bacon on the bar, Cullen took both belts, then picked up Jesse's gun. "Pick your pa up and get him out of here. Take him home and he'll be all right," he ordered, while covering them with his Colt. "There ain't gonna be no killin' here today. And if you're smart, you'll just forget about gettin' even for your brother's mistake. He made a play that didn't work out for him. Don't you make the same mistake." Still numb with shock from the way the confrontation with McCabe turned upside down, Joe and Samson helped their father to his feet. Jesse, unsteady and confused by the blow to the bridge of his nose, staggered out the door with the support of his sons. They managed to get him up in the saddle, and he promptly fell forward to lie on his horse's neck. Still covered with flour, he looked like a ghost lying there. Watching the process from the boardwalk in front of the store, Cullen said, "I'm gonna leave your weapons with the sheriff and tell him to let you have them back tomorrow." There was no reply from either of the boys, and Jesse was still too groggy to respond. Cullen continued to watch them until they rode out the end of the street. It occurred to him then that he hadn't taken their rifles from their saddles. *I hope to hell they don't think about that,* he thought.

"I reckon you're gonna need some more flour," Thornton commented, standing in the doorway of the store. "Maybe some bacon, too."

"Reckon so," Cullen replied, "flour, anyway. The bacon looks okay. I'll just cut that bullet hole out of it—might flavor it up a little bit."

"I'll tell you what," Thornton said. "I won't charge

you for another sack of flour. That coulda been a bad situation back there, and I wanna thank you for preventing a gunfight in my store."

"'Preciate it," Cullen said. "Now, I expect I'd better get movin'. I'm takin' the road outta here to Austin, and that's the same road they just took to go home. If you don't mind, you can get me another sack of flour and I'll take these guns to the sheriff while you're doin' that." He started walking down the street at once and called back over his shoulder, "Sorry 'bout the mess I made in your store."

Still standing in the door, Thornton looked back inside. "Don't worry about that," he said, "Clara's already sweeping it up."

Sheriff Calvin Woods was just in the process of locking his office door as he hurried to investigate the shot he had heard several minutes before. Seeing Cullen approaching, he feared it was to report another killing in his town. When Cullen told him what had taken place, the sheriff also expressed his appreciation to him for avoiding a shoot-out with Jesse Tice and his sons. Cullen left the weapons with him, then returned to the store to tie all his purchases on his packhorse. Ronald Thornton stood outside and watched while he readied his horses to ride. When Cullen stepped up into the saddle, Thornton felt prompted to comment. "It looks like Jesse Tice ain't gonna let it rest till he either gets you, or you cut him down."

"It looks that way, doesn't it?" Cullen replied. "I reckon killin' a man's son is a sure way to make him an enemy." He wheeled the big bay away from the hitching rail and set out for Austin.

Thornton's wife was waiting for him when he came back in the store. "Well, you don't know any more about that man than you did before, do ya?" She shook her head impatiently. "You and Leon Armstrong are gonna have to get together to gossip over McCabe's visit to town today, I suppose," she said, referring to the many discussions the two had already had, trying to figure out the man's business. "I'm not sure I like to see him come in the store," she concluded as she pointed to a bullet hole in the floor. "It seems like everywhere he goes, somebody starts shootin'."

"In all fairness, Hon," Ronald pointed out, "it's people shootin' at him, and not the other way around."

"I don't care," she said. "It like to scared me to death. I was sure one of us was gonna get killed, and right now I've gotta go to the house and change my drawers."

Thinking it not smart to take another chance on a showdown with Jesse and his boys, Cullen nudged Jake into an easy lope as he set out on the road to Austin. He remembered all too well the day he was forced to shoot Sonny Tice. At the sheriff's urging, he had hurried out of town, only to find that the trail to the Tice ranch forked off the road to Austin a couple of miles north of Two Forks. He had managed to pass that trail before they found out he was heading to Austin. It was his intention to do the same today. As he rocked in the saddle to Jake's easy gait, he kept a sharp eye on the road ahead of him. In a short while, he came to the trail leading off to the west and the Tice ranch. He rode past it with no incident, so he hoped that would be the end of it. Time would tell, he told himself, but he was not going to count on it. He had not only killed Jesse's son, but what might be worse for a man like Jesse Tice was the fact that he had made a fool of him twice. There was also the matter of three horses Cullen had taken from the ambush site. *There ain't no doubt,* he told himself, *that old bastard has plenty of reason to come after me.*

CHAPTER TWO

It was time to be thinking about some supper by the time he rode into the capitol city of Austin, but he decided it best to take care of his horses first. So, he rode past the capitol building to the stable at the end of the street, operated by a man he knew simply as Burnett. He stepped down from the saddle at the stable door. Having seen him ride up, Burnett walked out to meet him. "Mr. McCabe," he greeted him. "You ain't got no horses to sell this time," he said, glancing past Cullen to see only the one packhorse.

"No, I reckon not," Cullen answered. "Ain't run across any lately. I'd like to leave these two with you overnight. And I'd like to sleep with 'em, if you don't charge too much."

"Sure," Burnett said with a wide smile. "I reckon I charge a little bit less than the hotel does, unless you want clean sheets." He chuckled in appreciation for his humor.

"I 'preciate it," Cullen said. "Maybe you could recommend a good place to get some supper. Last time

I was in town, I ate in the dinin' room of that hotel near the capitol, and it wasn't to my likin'."

"You shoulda asked me last time," Burnett said. "I woulda told you to go to Pot Luck. That's a little restaurant run by Rose Bettis between here and the capitol building. That's where I go when I take a notion I don't wanna cook for myself, the Pot Luck Restaurant."

"Restaurant," Cullen repeated. "That sounds kinda fancy." He thought of the place where Michael O'Brien had taken him to breakfast before and all the diners dressed up in suits and ties. Since Burnett said it was back the way he had just come, he commented. "Sounds like I shoulda noticed it on my way down here."

Burnett laughed. "Nah, Pot Luck ain't fancy. It's anything but. It's just a little place next to the hardware store. I ain't surprised you didn't notice it, but if you're lookin' for good food at a fair price, then that's the place to go."

"I'll take your word for it," Cullen said. He followed Burnett into the stables, leading his horses. He unloaded his packhorse and stacked his packs in the corner of a stall. After checking Jake's and the sorrel's hooves, and finding them in good shape, he asked Burnett what time he should be back before the stables were locked up for the night.

"You've got plenty of time," Burnett assured him. "I don't usually leave here till after seven o'clock. I ain't got a wife to go home to, so I ain't in any hurry to go home." Cullen told him he would surely be back before then and started for the door. "Tell Rose I sent you," Burnett called after him.

He found Pot Luck next to the hardware store, and he was not surprised that he had not noticed it when he rode past before. A tiny building crammed between the hardware store and a barbershop, the name POT LUCK RESTAURANT was painted on a four-foot length of flat board nailed over the door. A little bell over the top of the door announced his entry when he walked in and paused to look around the small room, half of which was taken up by the kitchen. A long table with a bench on each side and a chair at each end, occupied the other half of the room. A man and a woman, the only customers, were seated at the far end of the table. They both stopped eating to stare at the man who appeared to fill the doorway completely. A short, rather chubby woman standing at the stove, whom he assumed to be Rose, turned to greet him when she heard the doorbell. She paused a moment when she saw him before she brushed a stray strand of dull red hair from her forehead and said, "Welcome. Come on in." She watched him as he hesitated, still looking the place over. "Since you ain't ever been in before, and you ain't, 'cause I'd remember you, I'll tell you how I operate. I don't have no menus. I just cook one thing. It ain't the same thing every night, but I just cook one supper—just like your mama cooked for you. Tonight, I'm servin' lamb stew with butterbeans and biscuits, and you won't find any better stew anywhere else in town. So you decide whether you wanna eat with me or not." She waited then for his reaction.

"I don't recollect if I've ever had lamb before, but I reckon this is a good time to try it," he decided.

"If you don't like it, you don't have to pay for it," Rose said. "'Course, that's if you don't eat it."

"Fair enough," he said.

"Set yourself down and I'll bring you some coffee, if that's what you want." He nodded and she suggested, "You'd best set in the chair at the end, big as you are." He took his hat off, offered a polite nod to the couple at the other end of the table, then sat down in the chair.

The lamb stew was as good as she had claimed it would be, and the serving was ample for a man his size. The coffee was fresh and hot and she brought extra biscuits. The price was more than fair at fifty cents, considering prices for most everything were higher in a town the size of Austin. When he was finished and paying her, he asked, "Are you open for breakfast?" She was, she said, opening at six o'clock. "Then I reckon I'll see you in the mornin'," he said. "By the way," he thought to say as he opened the door, "Burnett, down at the stable, sent me here to eat."

The night passed peacefully enough as he slept in the stall with Jake, who snorted him awake at about half past five when the big bay heard Burnett open the stable doors. Knowing Michael O'Brien usually came into his office at eight, he decided he would buy himself some breakfast at Pot Luck before he saddled up for the day. He was sure he would prefer eating breakfast with Rose than going to breakfast with O'Brien at the Capitol Diner, where all the customers were dressed up like lawyers. As it turned out, Burnett went to breakfast with him and they took their time drinking coffee afterward. It was a rare occasion for Cullen, but he had to kill a lot of time before O'Brien would be in. Rose's breakfast was as good as her supper had been, so Cullen knew where he would be eating every time he came to Austin in the future. And that would depend upon whether or not he still had a job as special agent for the governor. He still could not know for sure how long the arrangement would last. Granted, he had received nothing but satisfied responses so far, but knowing it to be an unusual position with no formal contract, it could end at any time.

After leaving Pot Luck, he went back to the stable, loaded his packhorse, and rode back to the capitol building. He was still a little early for O'Brien, but Benny Thacker, O'Brien's secretary, was in the office, so he took a seat in the outer office and waited. He refused the offer of a cup of coffee from Benny, since he had drunk what seemed like a gallon of it at Pot Luck. He sat there for about fifteen minutes, conscious of the frequent glances from O'Brien's elfin secretary. He wondered why the shy little man seemed to be so intimidated by him. Then he recalled the last time he had been in the office. He had walked in just as Benny was coming out and they accidentally collided, the result of which nearly knocked Benny to the floor. Further thoughts were interrupted when O'Brien walked in the door. He started to give Benny some instructions but turned to discover Cullen sitting just inside the door when Benny pointed to him. "Cullen McCabe!" O'Brien exclaimed. "Just the man I wanna see. Have you been here long?" Before Cullen could answer, he asked, "Have you had your breakfast?" He hurried over and extended his hand. When Cullen shook it, and said that he had already eaten, O'Brien said, "Benny could have at least gotten you a cup of coffee while you waited."

"He offered one," Cullen said, "but I've had more than I needed this mornin'. Thanks just the same." Impatient now, he was anxious to get down to business. "Have you got a job for me?"

"Yes, sir, I sure do," O'Brien answered. "But first, let me tell you Governor Hubbard is well pleased with the success of this arrangement." He winked and said, "You did a helluva job in New Hope. He's started claiming that the creation of your job was his idea, even though it was mine right from the start. Nobody had even thought about appointing a special agent, who reports only to the governor until I suggested it." Without a pause, he went right into the reason for his summons. "This is a special assignment the governor wants you to investigate this time. So let's go on in and I'll let Governor Hubbard explain the job."

Cullen followed O'Brien into the governor's office and the governor got up from his desk and walked around it to shake hands with Cullen. "Cullen McCabe," Hubbard greeted him just as O'Brien had. "I'm glad to see you," he said. "I was afraid my wire hadn't reached you." He smiled warmly. "I'm glad to see you got it." He motioned Cullen to a seat on a sofa, while he sat down in an armchair facing him. "The job I've called you in for is one of special personal interest to me." He paused then to interrupt himself. "You're doing one helluva job, by the way," he said, then continued without waiting for Cullen to respond. "This is a slightly different situation than the problems you've handled up to now. We've got a little situation about a hundred and twenty five miles northwest of here between a couple of towns on Walnut Creek."

"Where's that?" Cullen interrupted, not having heard of it.

"Walnut Creek is a healthy creek that runs through the Walnut Valley. It's a branch of the Colorado River. I'm sending you to a little town on the west side of that creek, called Ravenwood. It was named for a man who owns many acres of land next to the creek, Judge Harvey Raven. He gave the land for the town to the county officials, along with about one hundred acres for county government business. Of course, the idea was to make Ravenwood the county seat. The problem, though, was that there was already a town of sorts on the east side of the creek, where a lot of settlers had farms and homes. They didn't like it much when the county took Raven's offer. Next thing you know, they started having trouble about the water rights. One thing led to another, and pretty soon there were some shots exchanged between the folks that built up Ravenwood and those that wanted the town left on the east side of the creek. So the east side folks created their own town and called it East City."

The governor rambled at length about the troubles between the two towns, a characteristic Cullen assumed common to all politicians, but he wondered what it had to do with him. "What, exactly, is it you want me to do?" He asked when Hubbard paused for breath.

"I'm getting to that," Hubbard said. "The problem in East City. It's become a town of saloons, brothels, and gambling halls. The mayor contacted my office. East City's crime is spilling over to the other side of the creek, so the folks in Ravenwood partitioned my office for help, also. I sent a delegation up there to meet with the city officials. They concluded that the town was justified in their complaints, but they couldn't recommend any plan of action to improve the situation. We sent a company of Rangers up there to maintain the peace. They set up a camp and stayed for three days. And for three days everything was peaceful. As soon as they left, East City went back to business as usual."

"Ain't there any law in the towns?" Cullen asked.

"Yes, there is," the governor answered, "in both towns. Ravenwood has a sheriff and East City has a marshal and a deputy. The problem is, the East City marshal seems to be in control of the whole town, and is nothing more than an outlaw, himself. And the town has become a haven for every other outlaw on the run in Texas. As far as we know, the sheriff in Ravenwood is an honest man."

"What do you expect me to do," Cullen asked, "if the Rangers couldn't fix the problem?"

The governor glanced at O'Brien and winked. "What you always do," he answered then. "What you did in New Hope and Bonnie Creek, look into the situation and see if there's anything you can do to improve it."

Cullen shook his head and thought about all Hubbard had just told him. "I don't know," he said, not at all optimistic about reforming two towns. It sounded to him that the governor needed a negotiator, and that label didn't fit him. The next best thing was to make one of the towns a permanent Ranger headquarters, and he was about to suggest that when O'Brien interrupted.

"Just ride up there and look the situation over," O'Brien said. "We trust your eyes more than the Rangers. If nothing else, you can at least report back with a more detailed presentation of the facts."

Cullen shrugged and shook his head again. "Well, I can do that, I reckon. It's your money. I'll see what I can do."

"Good man," Hubbard exclaimed with a grin. "I knew I could count on you. There's a check for your expenses already in the bank. You can pick up your money today. Think you'll be ready to leave in the morning?"

"I expect I'll leave today, just as soon as I pick up my money at the bank," Cullen said.

"Excellent!" Hubbard responded. "Come, I'll show you where you're going." He walked over to the large state map on the wall and pointed to two small dots that looked to be in the very center of the state. Cullen stood for a few minutes studying the route he would take, noting the rivers and streams. When he was satisfied with the way he would start out, he turned and said he was ready to go. "It's early yet," the governor stated. "If you'll need a little time to get ready to go, maybe you'd like to have dinner with me."

"Thanks just the same," Cullen responded, "but I'm ready to go now, soon as I pick up the money at the bank." He didn't think he'd be comfortable eating with the governor. He imagined it would be more awkward than it had been with O'Brien in the itol Diner. He shook hands with both of them k his leave after they wished him a good trip.

O'Brien and the governor stood at the office doorway and watched Cullen until he reached the end of the hall and disappeared down the stairs. "Might be a waste of time sending him up there," O'Brien commented.

"Maybe," Hubbard said, "but I've got a lot of confidence in that man. Besides, it's a helluva lot cheaper than sending a company of Rangers back there for who knows how long."

Visit us online at
KensingtonBooks.com
to read more from your favorite authors, see books by series, view reading group guides, and more.

Join us on social media
for sneak peeks, chances to win books and prize packs, and to share your thoughts with other readers.

facebook.com/kensingtonpublishing
twitter.com/kensingtonbooks

Tell us what you think!

To share your thoughts, submit a review, or sign up for our eNewsletters, please visit:
KensingtonBooks.com/TellUs.